THE
HOLLOW
BETTLE

THE POISONS OF CAUX

BOOK ONE

THE HOLLOW BETTLE

SUSANNAH APPELBAUM

illustrated by Jennifer Taylor

Alfred A. Knopf · New York

THIS IS A BORZOI BOOK PUBLISHED BY ALFRED A. KNOPF

Visit us on the Web! www.randomhouse.com/kids

Educators and librarians, for a variety of teaching tools, visit us at
www.randomhouse.com/teachers

Library of Congress Cataloging-in-Publication Data
Appelbaum, Susannah.
The Hollow Bettle / Susannah Appelbaum. — 1st ed.
p.   cm. — (Poisons of Caux ; bk. 1)
Summary: Eleven-year-old Ivy Manx sets out with her new friend, a young "taster," to find her missing uncle, an outlawed healer, in the dangerous kingdom of Caux, where magic, herbs, and poisons rule.
ISBN 978-0-375-85173-5 (trade) — ISBN 978-0-375-95173-2 (lib. bdg.) —
ISBN 978-0-375-85354-8 (e-book)
[1. Poisons—Fiction.   2. Uncles—Fiction.   3. Fantasy.]   I. Title.
PZ7.A6445Ho 2009
[Fic]—dc22
2008022626

The text of this book is set in 12-point Caslon.

Printed in the United States of America
August 2009
10 9 8 7 6 5 4 3 2 1

First Edition

to my father,

the Winds of Caux

If you drink much from

a bottle marked "poison," it is almost certain to

disagree with you, sooner or later.

—Alice's Adventures in Wonderland
Lewis Carroll

Contents

Part 1: Of Poisons and Tasters

Part II: Elixir

Part III: The Winds of Caux

Part IV: Templar

Many things begin with an end, and the story of Caux is no exception. In this case, it was the end of a life.

A very long time ago, a girl was poisoned. Her death held the distinction of being the very first poisoning—a new and horrible crime, one that was mysterious and beguiling. Unfortunately for both the girl and her country, her father was the king.

A shadow fell over the realm. The king turned his back on Caux and doomed his people to a life of misery under the Deadly Nightshades. A life of poison. Few still remember their king, Good King Verdigris, who—it is whispered—might someday return.

🌿 🌿 🌿

Part 1

Of Poisons and Tasters

The bereft souls from whom nature has withheld the legacy of taste have dour expressions upon their sallow faces, their countenances speak of deprivation, and they are forced at every turn to wonder at their plate—is it . . . poisoned?

—The Field Guide to the Poisons of Caux

Chapter One

Mr. Flux Arrives

I t's an astonishing feat that young Ivy Manx was not poisoned during Mr. Flux's tenure as her taster.

These were corrupt times in Caux, the land being what it was—a hotbed of wickedness and general mischief. The odds were stacked against anyone surviving their next meal, unless they had in their employ a half-decent Guild-accredited taster. A taster such as Mr. Flux maintained himself to be.

The day of Mr. Flux's arrival was a day like any other, devoid of goodwill and cheer (and befitting the taster's disposition). A fire burned glumly in the grate within the small tavern Ivy called home, and beside it a few disinterested regulars took their drinks in tedious silence. Hidden in her secret workshop, Ivy Manx found herself hoping for something thrilling to happen—perhaps a particularly rousing poisoning. She had been ignoring her studies in favor of one of her experiments when Shoo cawed softly.

"Never you mind," Ivy admonished the crow. "Cecil will never know I was using his equipment unless you tell him."

She proceeded to strain an evil-smelling mixture through her uncle's sieve. Ivy worked with a look of great concentration upon her face, and when the task was finished, she set the vessel on a burner to boil. Almost immediately the syrup discharged a clingy cloud, and a sickly sweet smell filled the small room, forcing the crow to alight dizzyingly on a coatrack to avoid it.

This was greatly disobedient, she knew. Her uncle wished her to be a learned apotheopath—a healer—yet tinkering with her noxious brews was much more satisfying. Like most of Caux, Ivy preferred not the well-meaning herbs, but the darker, more potent ones. Apotheopathy seemed ancient to the ten-year-old, from a time when plants were used to heal, not harm. Her uncle's collection of dusty books and scribbled parchments made her yawn—both to Cecil's and Shoo's great disappointment.

"There. Let's see what that does when it's done."

As she stepped back in the workshop, Cecil's top shelf caught her eye. He was still in the habit of putting his secrets up high, thinking they remained safely out of her reach. There was quite a lot to see, for as Ivy knew, there is no such better display of a person's ideals and deficiencies as a bookshelf. (Cecil tended toward being an untidy person and the shelf illustrated this fact well.) Her eyes narrowed at the sight

of the small leather case that contained his apotheopathic tinctures.

She pushed over a three-legged stool, and as Shoo grew ever more agitated, Ivy climbed up, reaching.

"Just a peek, Shoo. It's his remedies. Clearly, this counts as studying."

The black crow, longtime resident of the Hollow Bettle, knew better. The ampoules were strictly off-limits at this point in her studies, and the crow began pacing excitedly. With her uncle set to depart the tavern in the evening, Ivy was reminded that this trespass would better wait until then.

"But he'll take them with him," she told Shoo. "And, if you're lucky, you, too."

The stool was proving to be insufficient. Ivy considered climbing up the rickety shelves themselves. She wanted nothing more than to examine the delicate glass-stoppered medicines within the case and had long ago given up asking. First she must complete the long memorizations of herbs and plant lore—so completely bookish and boring.

"Anyone can produce a potion that will make you sick," her uncle would remind her, his eyes gleaming with enthusiasm. "But it takes much learning to use plants to cure! Which would you rather be, then, a common poisoner or a respected healer?"

Interestingly, Cecil never seemed to wait for an answer.

Testing a bowed shelf for sturdiness, she gingerly began scaling upward, with Shoo now flying about the room squawking excitedly.

Ignoring the bird, Ivy was quite nearly there when the worst happened. Her foothold gave way and the entire contents of the overburdened unit—her uncle's medicinal books and priceless notes, his scales and workshop essentials, important-looking mahogany boxes containing powders and infusions—all came crashing down, nearly taking Shoo with it.

In the silence that followed, Ivy and the crow waited nervously for Cecil's appearance. Her straw-colored hair and flushed cheeks were streaked with her uncle's pitch. She brushed something white and gritty from her shirtsleeve while considering what an appropriate punishment would be—and wondered if he'd forbid her from her experiments. (Just how this would be enforced in his absence she wondered, too.) Shoo, rumpling his sleek feathers, settled in front of the narrow door that let out into the tavern area.

"Don't be in such a hurry. He'll hold you responsible, you realize."

When a remarkable amount of time had passed and her uncle had failed to respond, Ivy grew curious.

The workshop door was veiled from sight by dust and shadow, a sly entrance cut in the middle of an enormous blackboard in residence upon the tavern's far wall. It was further obscured by the simple fact that the shadowy wall was never regarded—the menu on the blackboard was long obsolete. When Cecil was seeing his patients or when the workshop was hosting Ivy's nefarious experiments, a sharp eye might discern a flickery crack of amber light slicing through the darkness. It was here that Ivy put her eye, wondering what might be keeping her uncle.

It was fortuitous timing. Ivy watched as a scrawny and particularly unimpressive stranger crossed the threshold, pausing right in front of her to scrape the caked mud from his tatty boots. He exuded from him a sour sense of disinterest, and clinging to him, although unseen, was an odd sort of melancholia—the kind that affects the bearer not at all, but those who behold him feel instantly cheerless.

Having just passed through the Bettle's creaky front door, Mr. Flux—for indeed this was he—made a beeline to the bar. He ordered and consumed an unusually expensive brandy and then quickly ordered another, requesting Cecil leave the bottle before him.

Surveying the room, Ivy gave the lone traveler five minutes in the midst of this group of scoundrels and found herself eager at the prospect of his gruesome end.

"At last," Ivy whispered to Shoo. "Something exciting."

The room grew deeply quiet; there was nothing but the sound of coals settling, shooting off a vicious whip of sparks. The tavern's regulars, with a great distrust of outsiders, ceased their chatter. Ivy watched the stranger smirk as he took a bored look around the silent room. His pasty face, tinged an odd yellowish hue, was half hidden by an unusual hood. With no one to meet his eye, he returned to an idle consideration of his glass.

Ivy was perplexed. The rule of the land was poison or be poisoned, and such a haughty entrance seemed to shout out for a lethal dose of attention. Yet everyone seemed intent on avoiding the man's eyes—a few chairs creaked uncomfortably, and Ivy frowned as Curtains, one of the tavern's more notorious regulars (and one of her best clients), sidestepped it to the door.

She examined Mr. Flux more closely. Something about the man's threadbare cloak seemed familiar, although even in the dying light of the tavern it was plain to see that the robes were ill kept and patched with an unsteady hand. Ivy tried to place it. Her thoughts turned to her neglected studies, and with a start, she realized what it was she was seeing.

"A graduate of the Tasters' Guild—Shoo, can you believe it? A real taster, here at the Hollow Bettle!"

Indeed, it was so—Mr. Sorrel Flux was the first Guild-accredited, educated palate to call upon the services of the small forgotten tavern. A true taster! Theirs was normally the territory of the rich and royal, and surely only the very well-to-do might employ one.

Yet there was something oily about Flux, and his carefree

way of pouring her uncle's fine brandy down his gullet seemed to be anathema to a taster's training. His collar was askew—and worse, stained with marrow and puddles of grease. Much less refined than Ivy thought a taster should be, he looked as if he'd been dragged by his scruff through a thornbush.

Since her uncle cared little or nothing for the Guild or its graduates, she waited expectantly for Cecil to show him the door. Instead, to Ivy's great astonishment, they began conversing in low, hushed tones.

Ivy pushed Shoo aside for a better look, receiving an indignant squawk.

The taster's eyes alighted upon a high shelf behind the bar. There a stocky bottle made vague with dust and grime sat alone. Inside, amid the amber brandy, a twinkle of red from a small stone.

"Perchance that be your bettle, sir? Of which you've named your fine establishment?"

Cecil followed the taster's gaze. "That it is."

"Priceless, they are."

"I suppose. To some," he allowed.

"To those who wish to ward off the ill effects of poison," Mr. Flux scoffed. "May I?"

As the taster licked his thin lips, Cecil retrieved the bottle from its perch and placed it upon Mr. Flux's yellowed palm.

"What an odd twinkle it possesses! I see now how one might think it hollow—although, of course, that's an utter impossibility."

The bottle clinked appealingly as Flux angled it for a better look. He fingered the coil of golden wire that sealed it. A moment passed, at the end of which the taster put the bottle down haltingly, tearing his eyes away, swallowing what remained in his chipped glass.

"If you don't mind—" Cecil was attempting to return the bottle to its shelf, but the taster's fingers still gripped it tightly.

"Yes, yes, of course." Mr. Flux dismissed the bottle with a wave. "I see now it is but a clever fake," he said. "A hollow bettle! A fine example of wishful thinking."

Mr. Flux was close enough for Cecil to smell his sour breath and appreciate a protruding vein in the man's left temple—a proximity that Ivy's uncle wished to change immediately. He was prevented from doing so by the following statement.

"Word has it, you're off to cure the king," the taster hissed.

Cecil froze, bottle in hand.

"Perhaps," he finally allowed.

"Never mind that none have succeeded before you. Yours is not their unfortunate destiny, now, is it?"

From the workshop, Shoo let off a low throaty call. Ivy's uncle had said nothing of the dangers of his travels.

Suddenly business-like, Mr. Flux produced a packet of papers, which he proudly called his credentials.

"You'll find everything in order," he assured Cecil in his nasal voice. "Normally my fee is—well, how to put this? Unaffordable." His eyes strayed back to the red bettle. "But in light of your honorable errand, I find it my duty to be of whatever service I might in your absence. In times like these, I'm sure you'll agree, the well-being of the little girl is of great concern. I am, of course"—and here he allowed a slight crooked grin to rise unsteadily upon his face—"Guild-accredited."

It was the way Flux spoke the word *Guild* that sent an odd prickle up Ivy's spine, and a profound feeling of dread settled in—as sure and heavy as the dander upon Flux's weak shoulders. The feeling, not at all a pleasant one, would remain there in its way for quite some time.

It was quickly decided.

For a surprisingly small fee—a few minims and a scruple only—Mr. Sorrel Flux would reside at the Hollow Bettle and assume tasting responsibilities for Cecil's niece. Since the apotheopath expected to be gone no longer than a week at most on his errand, it was arranged.

Sadly for Ivy, it was the case that the well-timed arrival of Mr. Flux heralded an important departure. The day that Mr. Flux arrived inquiring about a position was the day Ivy's uncle Cecil left, unhappily, not for a week as he had planned, but for good.

In his hurry, Cecil Manx overlooked some of Flux's more obvious failings. He also neglected to tell the taster anything of his niece Ivy—after all, the man had not asked. And in this, it could be said that Mr. Flux had sorely underestimated the talents of his charge.

As Flux had arrived across the threshold of the Bettle, his incurious nature allowed him to overlook a crooked panel, with a flourish of red ink, that clacked beside the front door.

Poison Ivy

Inheritances hurried

Rivals disposed

Revenge awarded

~Starting at 5 minims~

And since Ivy Manx held the questionable taster responsible—rightly so or not—for the disappearance of her uncle, it was an astonishing feat that Mr. Flux survived what was to be his entire year of tasting for Poison Ivy.

Chapter Two

Poison Ivy

It was generally assumed at the Hollow Bettle that Cecil Manx's excuse for his inexplicable tardiness was his own death. It made natural sense to everybody—everybody but his niece—that Cecil had succumbed to poison along the route his impulsive errand had brought him.

Ivy would hear none of it, while her taster preferred not to raise the subject lest his desirable position somehow be lost. The only problem with this agreement—immediately presenting itself upon Cecil's departure—was the simple fact that Mr. Sorrel Flux was a taster of dubious quality and talent. He seemingly could no sooner detect poison in a bowl of the Bettle's famous hundred-year soup than stretch out his scrawny arms inside his shabby cloak and fly.

"Cabbage," he pronounced Ivy's lunch shortly after Cecil had left. It was his first and only attempt to taste for the young girl.

"But this is *beet* soup!" Ivy answered, incredulous.

Four bugs with four hundred feet.

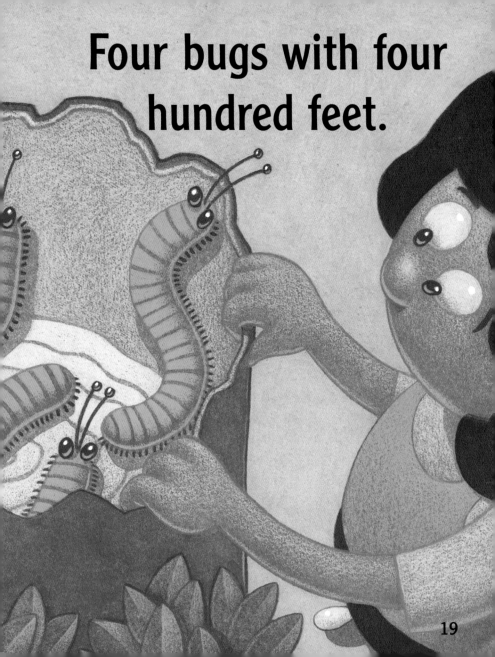

"Yes, of course. Just as I said. And it's quite fit to eat," he called over his shoulder—making fast progress up the stairs to her uncle's chambers with his small roll of possessions.

Ivy wondered almost immediately if he was indeed a graduate of the revered Tasters' Guild.

Mr. Sorrel Flux dressed in the robes of the Guild, although ill fitting and worn, and he liked to pepper his phrases with references to the secretive school for anyone within earshot. But Flux was, simply put, an awful taster who couldn't save anyone's life but his own, and this he did purely through inactivity and insubordination to his taster duties. He ate very little, and only for himself, and even then with a look of distrust and trepidation on his unpleasant face. Given these habits, it would be of no surprise to learn that he was of quite a scrawny build. That, coupled with the yellow cast of his skin, made him, with very little stretch of the imagination, resemble a plucked chicken. Mr. Flux was furthermore entirely unapologetic in his inabilities and quite soon revealed another annoying trait: a penchant for napping and idleness.

So it was on one subject alone that the two of them agreed: they would talk to each other as little as possible, and then only about vagaries.

Conveniently, there had been nothing of an introduction between taster and charge—Mr. Flux simply referred to her almost immediately as "the little menace." (The taster did, however, stumble upon the old crow's name, purely by accident, as he repeatedly swatted it away from his morning porridge.)

Their conspiracy of silence was broken only twice.

The first was early in his stay, when Ivy wondered whether Mr. Flux might have had any word from her uncle. Mr. Sorrel Flux replied—truthfully—that he had not. Inwardly, the taster could not have cared less about the girl's uncle, except where it concerned the comfort of his feather bed or his taste in nightshirts. Mr. Flux was of the opinion, anyway, that it was unlikely that the foolish man had gotten far—his journey's commencement was ill timed to the start of Caux's dangerous Windy Season.

This prompted the second, and last, conversation.

It was a simple request. Ivy warned him away from her garden.

Ivy's satisfying garden grew behind crumbling stone walls thick with moss and knotted branches and buzzed loudly with honeybees. Poisonous plants grew right beside their natural antidotes, with chipped slate announcements (in curly writing) labeling each in the old tongue. With Ivy's care, the herbs grew to great beauty and potency. With Shoo's help, the garden was not bothered by pests; he could be found—without any sense of irony—perched upon a stricken scarecrow.

Understandably, for the uninvited, Ivy's garden was a place of grave danger.

Sorrel Flux knew himself to be uninvited, but Ivy's warning had piqued an uncharacteristic interest in his languid brain. One day, in a fit of exertion, he found himself beside the overgrown walls. Hearing something, he peered in.

A picture of sweet sadness met his eyes. Ivy had been weeping over a crop of feisty snapdragons—her uncle particularly delighted in them—and as she sat there crying quietly upon the earth, not a soul could resist being moved by the young girl's plight.

Not a soul, that is, but Mr. Flux.

Mr. Sorrel Flux's heart, in fact, which pumped its limp business inside his chest, was just as hard and calloused as the rest of him. It was stony and small, and if someone had plucked it from his body and thrown it at you, it would have certainly left a bruise. Because of this, Mr. Flux was entirely incapable of shedding a tear—except perhaps for himself—so Ivy's current lonesome state left him entirely dry-eyed.

Dry-eyed and thirsty.

As he made to leave, he was distracted by a different sight. Mr. Flux was not in possession of even the slightest green thumb, but his eyes were drawn to the curious nature of the plants within the old walls. The foliage seemed to positively sparkle and pulse with an odd, shivery force, and the taster wondered at once if he were not the victim of a bottle of bad brandy. The plants trembled, as if with a chill, and Flux couldn't escape the idea that they might extract their pale, sodden roots from the soil and start scurrying about. He blinked several times and rubbed his eyes thoroughly, and to his relief, the effect was gone.

But the experience served as a reminder that the tavern that Ivy Manx called home had some fine brandies from which to choose, as well as a hearty assortment of hard ciders and something called applejack that was better suited as fuel for the tavern's few and flickery lanterns. With this, Sorrel Flux departed the garden for the tavern, where he spent the rest of the day recovering from his stroll.

The next morning, Ivy recognized telltale signs of his adventure. Flux's first and only visit to her garden resulted in a persistent rash. It began as blisters and soon formed red itchy welts, concentrating themselves upon the taster's heavy-lidded eyes but soon spreading merrily about his entire face. The punishment for his excursion was straightforward—the glossy vine that clung to the garden walls was none other than Ivy's namesake. And since none of Cecil's poultices seemed to alleviate his discomfort, he resigned himself further to bed. Here he breakfasted and lazed away the day, occasionally calling on a little wooden whistle for Ivy to prepare for him a tray of assorted brandies.

Sadly, Mr. Flux never felt entirely well again for the complete year he lived there. The yellowish cast his skin possessed upon arrival became more pronounced, spreading alarmingly to the whites of his eyes. He complained of sharp pains while reclining in bed. (Shoo had taken to introducing Ivy's silvery pushpins into his mattress while he slept, and it resembled more a pincushion than a pallet.)

In fact, never once did Mr. Flux think of leaving the Hollow Bettle for more predictable digestive arenas. In a thin convalescent's voice, he would remind the Bettle's lone maidservant that the Tasters' Oath to which he'd sworn prevented his departure.

He must stay with his charge to the bitter end.

It was Ivy Manx's hope that that end would come soon, and from this wish was finally born a plan, a dangerous plan, which she decided to implement only after it became sadly clear that her uncle was not coming home.

Chapter Three

The Deadly Nightshades

L ooking down at the world of Caux, say, from a passing cloud, there is no telltale sign—no indication at all—of the mischief and malingering of its inhabitants. Why, Caux from up here looks positively cozy—snug within its borders of sea and cliff. Vast green plains and fertile rolling hills. Thick, fecund forests filled with luscious flora and fauna. Bustling cities. Clever castles. Winding rivers, picturesque trains, and, of course, glorious trestles.

But as we draw close, looking down now as a circling crow, there is hardly anything to spark the same surge of joy. From even here, high above the tallest trees, you can feel the land's misfortune—a poison that the citizens endure. You might feel it even pulling you in.

And were you to actually put your two feet on the ground, thus falling under the rulership of Caux's contemptible new king—King Nightshade—why, the world at your doorstep might not seem very bright at all.

In fact, positively dismal.

King Nightshade of Caux was a wicked and unhappy man. He was unhappy because he suffered greatly from a hideous affliction he possessed since birth. He was wicked because, well, he was unhappy. (Or perhaps he was just born that way—we'll never know for sure.) But from being shamelessly vile he derived great pleasure—thus forgetting momentarily his own unhappiness in the utter suffering of others.

The king maintained one wish, which was a simple one. He wished that his suffering—his dismal disfigurement— would disappear. He wished to be alleviated of his defect, and he thought that this might finally make him happy. Still wicked, but happy.

So he devised a plan and put the word out, in the form of a Royal Proclamation, that anyone who might cure him of his affliction would benefit greatly. He was intentionally vague, mostly because he was undecided about what form his reward might take. He was unused to acts of kindness, and so, incidentally, was the queen.

But it was finally announced that whosoever might provide him with a cure would receive a handsome fortune—his weight in gold and priceless bettles. And since bettles were beloved by the citizenry of Caux not for their beauty and rarity (and they possessed both), but for their supposed charms against poison, this was a tempting prize indeed. The king knew that most of the people of Caux who were presently alive preferred to stay that way.

But the punishment for failure, well, that was quite natural and easy for the Nightshades. Queen Artilla would see to their demise. She was, after all, quite famous throughout Caux for her spectacular acts of ruthless poisoning—a reputation she worked hard at maintaining.

King Nightshade enjoyed his power. Indeed, he had worked hard to take it away from his predecessor. It was an unusual day when he did not issue forth a Proclamation of some sort—whatever struck his royal fancy—and it would instantly become law. He was, after all, the king.

After assuming reign in what was generally believed to be Caux's most dismal day, his first act as quite a young king was to abolish at least one thousand years of learning in an enormous bonfire, targeting for the flames anything remotely connected to the previous king. He raided the famed Library at Rocamadour—the fire burned, it was said, for eight days and eight nights.

It so happened that the previous king was also a learned apotheopath, so what was thought to be a priceless collection of irreplaceable medical and herbal healing books was lost forever. With the Deadly Nightshades in the seat of power, apotheopathy evolved into poisonry quite quickly, and people soon foraged deeper in the forest for the darker, more potent herbs.

What followed was the new king's First Proclamation:

TO BE A PRACTICING APOTHEOPATH IS
ILLEGAL, PUNISHABLE BY DEATH.

At the time, when the news reached him that he was now an outlaw, Cecil Manx had merely shrugged. He was a man of many talents. He'd always wanted to open a tavern, and so he did.

It was hardly a secret, however, that he kept seeing patients in his back room.

Chapter Four
Soup

As it was unlikely that Sorrel Flux saw to any of the business concerns of the tavern, and as Cecil Manx never bothered Ivy about the taxes, it was safe to say that for the entire year her uncle had been gone, not a minim had been sent to the king's tax collectors.

There was a pile of correspondence behind the bar, and that was probably the best place to find the tax bills—but it's hard to look for something you don't know is missing. Besides, Sorrel Flux was often found warming his bony hands beside the fire—which, if it was not warm enough for his liking, he would ignite with a handful of paper nearby. It was in this way that the Notice of Default and Intent to Collect went up in smoke.

When it came to taxes, King Nightshade was ruthless and efficient.

His sentries, in fact, were waiting outside for first light

when they saw a candle flickering in the young girl's room above the tavern before dawn. This was interesting to the group only insofar as it momentarily distracted them from their hunger. The men knew taverns to be occasionally a place of good food and drink, and they had been without either for the entire night. The glow vanished almost as soon as it appeared, and the sentries returned to the grumbling of their stomachs.

Ivy was executing her dangerous plan. If her uncle would not come to her, she would go to him. An entire year had passed— a miserable year, one filled only with the tedium of Flux's company. She was now eleven, and Ivy had no plans on growing any older without her uncle's company. Besides, the thrill of experimenting on her freeloading taster was gone, but as a parting gift, she had slipped some of her famous sleeping draught into his nightcap. A double dose.

Ivy was headed to the tavern with an audacious theft in mind. It was her intention to relieve the Hollow Bettle of the very jewel for which it was named. She paused in the low hall, straining to hear any sounds from the taster's quarters.

Cecil Manx's mill house was resplendent with little hidden passageways, and in the dim morning Ivy used one that led her down a set of irregular stairs. She soon found herself just where she needed to be: at a small door behind the Hollow Bettle's bar.

Ivy quietly opened the little door and discovered, to her complete surprise, that she was not the only thief in the room. Two other souls populated the tavern presently, and further to the young girl's dismay, one of them was quite easily recognized (even at this early hour) as the unpleasant man who had been nothing but ill tempered and poor company to her for this past long year. Mr. Flux looked wide awake, she noticed, in defiance of her robust sleeping potion—a first, if ever there was.

The taster's companion—for they seemed on quite familiar terms—was even more inexplicable.

He wore an objectionable amount of facial hair and towered over the taster. His eyes were deep-set and dark. And, most disconcerting, he seemed to speak—the few times he did—in guttural grunts that Ivy could make nothing of but somehow Mr. Flux comprehended with practiced ease.

Ivy was no stranger to madmen—especially drunken madmen—but something about this friend of the taster's made her hesitate. The bettle, in its bottle of brandywine, was on a shelf right above her, but to get it would require her to climb on a nearby cask and stand for a moment in plain view. This was unacceptable, considering her company.

Fortunately, the two trespassers were embroiled in what seemed to be an argument and hadn't noticed the girl in their midst. There was some pluck in the small taster. His diminutive stature brought him merely to the dark man's collar, but his contempt challenged even the mighty. Mr. Flux was un-characteristically animated—Ivy was so accustomed to seeing him in his nightdress with nothing but a collection of chipped glassware as company. He was stamping his foot and repeating himself intently, slower now, as if discussing a lofty topic with a child.

"I don't care what the orders were; I'm telling you we'll do it my way—who's been living in this dump until the word came down? I've been here for an entire year, waiting!"

The tall man uttered something menacing, and although Ivy could understand none of it, she felt a chill run down her spine. His voice and presence had none of the same effect on Sorrel Flux, who was by now so enraged his arms were flapping about his sides.

"I won't waste my breath on you any further. Do as I say," he snarled through gritted teeth, "or I'll be forced to discuss this with the Director."

But the argument would not soon see itself resolved—at least not today at the Hollow Bettle—since before another word could be exchanged, the tavern's door was rudely separated from its hinges and made suddenly into not a door at all, but a welcome mat for twenty of King Nightshade's most hungry sentries.

Ivy used this moment to procure the bottle of brandywine from the top shelf, slipping back down to her hiding spot just as quickly again to watch the newest arrivals.

"Good day," declared the captain of the group as he stepped forward from among his men. He was an ambitious gentleman—at least for the next fifteen minutes—with an influential family made up mostly of tradesmen, influential enough to get him several dubious promotions to the level he now found himself at in the Nightshades' army. His name was Turner Taxus.

"Can I help you?" Sorrel Flux demanded, successfully turning his outraged tone into something more akin to sweet cheer.

"Are you the proprietor?" Turner Taxus asked in his most official voice. "One"—he consulted a sentry next to him—"Cecil *Minx*?"

The taster sensed in the situation perhaps a way to profit, and his pasty face, as if made of putty, expertly molded itself into a hospitable one.

"Welcome! Welcome," he cried, gesturing about the bar. "I say. Can I perhaps get you gentlemen something to drink? You must be thirsty after breaking down that door—or at the very least hungry for something warming and restorative." He stepped in front of his companion, who was trying, in any event, to keep to the shadows.

"Very well. Here you are." Turner Taxus slapped a parchment roll into Mr. Flux's hand with the precise air of a bored official.

"What's this?" The taster recoiled. Things wrapped with

the king's colors and sealed with his wax seal rarely contained good news.

"A copy of the Crown's Notice to Collect; I trust you received the original. It says either you pay the taxes due to King Nightshade, with a generous amount of interest, or you surrender your establishment to him immediately. Wherein he installs a new tavern keeper." Turner Taxus's long face was stony. Repossessions such as these were completely beneath his status, he felt, and giving anything more to them than necessary was a waste of his valuable time.

"Ah—you have made the understandable mistake of assuming me to be a property owner. I admit, I betray an air above my station. I am merely a *servant* to the proprietor, my dear man. Of the *Guild*, I dare add. I hardly am qualified to accept such a document." He tried to unhand the awful parchment and return it to the sentry. "Your scroll."

Having no luck rescinding the decree, Flux relieved it onto the sawdust floor and with the tip of his boot pushed it at the man in uniform, taking a step backward.

"I'll just leave you to your business. I'm sure the fellow's around here somewhere—and if not, I know where his bony little girl is sleeping—"

While Flux was spitting out the directions to Ivy's bedroom, his eyes wandered to behind the bar. Ivy was now completely within his sight—he need only glance down to spot her. But his eyes were looking to the top shelf, drawn to his prize.

"Mind your head at the top of the steps—although those helmets must be good for something. And do watch out for that bird; he's been trained to go for the eyes. . . ."

Then he froze, seeing only the dust shadow where the bettle once was. From where Ivy sat, Flux looked monstrous, and she pushed back further into the shadows. Towering over her, at last he lowered his yellowed eyes and found her easily. A particular smirk slid across his unpleasant face. As Mr. Flux turned back to the captain, Ivy braced to be turned over to the king's soldiers.

"But wait! Where are my manners? You should really try the soup—it's famous, you know—before you go on with the tedious details ahead of you."

At the mention of food, the sentries perked up. Sorrel Flux stepped back by the fire and lavishly gestured at the large kettle filled with the hundred-year soup.

"It's been cooking on this fire uninterrupted for over a century. Every day something is added to it—more potatoes, parsnips. A ham bone, an oxtail. Truly an adventure in both history and taste!"

Turner Taxus wasn't as hungry as his men—he had prudently brought along a bagged supper for the trip and eaten it in a quiet moment with his taster in the wee hours of the morning. But he was aware that it smelled quite delicious: rich and hearty—a good morale booster. He remembered that a leader is only effective if he has the admiration of his men.

While Taxus mulled this over, Sorrel Flux signaled his dark friend with an almost imperceptible nod in the direction of Ivy's hiding place. Keeping to the shadows, the man began creeping her way, breathing appallingly, with what could only be thick spittle stuck to the corners of his mouth.

Turner Taxus raised his gloved hand to his men and beckoned.

From behind the sentries, somewhat meekly, emerged a young man—barely old enough to be wearing tasters' robes. They were, Ivy was happy to see, quite a better example of those worn by her own taster—the black cloth was new, crisply ironed, the collar (really, more like a bib) white and untainted. In their presence, Sorrel Flux somehow looked even more shabby and ill kempt.

"Taster," Turner Taxus commanded, "taste, if you will, this soup."

Sorrel Flux stirred the pot invitingly with a long wooden spoon.

"Please step away," Taxus added, "and let my taster work."

Flux did, with flourish.

The young man approached the hearth. He couldn't have been much older than she, Ivy guessed, and although he was doing his best to maintain a demeanor of professionalism and scholarship, she noticed he seemed slightly unsure of himself.

He cleared his throat and ladled himself a serving into a plain earthenware bowl. He leaned in and sniffed. He sniffed again—this time quite loudly—after which he looked upward, as if playing the odors about on his palate. Thoughtfully, he brought the bowl up to his mouth as Sorrel Flux eyed him with undisguised contempt from beneath heavy eyelids.

The young taster allowed a small drop, really no bigger than a child's tear, to pass over his lips and onto the tip of his tongue.

All of his taster training, many long years of study at the impeccably credentialed Tasters' Guild, came down to this. True, he hadn't been the best of students. Nor had he graduated anywhere near the top of his class, making him almost unemployable. But he had somehow landed this impressive charge—for a first assignment it was a good one. He was unaware of the reputation of the Taxus family, which was one of immense thriftiness and militant frugality. They were just as happy to hire him at a discounted wage as he was to accept the position. Unfortunately, you almost always get what you pay for.

Rowan Truax, for that was the young taster's name, let the droplet play about all areas of his tongue—past the tip, onto both sides, and over to the back of his mouth. He played the complex flavors over his taste buds—hints of sweet and sour, salt, and even bitter (the flavor of many poisons). Tasting nothing untoward, he turned to his charge and pronounced the kettle of soup fit to eat.

"Fit to eat!" Turner Taxus repeated to his twenty hungry men, with an air of generosity—as if he'd cooked it himself.

The sentries could help themselves no longer and all surged forward to quell their hunger pains. Sorrel Flux bobbed and weaved through the group, exchanging syrupy pleasantries—all the while monitoring the back of the bar.

Ivy, bottle with bettle in hand, only just managed to retreat through a grate below a large crock of pickled eggs before the dark stranger was upon her. She would not likely soon forget the throaty splutter he made as she slipped away.

Chapter Five

Aqua Artilla

he Field Guide to the Poisons of Caux—the perennial best selling reference book that, for obvious reasons, was required reading by anyone alive in Caux wishing to stay that way— lists just one undetectable poison. Oddly, it was sold, with a wink, as perfume.

It was created in honor of—who else—Queen Nightshade, by the Royal Perfumer, a man named Mawn. He called it Aqua Artilla. Befitting the queen, it contained, amid its secret ingredients and cloying scent, a mixture of potent and deadly toxins. The queen not only wore a trace behind her ears and upon her royal wrists, she carried a few drops of it in her favorite hollow ring for her murderous impulses.

It was a great success in Caux. It made a name for the Royal Perfumer and made his fortune as well. And since Mawn touted it as impossible to duplicate without his secret formula, his fortunes grew and grew.

Ivy had come across a bottle of Aqua Artilla only once, not long before Cecil's departure. But once was all it took.

She set out to crack the secret formula and stayed up late to do so, Shoo pacing the sturdy table alongside of her. Nights passed, but the formula proved harder, or Mawn cleverer, than she'd expected.

Ivy worked feverishly, inspired as never before by the queen's poisoned perfume, yet her first attempt at Aqua Artilla ended in a thick lacquer. The next, a noxious epoxy. It was a stringy, vicious-looking brown and clung to the sides of the copper pot. In the morning it had hardened and she was forced to throw the entire thing away—hoping that Cecil wouldn't notice his missing basin. The next day, she managed to produce something akin to chewing gum.

One rude brew after the other boiled and bubbled in her little workshop.

She tried it every which way she could imagine, culling from her garden some of the most truly awful roots and herbs, a choice mushroom, a suspicion of garlic, even some honey from the bees that feasted upon her poisonous flowers. And then, in what she considered a stroke of genius, she snuck into the bar quite late and helped herself to her uncle's prized brandy from its high perch. It was time to try a different distilling agent.

The coil of golden wire came off the stopper quite easily,

she found, and the stone bettle inside clinked as she poured all of the aromatic contents into the basin. At first she thought she had found the secret ingredient, for now her tonic smelled and looked just right. She poured out a small sample, and holding the vial, she cast about the room eagerly for something to try it out on. With a squawk, Shoo wisely flew out the open window.

The crow needn't have worried. The syrup smelled just right but seemed to do perfectly nothing. She carelessly tossed aside the small vial, but as she set about stowing away the remainder of the infuriating infusion, she heard Cecil returning to the workshop. Hastily, Ivy returned her failed Aqua Artilla to the very same brandy bottle and artfully restored the golden wire to the bottle's stopper.

"What are you doing with that bottle?" Cecil's brow was raised in surprise.

"Dusting." Ivy smiled, and with practiced distraction, she presented her uncle with the small vial of her failed Aqua Artilla.

"Here," she said. "I got the smell right this time."

Away went her pots and pans, and she turned her attention instead to making customers for Cecil.

Now, as an apotheopath, Cecil was indeed an effective healer.

If practiced properly, this illicit brand of doctoring had astounding results. Yet as with everything, there were failures.

And when confronted with one, Cecil believed a patient could be well served by a simple dose of sugar syrup.

Shortly before the arrival of Mr. Flux, Cecil had been making such assurances to one Mr. Rankl, a ruddy pear-shaped man who suffered from a particularly incurable case of gout. None of the ancient medicines was working for Mr. Rankl, and Cecil found himself hopelessly confounded. So, with the cheerless eyes of his patient upon him, Cecil reached for his fail-safe sugar syrup—only in his carelessness he grabbed the wrong vial. This ampoule was the discarded result of Ivy's Aqua Artilla distillation, the very one she had presented to him not long before.

After administering the potion to Mr. Rankl with his usual seriousness, Cecil soon realized his mistake. The room was thick with the telltale smell of the queen's perfume! Try as he might to maintain a look of professionalism upon his face, he could not. He soon twitched and spasmed with a morbid anticipation, a fine bead of sweat trailing down his forehead.

Luckily, the goutish Mr. Rankl noticed none of this.

For the first time in quite some years, he was walking about the room without an insipid dagger in his left big toe. In fact, he was such a picture of health he declared himself to feel a man half his age. The patient flushed and sparkled with enthusiasm. He declared his many appetites returned, and talked of taking a wife—but would begin his celebration with a good bowl of the Bettle's rich soup.

Cecil had no choice but to agree that Mr. Rankl's incurable case of gout was cured. The results of Ivy's tonic were nothing short of miraculous, and he resolved to keep the elixir on hand for a time when his medicinal talents might fail him. Since he was a very good apotheopath, he would hardly ever use it.

The same, however, cannot be said of Mr. Flux, who—quite unbefitting a taster—had in his possession a small garish bottle of the real thing. He found it quite easy to administer the Aqua Artilla to the Bettle's kettle of soup and from there to a roomful of Nightshade sentries.

Chapter Six

The Field Guide

Sorrel Flux's other possession, more befitting a taster, was a copy of the *Guide*, as it was commonly called. The leather-bound book was impossibly thick, edged with gold leaf, and riddled with myriad thumb tabs. There were several sets of ribbons sewn directly into the binding for marking interesting pages, and the contents were helpful and all-encompassing. About the author little was known except—at least according to the book's cover— that he was a man called Axlerod D. Roux, who over the years had proved to be a recluse of such renown that many had come to doubt his very existence. The *Field Guide* was Flux's only book, and for the most part it went unread. His mind was not one to wonder at something and turn to a book for an answer. He felt, were he to be asked, that there was little of interest in books at all, and he would not shed a tear if a calamity struck his vision and rendered him unable to read.

It was in this way that for the entire year Sorrel Flux had spent in the tavern, he had no idea that there was a hidden back room. Since the entrance to Cecil's office was disguised—apotheopaths were punished with death if caught—by the enormous slate chalkboard and since there was no doctoring occurring in Cecil's absence, there were few visitors to the office for Flux to regard.

If he were the observant type, he might have sensed the upstairs of the mill house was out of proportion—rather much larger than the downstairs. But that might have been easily dismissed by the suggestion of a large kitchen, for Sorrel Flux not once ever deigned to enter the room. His haunts were few and, as we know, concerned either libation or dormancy.

Ivy, meanwhile, was intent on getting away from Sorrel Flux, and from his intimidating companion, as quickly as possible. She scrambled through the twisty tunnel that served as a shortcut from the bar to her uncle's messy den. She was very certain the bearded man could not follow her—at least this way—since he was decidedly larger than most men and she herself fit snugly in the passage. Sorrel Flux was another story. He was about the right size and gave the impression of being able to compress his body into tight spaces if need be. She could see him fitting himself tidily into a shoe box if it could benefit him somehow.

Either way, it wouldn't be long before they sounded the

alarm: there were at least twenty of the king's men and one scrawny taster—make that two—and the odds of their discovering the hidden entrance were in their favor.

She pulled herself out of a cupboard and into the workshop, where she hurriedly searched the tabletop for something in which to stow the brandywine bottle. Small vials of her early failed Aqua Artilla clattered in her wake—several falling to the floor and shattering. The air was suddenly thick and rancid.

Under Cecil's desk she finally found a tattered black satchel, the type favored by men of the medical profession, and removing a stack of ledgers, she gently placed the brandy bottle—and the bettle—inside. She swept an area clean atop his writing table. Small dusty notes in Cecil's elegant script scattered to the floor—the result of years of his medicinal observations—along with bits of string, candle remnants, an odd river stone. An upended bottle of ink puddled to one side of it all.

She heard a splintering of wood coming from the passage and, with a start, jumped upon the sturdy desk her uncle's elbows had polished clean.

"Shoo!" She called for the crow. She looked frantically around, but his usual perch was empty.

It was then, amid the thudding and vague curses Ivy easily attributed to her taster, that she looked down. Beside her foot, in an area of Cecil's desk that hadn't seen the sun in a year, Ivy saw it. A small brown case of soft leather, the one from high upon his shelves. It was unmistakable—she had, after all, for years tried to get her hands on the delicate ampoules. She scooped up her uncle's medicines, tossing them into the apotheopath's satchel, and then, with barely a look behind her, stepped out the small window into the early morning, quite alone.

With the appearance of the sentries at the only home she knew, Ivy naturally had some concerns about her future. Leaving the tavern behind, she would turn to the help of an old friend. Behind her in the workshop, discarded in her hurry, was Ivy's own dog-eared copy of the *Field Guide*. It was open to the first page, in which ropy letters and thoughtful curlicues formed the inscription:

Thanks for all the fine advice!

Your neighbor,

Axlerod "Axle" D. Roux

Chapter Seven

The Worse of Two Tasters

The Windy Season was not yet upon Caux's suffering residents, but that morning a young wind was channeling itself down the valley by way of the river Marcel, slapping errant waves and spewing spray in its wake. It angered Cecil's old mill wheel, which spun dizzyingly in the rapids. It upturned rows of strange and suspicious potted plants on Ivy's terrace. The old hickory tree, with its dancing balls of mistletoe, creaked and groaned.

There was one structure, aside from the stone mill house, impervious to this wind. At a narrow part of the Marcel, just down from the mill, sat an old iron train trestle, and it girdled the frothy brew impassively.

It was a small trestle as train trestles go—but a proud one. It had stood there for many years longer than anyone could remember and was part of the rail system that brought trains from the Northward Corridor down along the Marcel and on to the old capital city Templar. Because the city of Templar fell out of favor with King Nightshade—it was too old and reminded him of the previous monarch—not a lot of trains found themselves crossing this trestle. Except once a year, when the Royal Cauvian Rail was commanded south again to the walled city, where the royal family waited out the dangerous winds in the ancient stone castle.

If you looked very carefully, you might catch the warm light of a lantern underneath the bridge burning at most times of the day or night. For beneath this trestle sat the reclusive trestleman and famed author Axlerod D. Roux. On most days, he could be found working thoughtfully on the thirteenth edition of his famed *Field Guide,* but today he was looking out at the dark air. He was a wise man. He knew that there were great forces at work in his tiny little corner of Caux.

Outside, in the uninvited wind, Ivy Manx discovered she was not alone.

The little window of Cecil's back room let out on their woodpile—made up mostly of discarded oak casks and a few pallets. The weather brought with it little of the daylight she'd expected to see, and after pulling the apotheopath's bag through the window behind her, she turned to spot in the dimness someone rounding the corner.

To her great disappointment, this person was clothed in dark tasters' robes, which were flapping vigorously in the wind. He was rushing at her, almost frantic in his pace. Ivy only had time to cringe, clutching her uncle's satchel, fearing Sorrel Flux upon her.

But his dark hood suddenly flew back in his flight, and with it came a shock of brown curls, and she instead recognized the other taster from the tavern, the sentry's boy. His young features were heightened in his panic. He ran blindly, and he hadn't seen Ivy at all, nor the stack of old barrels she stood upon. This resulted in his colliding noisily with both of them.

"*Shh!*" they admonished each other while looking around the corridor.

Ivy glared at the boy in the moment that followed.

"Why don't you watch where you're going—or do you want the entire king's army coming to see what all the racket is?!"

"I'm sorry, it's these robes. I couldn't see anything." He tried to hug them tighter around him but was thwarted by the wind. He looked simply miserable. "But I think you need not worry about the sentries."

"Why's that?" Ivy asked suspiciously.

"They're all dead—every last one of them. It was the soup."

"What? The soup! That's impossible." Ivy had been making the Bettle's famed soup for the past year, and she said so.

"Well, you've killed twenty of the king's sentries."

Here the pair met with their first disagreement.

"I killed twenty—why, who was it that *tasted* it?" Ivy lowered her voice but increased her glare.

The boy sagged.

"You're right, of course. I'm a miserable taster. I've killed my very first charge!"

"Well." Ivy was feeling bad for the boy. She thought she knew quite clearly who was responsible for the poisoning, and it wasn't him. "Tough luck." She sighed. His misery was catching.

"Yes, yes, it is. Do you even know how many years of school I needed to complete to become a taster? And for what?"

The wind groaned, and a cluster of the casks fell from their perch.

"Where are you going?" the taster asked hopefully.

With this question, Ivy was reminded again of the reality of her plight—the sentries were only one part of the equation, where her former taster and his unsavory friend were the worst of it.

"Aren't you supposed to stay by your charge or something? And wait by the body? Isn't that part of—"

"The Oath." He sighed again.

At another time, Ivy might have enjoyed talking further to this young man—only the second taster she'd ever known and by far a more promising conversationalist. But at present, the man her uncle hired to save her life was intent on just the op-posite, and that fact alone necessitated haste.

Still, she felt a slight responsibility for the boy's predicament—Sorrel Flux was her taster, after all, and surely the reason behind the poisoned soup. And the young taster looked so troubled.

"Oh, fine. Come with me, then. But hurry—and mind your robes!"

It was then that Ivy set out on what was to be the begin-ning of her astonishing story, accompanied by what very well might be the worse of the only two tasters she'd ever met. Per-haps in some ways she might have been safer with the ruthless Mr. Flux.

Chapter Eight

Rowan Truax

Rowan Truax was indeed a bad taster. But it was no fault of his own. He was born in the north, where the land is very flat and a dark, rich black. His parents, and their parents before them—as well as all his neighbors and friends—were farmers. His father farmed mostly pigs, and as anybody knows, the smells of pigs and perfume are nothing alike.

Poor Rowan's sense of smell was doomed from birth, for really, the only way to live a happy life on a pig farm is to not be able to smell a pig farm.

Yet he was a boy of adventure, as many are, and he dreamt of seeing lands other than the flat ones he grew up on (in particular, he dreamt of mountains). The life of a taster would offer him that excitement, as well as the only acceptable alternative to the life of a farmer in his father's eyes.

When he applied to the famed Tasters' Guild, he

neglected to inform them of the ruinous nature of his father's profession upon his tasting abilities, and because Rowan was one of those rare people who were gifted with a carefree nature and some sort of inexplicable fortune, he was accepted to study in Rocamadour—the city of the Guild's headquarters. Indeed an honor for the son of a pig farmer.

Turner Taxus seemed an acceptable employer (Rowan had nothing by which to compare him), and his demise left the young boy despondent at the thought of his flashy career coming to such an abrupt end. He hadn't yet found his feet upon any mountain! There was more—so much more—to see of Caux (he dared not dream of other lands), and he was not one to sit around waiting for a punishment to be meted out—Oath or not.

Back in the dining room, it had become immediately apparent that the other taster—the oddly yellowish one—had not been interested in holding Rowan accountable for his missteps. This was unusual taster behavior indeed. In fact, the strange man had vanished before Rowan could grasp the situation in which he found himself. Soon his own feet had run out the very same door he'd come in by—as if with a will of their own.

And as luck would have it, the young renegade taster chose for his escape route the path that would soon take him to the top of the highest mountains in Caux and places, too, not found upon any map.

There was a small uninhabited footbridge north from the Hollow Bettle, not worthy of a trestleman. It was the only way to cross the river in relative safety and was, in fact, used by many a tavern regular. But Ivy Manx, bag in hand, had other ideas about safety. She directed Rowan south, to the train trestle. They crept and ran along the river's edge.

This was the arena of her childhood playground. At any time of day or night, Ivy could make this walk with confidence. The Marcel was quite narrow here and the views pastoral when not under assault by gale-force winds. Across the river, above the white limestone banks cut by the water, began Southern Wood.

Sorrel Flux, having not spent his childhood playing by the riverside, was not as sure-footed on the limestone banks of the Marcel. (His unremarkable youth was spent recovering from a series of fevers.) He was an awkward outdoorsman at best, probably owing to his preference for fireside warmth, and shunned even ice in his drink—preferring everything on the tepid side. Anything damp, besides his cocktail, made the sinuses in his rather large nose act up. He was a man of very definitive likes and dislikes, to say the least.

Trudging against the wind to the footbridge was easily something that fell into the category of dislikes.

The awful wind was howling at him every step of the way,

at times pushing him several steps back. Progress was slow when haste seemed most urgent. Even with the help of his advantageously large associate—who stood behind him anchoring him to the earth—he seemed to not be getting far.

It was his guess that the young girl, and the bettle with her, was headed this way. But at the little bridge, made from plank and rope and whipping altogether dangerously in the strong wind, Sorrel Flux began to have second thoughts. He'd never found himself near such angry water.

Looking at the bridge, he knew the crossing would be treacherous. He thought at first to send his associate across in his stead, but that would leave him right where he was without protection from the elements.

Mr. Sorrel Flux was beginning to tire of the entire situation. The morning had not gone as planned. And as he was a man to quickly find fault—but never with himself—he cast a dark look at his companion.

"You there," he shouted in as loud a voice as he could. "You need to get the girl or there'll be serious consequences," he squawked.

The bearded man agreed with him.

Before Sorrel Flux could add another injurious comment to his first, the shadowy man was gone—leaving the sorry taster nothing to hold on to besides the flimsy rail of the small bridge.

As Ivy Manx ran along with the wind at her back, she took a moment to think about everything that had happened to her this morning. The pit of dread in her stomach grew as she remembered finding her uncle's medicines. It was completely unlike him to leave them behind. Wouldn't he need them to cure the king?

Yet she had managed to collect her uncle's bettle before it was stolen, and she intended to keep it safe and sound until she could proudly return it to him, wherever he might be. She allowed herself a small moment of congratulation as she hurried.

Had she known, as she ran from the thieves, that it was not the bettle they wanted—it had merely been a tempting distraction—she might have picked up the pace a bit. Sorrel Flux hadn't spent an entire year suffering the whims of Poison Ivy for naught. No, it was not the bettle that he and his associate wanted.

They wanted her.

Chapter Nine

The Trestle

"Which way now?" Rowan yelled to Ivy, who was coming up behind him.

They had reached the embankment where the train tracks rose to cross the river. It was here that the earth dropped off to become the troubled waters of the Marcel below.

"Up," Ivy indicated.

There was a series of footholds where you could boost yourself up onto the tracks—an act at which Ivy was quite accomplished. Rowan, however, was not. It wasn't that he was lacking in athleticism as much as his robes were getting in his way. Each time he lifted a leg to climb, he managed to catch the inside of the garment, treading up the inner lining—an effect that made his neck jerk down in a way that any other time Ivy might find comical.

Not so now.

The sun still refused to arrive; Southern Wood was a massive looming darkness across the river. But where the Marcel cut its ancient path, a patch of lighter sky broke through. It was there that Ivy had seen something silhouetted, moving quickly in their direction from the footbridge.

"Get up!" Ivy cried to the taster frantically. She stooped to give him a boost, regretting inviting him along.

A taster's robes are a curious set of things.

Not only are they a statement of status, if you go in for that sort of thing, but there is a bit of superstition that surrounds them. They are given to the new tasters upon graduation by the reclusive and highly intimidating Director of the Guild, Vidal Verjouce. It is a secret ceremony called the Epistle, and since their many years of schooling are left to the subrectors, the Epistle is the only time the new graduates encounter the Director. Which, they all would agree, is a highly fortunate thing, as the Director's face is one so terrible to behold.

The robes are not meant to be manhandled in the way Ivy was at present; they are to be respected the way one might admire the fine plumage of a peacock or bloom of a morning glory. One is expected to refrain from sullying them and mend or darn any unpreventable rips or tears immediately. The robes represent the office of the Guild and should be treated accordingly.

Although Rowan Truax was finding his robes to be entirely unhelpful at present, he was a graduate of the Guild and as such was finding himself quite annoyed at their current treatment.

"Get off!" he shouted at her as she practically pushed him up the rocky slope. "I can do it myself!"

Ivy stole another look over her shoulder—there was nothing now but darkness on either side of the river. Rowan took it upon himself in this moment to swing his robes up and over his shoulder, revealing a baggy set of unofficial long underwear. Flushed with indignity, he was up on the tracks in a flash and with his newfound freedom reached down for Ivy.

It was at precisely the moment that Rowan's hand encountered Ivy's, and she was halfway hiked up the earthen wall, that a second one grabbed her ankle.

This grip was not nearly as friendly as Rowan Truax's, the hand much larger and ruthless. It belonged to Sorrel Flux's companion, of course, and Ivy knew at once that in a tug-of-war, he would win. There was something altogether frightening about his touch, but that was tame when compared to his merciless eyes. The wind was blowing his black beard in every direction, and he looked much larger and more unsavory than ever before. From his throat issued a deep and utterly fearsome babble, and a mad froth foamed from his lips, adhering to his whiskers.

This was a real calamity. Ivy looked up at Rowan, unable to move and frozen in fear.

"Kick!" he called down to her. "Kick your legs as hard as you can!"

It was fortunate for Ivy that Rowan's advice was excellent—and that he'd shouted it before examining their assailant. For as he did so now, peering down past Ivy amid the snarl of untamed hair, Rowan's courage flickered and then died in his heart. The man's mouth was black and hollow and missing something of great import. He was without his tongue.

Rowan's wrist went weak.

And then, from the north, up the tracks across which Rowan was lying, came suddenly a distant yet insistent clanging.

Ivy, having spent eleven years beside a trestle, knew exactly what was coming their way. Even if it were the policy of the Royal Cauvian Rail to avoid pedestrians—it wasn't, by decree of King Nightshade—the train was much too close to make any sort of emergency stop. If she didn't somehow manage to free herself—even with all her wriggling, the grip on her leg was increasing—Rowan would soon be hit by the approaching train, and she would fall right into the arms of her pursuer.

But salvation came in the form of a streak of shadowy feathers. Emerging from the murky morning came old Shoo, flapping wildly. The crow flew upon the large man in such a fury that he appeared a coal-black tangle of jagged edges and flashing talons. He sought the man's eyes with his beak and slashed at his flesh.

"Shoo!" Ivy called to her uncle's crow. "Watch out—be careful, you brave old thing! *Shoo!*"

Ivy felt the dark man's grip loosen ever so slightly upon her leg, and in no time she was kicking mightily. For a brief moment she thought she might be free, but she saw then the thick arm of her assailant thrash out and unkindly swat her old friend. Shoo was brutally flung to the earth— several downy feathers left floating lazily behind—and to her horror, he remained there quietly, unmoving.

"Shoo!" Ivy called against the din of the approaching train.

She summoned up a year's worth of frustration—picturing the yellow face of Sorrel Flux—and produced an impressive burst of energy. With her free foot squarely on the stranger's face, she pushed off and onto the tracks.

Ivy and Rowan stood up as the train from the Northward Corridor—on time, it would please the king—rounded the slight bend and cast its enormous flickering headlamp upon them. Peering about frantically, she finally located the dark creature. Her heart broke to see Shoo lying impossibly far down the embankment. She could never get to him.

"Uh, hello?" Rowan called—the train's lamplight on his young face getting progressively brighter. "What now?"

At one time in Caux, to travel by train was simply the very best way to see anything and everything at all. Under King Nightshade, things like leisure and holidays were forgotten—or made illegal—and the trains, although still somewhat spectacular, were not what they once were.

So that is how Ivy and Rowan came to face a train once called the Pimcaux Haste, formerly the crown jewel of the RCR's fleet. But, like an aging showgirl, the train was but a shadow of its former self—and rechristened by the Nightshades as the Hollyhock after an innocuous, if somehow mildly toxic, garden weed. The Hollyhock was bearing down on them in a determined way.

With few options, and illuminated in an amber lamplight as bright as the rising sun, Ivy and Rowan turned and began running across the trestle—an unfriendly path over tracks and ties with gaping slits of open air between. Slits that Ivy knew were big enough for even Rowan to slip through.

They sprinted as best they could—Ivy was more accustomed to the task and was making better progress against the train. The pathway required that the two take large leaps over each dangerous opening between the ties, and it was better to not look down at the Marcel below. Ivy's feet found their way on their own, which was fortunate, for her mind was still beside her longtime companion. The last sight of him made her more anxious than ever—the only movement she could see was the wind playing against the feathers of Shoo's once-proud tail.

They were out now far over the water in the rib cage of the rusty trestle. The sound of the oncoming train was louder, echoing across the river unbearably. The design of the bridge was one with little room for pedestrian passage. It looked unlikely that they'd find a place to safely let the train pass unless they slipped out between one of the giant trusses and held on for dear life—something Rowan preferred to not consider.

Rowan Truax was a taster, albeit an uncollared one now, and was not accustomed to thinking quickly on his feet. Tasting, by definition, is slow and steady, requiring deliberate contemplation. A morsel in the mouth can reveal an entire symphony of flavor, with some coaxing.

But Rowan knew that he was running not only from the steely mouth of the Hollyhock, but from the Tasters' Guild itself. The Guild would not tolerate his departure from his charge and meted out harsh punishments to tasters who fled.

"Is it far?" Rowan called to her as they ran. There was no hope of any conversation, though, with the rumbling behind them.

He turned at once to look at the light—something not at all wise—and by the time his eyes readjusted to the dimness of his path, he realized Ivy was gone. There was simply no sign of her at all.

He ran blindly for a few more steps until he lost his footing . . . and felt himself slipping through.

Chapter Ten

Axlerod D. Roux

This particular train trestle differed little from most in Caux in style and substance. It was built upon fortified stone piers and could endure easily not only the weight of a passing train, but the seasonal assault of floodwaters. On either side, iron gridwork rose tastefully into sweeping arches, which for the most part gathered ivy and sheltered pigeon roosts.

And, of course, it was here that one might find—if one knew where to look—one of Caux's trestlemen.

So it was that the young taster was pulled just in time through a miniature version of an altogether normal front door, the kind you might pass on a Sunday stroll through any of Caux's once-genteel cities. It was a tight squeeze. He hardly had time to wonder at what a red-lacquered door was doing in the middle of a train trestle, but indeed, there it was, situated cozily against the rusted partition. A small brass knocker, a minia-ture peephole, a potted plant.

He hurtled to the other side safely, rolled—or was he pushed?—down a small set of stairs, and lay crumpled upon a polished wooden floor on the underside of the trestle. Ab-sently, Rowan noticed the floor had a nice beeswax scent to it.

With the train gone now and the roar of it only a memory in his ears, the room seemed golden with silence. After a mo-ment or two, as his hearing returned, Rowan perceived a crackling fire. He sat up, curious as to what such a door, a fire, and a well-waxed floor were doing beneath a bridge.

The room itself was remarkably well appointed, Rowan thought, although there was the question of scale. It seemed normal in every aspect, except for Ivy, who was sitting on a worn and altogether comfortable-looking leather armchair. She seemed suddenly very big—or the chair quite small. And whatever was in the tiny mug steaming beside her smelled ut-terly delicious; Rowan found himself wondering when he might be asked to have some, too.

And with that, he realized they were not at all alone.

"Oh, courage, courage!" proclaimed a man unlike any Rowan Truax had ever encountered. He was, for one, ex-tremely small. Smaller than Ivy by a great deal. And old—was he old! His face was framed in a mane of gray bushy hair, com-peting in an unruly way with his lengthy beard, which ended in a blunt line as if someone had taken an ax to it. His head was topped off by a dark hat with a shiny brim—a watch cap, Rowan decided—the kind you might see on a train conductor in an old photo. The rest of him, too, was in a similar blue-black sturdy wool suit with silver buttons running up and down the chest. His eyes were unduly watery, and over them he wore an old pair of wire-framed glasses that pinched themselves in place to the bridge of his nose. And stranger still, since Rowan had never before met a trestleman, his face looked entirely and distinctly familiar.

"Did you bring it?" the trestleman was asking Ivy urgently.

"Axle—Shoo's out there, hurt—"

"Did you bring it?" Axle interrupted.

Ivy nodded, indicating the bag, now by her feet.

"Well, that's a relief, then." He sighed. In his small hands was a mug he now suddenly remembered. "Here." He thrust the drink at Rowan offhandedly, and Rowan minded not in the least. It smelled buttery and vaguely like cinnamon sugar.

"Let us see here. . . ." The man was digging through Ivy's satchel, spreading odd pieces of parchment and various forgotten ornaments that tend to gather at the bottom of dark bags.

"Yes, here."

He held the bottle tightly to his chest, and Rowan caught a quick flash of red in the firelight. For a moment, as the bettle blazed, an odd sort of light shone upon the trestle-man's face.

"This, you're sure, is all of it?"

"Except for what I gave Cecil, yes. But why, Axle?"

Rowan, with his mouth fortified by the hot drink, found it working without his intention.

"I can't *believe* it! You're Axlerod D. Roux! I'd know you anywhere! *AWWoww!*" The taster, in his excitement, had jumped to his feet—only to hit his head rather forcefully on a low ceiling beam, spilling the contents of his mug on his white collar.

The trestleman examined the young man in his home with no small amount of displeasure. Tasters reminded him of poisons, which reminded him of the state of the world in which he lived—albeit quietly. His was the time, before the current king, when meals were an occasion of joy, not trepidation. He preferred Caux as it once was—really, not that long ago in trestleman terms. To have a taster from the Tasters' Guild present in his own home was a great inconvenience, and a true test of his graciousness.

Rowan was frantically feeling about the front of his robes. There are many, many hidden pockets for things that tasters find important, such as a little pen and pad of paper, a small golden fork and spoon, a tongue scraper. Rowan found what he was looking for and drew out with some flourish a well-worn copy of *The Field Guide to the Poisons of Caux*. He riffled to the back page and produced for his uninterested companions a sepia-toned photograph of the author and pointed to it excitedly.

"It's you!" And then to Ivy, "It's him! Axlerod D. Roux!

Although you seem somehow smaller in person and less blurry." And upon further recollection, "I thought you lived in Templar."

He looked from the girl to the trestleman eagerly.

"Really." Ivy rolled her eyes. "Pull yourself together! It's just Axle." Ivy, having been in the enviable position of growing up with a trestleman for a playmate, was unimpressed with Axle's reputation of distinction.

"You are my *favorite* author in all of Caux!" Rowan blurted, ignoring Ivy.

At this, there was a slight softening around the trestleman's eyes. Perhaps this taster wasn't as bad as he thought. He certainly seemed well educated. Perceptive.

Ivy sniffed. Her mind was elsewhere, and even the revitalizing powers of a trestleman's hot buttered cider could not lift her spirits. Giving Rowan an unforgiving look, she turned to the trestleman.

"Axle, Shoo looked horribly hurt! I left him out there with that . . . that—" Ivy shivered.

"Outrider," Rowan finished her sentence dully. His own mood was instantly dampened by the memory of their tongueless persecutor. To make matters worse, he couldn't stand up properly in this small house and being in the shadow of his idol was very disconcerting—all of which made him slightly flushed, to his great chagrin.

"Outrider?" the trestleman asked at once—sharply.

"What's an Outrider?" Ivy asked. Annoyed, she realized Cecil might have a point about the importance of studying.

"An Outrider." Rowan cleared his throat as if back in the classroom. "An Outrider is a 'disgraced former taster—made to serve the Guild and its Director for past misdeeds. He shall be forever dishonored and punished in a secret procedure called a' "—here Rowan gulped—" '*degulleting*. Or the surgical removal of the tongue.' "

"Is this true?" Ivy wondered.

"Of course," Axle replied. "I wrote it."

"*That* was an Outrider?" asked Ivy. The memory of kicking his face seemed even more pleasing with his newfound importance.

Rowan was somber at the thought of how much he currently enjoyed the use of his own tongue. "I first noticed him in the tavern, although he kept to the shadows. He was with another taster—or at least someone wearing some old ragtag robes. . . ."

"Flux," Ivy told Axle.

"Flux with an Outrider—how very . . . interesting," Axle muttered, more to himself than his present company.

"They were after Cecil's bettle—I came down just in time!"

"Well done!" Axle again held up the gleaming amber bottle. The jewel caught the light from the hearth, and again the threesome was dazzled by it. The red stone was lozenge-shaped and appeared to be about the size of Ivy's thumb, smooth and facetless. The amber fluid flickered like liquid fire.

"It's . . . it's a wonderful specimen," Rowan allowed. "So unusual—that flaw." It was cracked in a way that made it look hollow, and Rowan hoped he sounded appropriately knowledgeable. He had in him ingrained from the Guild a deep respect for the jewels—as signifiers of power and prestige, as charms against poison—and although he never, in fact, had held one, he was quite certain that they weren't supposed to break.

"Indeed." Axle nodded.

"But—" It was Rowan's intention to pursue the bettle's strangeness further, when Ivy interrupted him.

"This one here"—Ivy indicated the taster—"killed off all twenty of King Nightshade's sentries!"

"Is that so?" Axlerod, who was decidedly less of a fan of the current king than just about anyone could be, was beginning to like his newest guest.

The trestleman looked at his friend Poison Ivy. He took a deep breath. An Outrider in his small corner of Caux could mean only one thing.

Chapter Eleven

The Cinquefoil

To consult Axle's *Field Guide* for clarification on the children's current host, you would be quite stymied. Here it is maddeningly incomplete, perhaps from a sense of humility that most trestlemen share, and lists the following simple characterization:

trestlemen (n. pl.): an ancient breed of tinkerers found beneath many of Caux's train trestles and usually near water

But make not the mistake of thinking all trestlemen are alike—for that would be like thinking all children to be similar simply because they are smallish, and playful, and generally smell nice.

Indeed, Axlerod D. Roux, like all trestlemen, was undeniably small. And quite old. An older race would be hard to find within the boundaries of Caux, or elsewhere. And they are known far and wide for their profound respect for the solitary life. In almost all respects, they are a breed of clever inventors, with each trestleman's expertise being as unpredictable as the next's.

But one of the most surprising things, especially in this day and age, is what simply wonderful cooks they are. If you ever find yourself at a trestleman's table, you are a lucky soul indeed.

So it was over a bountiful breakfast that Axle sat with his good friend Poison Ivy and the runaway taster Rowan Truax. After assuring the pair that Shoo would be tended to when all was safe, Axle refused to discuss anything further until everyone was seated in front of a generous plate—which he produced somehow in no time at all.

There were honeyed clusters of puff pastry, oozing with fresh vanilla cream and dusted with sugar. Stacks of fruited pancakes dripping with melting butter and warm syrup. Pitchers of frothy hot chocolate and steamed cider. Buttery, flaky ham biscuits. Hot, savory corn scones filled with rich gravy. Tiny, delicate eggs, hard-boiled, in a variety of subtle shades of purple and blue—carefully piled in a simple pottery bowl, with small highly scented violets bursting out from in between. And in the middle, a single beautiful wildflower.

They couldn't wait to dig in, and each filled up their little plates—stacking the delicacies sky-high. But the small yellow wildflower—with its delicate scent—distracted Ivy.

"Axle, that flower," Ivy said suddenly, forgetting her mouth was full. She peered in closer, squinting. "Is that what I think it is?"

Ivy stared at Axle wide-eyed, and Axle, in turn, looked quite pleased with himself.

"What?" Rowan asked the pair, who seemed to be wasting their time on a small yellow flower rather than savoring the delicacies before them.

"It is indeed!" Axle cried.

"Wow!" Ivy leaned in to smell it. "How did this happen?"

"It bloomed just this morning." Axle's eyes sparkled.

"A cinquefoil!" Ivy sighed. "But what does that mean, Axle?" she asked, suddenly quite serious.

Rowan searched his memory of the *Field Guide* for any reference to a cinquefoil.

"Um. Excuse me. But isn't that flower . . . criminal? I mean, prohibited by Proclamation of King . . . *er* . . . Nightshade?" Although he couldn't say why, Rowan felt suddenly foolish using the king's name at such a feast.

"You have much to unlearn, taster." The trestleman's eyes flashed, and Rowan instantly regretted speaking. But Axle relaxed momentarily, the effort of his bitterness exhausting him. He sighed deeply.

"The cinquefoil is a noble flower. It was chosen, after all, to be upon the Good King Verdigris's own crest. And, in turn, became the symbol of every apotheopath. Now, like apotheopaths, they are a thing of great rarity."

"I've never even seen one bloom!" Ivy added.

"The thing about this flower, the cinquefoil, is its peculiar nature. Plants—all plants—have secrets. To unlock them is power, as the apotheopaths knew. Many plants seek out specific conditions. We know certain mosses favor the north sides of trees—surely a helpful fact for anyone lost in a forest. But did you know some grow where gold is buried and can make your fortune? Others bloom only in ghostly moonlight, guarding lost or buried secrets. And some plants, well, some can even make you king. But the little cinquefoil is truly rare." Axle looked from Ivy to Rowan and continued in a hushed tone.

"Ivy has never before seen one bloom, because the cinquefoil only grows in the presence of magic."

Rowan looked around, as if he might spy some magic himself.

"Apotheopaths?" he repeated the word thoughtfully. He knew them to be quacks, snake-oil salesmen at best. The Tasters' Guild had taught him over the years how dangerous a trip to these hacks could be—they were hardly respected physicians, after all, preferring instead to rely on ancient teachings, consult books in the old tongue, and gather their medicines from the countryside rather than an approved druggist.

"I was taught that apotheopaths were a sorry chapter from the history books—none exist today thanks to the diligence of King Nightshade," Rowan said quietly.

"King Nightshade's diligence is a discussion for another time. But I can't fault you for believing the teachings you received at the Guild—you are a victim of an education of half-truths. I can, however, offer to correct your misperceptions. Apotheopaths exist. But they are a dying breed—of which Ivy's uncle is one."

"Ivy's uncle is an *apotheopath*?" He whistled. "I thought he was a tavern keeper."

"Well, he's both," Ivy managed amid a mouthful of potato fritter.

"And a far better apotheopath than a tavern keeper." Axle smiled.

Rowan sat back to listen, determined to keep still. Yet he did notice that it was becoming increasingly hard for him to understand how the subrectors at the Guild could be so wrong.

Axle's eyes came to rest upon the amber bottle framed neatly in his tiny dining room window. "Rocamadour wasn't intended to be at all as you know it," he said flatly.

At the mention of the Tasters' Guild's dark headquarters, Rowan found himself shuddering involuntarily.

"What do you mean? It wasn't built for the Guild?"

"Of course not," said Axle, irritated. "It was built many, many years before there was ever a taster to taste a questionable meal. It *was* built as a school, actually, but the Good King Verdigris had a different sort of learning in mind."

"King Verdigris." Rowan hesitated. "I thought all his good works have been discounted."

"Is that what they teach you? I suppose it's not in King Nightshade's interest to teach his predecessor's history. He and Vidal Verjouce—your Guild's Director, but really a man in many ways more dangerous than your king—have seen to it that the legacy of the old king is buried and forgotten. As with most things he touches, Nightshade made Rocamadour into the dark and foreboding fortress it is today. At one time, the Good King Verdigris even held it up as his most treasured accomplishment—and that's saying quite a lot, as the man lived the length of many lifetimes, and from his hands came a great many things."

Rowan thought about Rocamadour, its dark clusters of stone buildings, its perpetual gray weather. The streets were thin and paved in cobblestones covered in a creeping moss that grew up and over most everything—even the massive black spire atop the cathedral. This was where most of the Guild's learning took place.

It was hard to think of the place as anything other than severe, and Rowan told the trestleman so.

"It's true. Although I haven't been there in a while, I can't imagine it's changed too much. But Verdigris meant it as a school of learning, where all distractions might disappear. Perhaps that is why it was built so. It was meant in its day as an academy for apotheopaths, a place to study the art of healing.

It was said to have the largest library in all the land." Axle glanced toward his study, sadly. He knew what little was left of that famous library could be found in it.

"I mentioned the fortress was said to be the king's greatest accomplishment, but I have my own favorites."

"Oh, Axle, do tell us about your favorites!" Ivy pleaded.

"Perhaps another time. Right now, we should help this young Guild graduate unlearn his years of schooling, and teach him the proper way to eat!"

And with that, the trestleman reached in and served himself an enormous plateful of cream puffs.

Chapter Twelve

The Doorway

The place where the world-famous Axlerod D. Roux did all of his important writing was a place to which even Ivy was not privy. His study was off the main room, with a pleasant view of the water—the river being one of his most favorite inspirations. The room was a largish one, with ample space for any trestleman, were it not for the incredible amount of literature Axle had amassed over his long years. Enormous hulking leather-bound books threatened to collapse their feeble shelves, and stacks of parchment and leaflets created odd pathways around the floor.

But there was a sort of order to things the longer you stayed in the room, or so Axle maintained.

The trestleman was helped immensely by an old invention of his, a crisscrossing system of pulleys and levers so confusing to the outsider—although there never *were* any outsiders—that one might conjure up any excuse at all to remain safely by the exit. These levers and pulleys advanced several sets of pincers attached to various lengths of accordion-like limbs, grabbing a book or magnifying lens at whim. The result was that Axle was never very far at all from a reference book or anything he might need in his research while he was seated at his handsome, sturdy desk.

Opening the heavy wooden door to Axle's study, Ivy Manx could not believe her luck. She had always wanted to see this room, and Axle, until today, had never invited her. Rowan, too, was in silent awe and held his breath in expectation. This was where it all happened—where his favorite author wrote! After breakfast they didn't think things could get any more exciting, but Axle had pushed his chair back from the table and stood—albeit not very high—and announced that he had something to show the children in his study.

"Come, come, come!" he called, making his way with great speed through tall barricades of reading material. He began flicking switches and levers, and the crisscrossing cables on the ceiling hummed to life.

He soon was lost to the towering literature.

"Axle?" Ivy called out, but the ceiling's drone was all that answered.

Picking her way slowly, she almost collapsed a tall stack of dusty books, which teetered distressingly high above her head and surely would have crushed her had Rowan not caught them in time. The ensuing cloud of dust caused the taster to sneeze loudly, sending a yellowed stack of old correspondence scattershot through the air. Ivy had hardly recovered when several books came flying by, at shoulder level, the pincers straining with their weight. She managed to dodge the first two—identical, ancient-looking texts easily as big as a trestleman—but the third nearly crashed into her at top speed. With an unfortunate grinding noise and an odd burning smell, the complex pulley system rerouted the book right over her head in the nick of time and off to the oblivious trestleman. At his desk beside the window, Axle received the deliveries distractedly and opened the top one from the stack. He looked over his shoulder impatiently.

"Ivy? Rowan? Do hurry!"

They arrived finally, and Axle began at once to flip through the enormous pages of the open volume. This would be hard going for anyone, but for a small trestleman it was a feat of athleticism. He muttered under his breath, and Ivy had the impression that he did this often. Finally, after resorting to the aid of one of his pincers, he found the page he was looking for.

"You asked me before about my favorite of Verdigris's creations."

He unhooked his wire-rimmed glasses from his nose and gestured with them at the open book.

"This one is it."

Ivy and Rowan peered in wide-eyed. Although the size

of the page was immense, the writing it contained was a tiny, ancient script. It was arranged in columns around a central image: a drawing, in the same hand as the lettering, in pen and ink.

"A door?" Ivy couldn't help herself. After the tales she'd heard from Axle over the years, it seemed a great disappointment that this might be the Good King Verdigris's crowning achievement.

Rowan, too, peered in closer.

The drawing of the door was quite well done, very realistic. The ink was a faded brown, and the door appeared to be one of quality, but plain, with very normal doorlike attributes. Wood. A set of insets, a pleasing polish. Hinges. There was a round knocker in the middle, made of metal—painted in what appeared to be real gold leaf. Perhaps the only thing missing was a doorknob, but that hardly made it something to marvel at.

Ivy couldn't disguise her disappointment. She was hoping for a moment that she might riffle through the rest of this enormous book—perhaps there were better things than doors to see. All the stories she'd heard over the years from Axle, as well as the tall tales from the motley set of tavern regulars she'd grown up with, made Ivy a girl with high expectations. A door, no matter how well drawn, would just not do.

As if reading her mind, Axle directed the pincer nearest to him to turn the page. Ivy's expectations rose—and then were

dashed. Sure enough, another door. Or was it the same door from a different angle? Ivy scoffed.

"The other side of the door?" Rowan asked. He was more patient, basking in the presence of the great writer.

"Exactly!" Axle couldn't contain his excitement. He seemed quite satisfied with himself.

"But, Axle." Ivy couldn't hold back. "You said that the Good King Verdigris created great things, things to marvel at. *This is just a door!* Show me this Rocamadour place! Got any drawings of that?"

Rowan bristled at the mention of the dark city of the Guild and thought how he'd be quite happy staring at either side of a plain old door instead. He looked in closer.

"Ah, Ivy. You are right—it is just a door. But there is an important question you need to ask yourself." Axle sighed.

"May I?" Rowan was hoping to turn back the page to get a better look at the first image. Axle nodded and continued.

"What do you think of when you see a door?"

Rowan gave a tug on the cable attached to the pincer, and obediently, the enormous page turned.

"I don't know. Something that's locked?"

"That's odd. There's no knob. And look—here. The pages after these two are missing! Look at the binding—someone's torn them from the book!" Rowan announced.

It was true—Ivy saw evidence of a hasty removal. Rowan,

whose favorite possession was his *Field Guide,* was aghast at such disrespect.

"Yes, these books were sadly mismanaged at one point." Axle returned to the topic at hand. "What else might you think of about a door?"

Ivy thought.

"Where does it *go*?" she asked.

Axle beamed.

"Exactly!"

The trestleman was perfectly satisfied in his response and didn't seem to notice the children were waiting for him to finish.

After an excruciating moment, Ivy burst out with the question on both her and Rowan's minds.

"Well?"

"Well, what?"

"Axle, the door. Where does it go?"

"Oh, I thought that was self-evident. To Pimcaux! The door goes to Pimcaux."

Chapter Thirteen

Pimcaux

"*P imcaux?*" both Ivy and Rowan echoed at once. Ivy remembered her uncle's tales of windmills and alewives, its pastures and . . . But this was impossible! Pimcaux was nothing more than wishful thinking on the part of Caux's grim citizens—a place filled with all the happy endings their dreary lives were missing.

"Axle, there's no real place called Pimcaux!" Ivy admonished.

The trestleman merely rocked back and forth on his heels and gestured at the enormous tome.

The children peered in closer to Axle's ancient book—Rowan still grasping the pincer's pull cord in his hand and Ivy on her tiptoes for a better look.

Perhaps it was the little cinquefoil—the Good King's flower—in bloom in the other room, working its magic beneath the trestle. Or perhaps it was the Good King's very own books at work, causing the cinquefoil to awaken. But either way—and these are questions for the sages to debate at another time (and Axle would happily oblige)—the two children found the enormous journals of Verdigris to be suddenly rather more than lifelike.

For one, the heavy golden knocker was emitting a shine of convincing reality against the old paper upon which it sat. Ivy reached out before she knew it and found it to be of satisfying weight and proportion in her hand. She held her breath and knocked.

The golden ring at first made a dull sort of noise against the image of the door—the kind you might expect from a paperweight. But when she knocked again, there was a noticeable change in timbre, and as Ivy and Rowan looked at each other in amazement, the knocking began to sound crisper, clearer, less of a thud and more of a rap, until the knocker tapped sharply upon something that looked like paper but very much sounded like wood.

Extraordinarily, Axle and his quaint study were now being taken over by shadow. The fine script on the pages reorganized itself into larger, more familiar letters but quickly dissipated like sand in the wind. This was of little concern to Ivy and Rowan. They heard the sound of whispering now, of a harsh insistent murmur, and in the silence that followed, the pages of the giant book began turning themselves at a devastatingly rapid rate—gone was the realistic door now, replaced with an enormous curtain of shadow.

As they peered still into the now-dark book, Ivy found she was holding Rowan's hand.

And then, suddenly, the dark shadow was gathered up by invisible hands and there was a brightening in the dimness—but still the scene was achingly hard to discern. A weak shaft of pale light on the side of a wrinkled old face. A hushed, choking sigh. A man seated on a throne of extraordinary beauty but with the posture not of a ruler—rather, of a man in defeat. He slumped, holding his head in his hand, nodding.

Behind him, still very much obscured in the twilight that infused the entire scene, was another man, a tall man. He stood before shelves of enormous books, a library of sorts; the golden letters of each volume glittered even in the low light. He was speaking in hushed tones, counseling his king. The words were unintelligible—harsh whispers on ill wind.

The king nodded, a slight nod, but hardly moved. His advisor straightened, and in doing so a beam of light caught his face. With a start, Rowan recognized him at once. A deep chill passed over the back of the young taster's neck. He was seeing the Director—his Director—as a much younger man. But even more shocking, he was seeing Verjouce as he was born, before he was blinded into the hideous specter he was now.

Vidal Verjouce's eyes were pale as water. And Rowan couldn't help but feel they were searching him out, even in this vision, scanning the corners of the stately room for eavesdroppers. He instinctually took a step back.

But it was not the children whom Verjouce's eyes finally set upon. In the corner, being dismissed by the king's sole advisor, was a small group of men—*trestlemen*, Ivy and Rowan realized. There, amid the shocked group, was Axle. They had come hoping to sway the king from his deep sadness, but Vidal Verjouce's hold upon him was already too tight. It was too late. The children were witnessing the end of the kingdom.

Verjouce counseled the king to send the visitors away, to banish them all—every last one of them—to a place where their particular nuisance could not be felt.

Ivy's heart ached as she watched.

But now the dark mists returned to the library, and even as Rowan tried his best to steal one last look at the youthful Axle, the vision darkened and soon the pair was once again in Axle's study—the whir of his pincers and cables above them.

"What sort of book is this?" Rowan managed. "If I had books like that at school, I might have studied more."

"Ah, but you did. Once, the library of Rocamadour was filled with similar magical books."

"Oh, Axle!" Ivy cried. "That was you! You were there—with King Verdigris!"

The trestleman was somber.

"What happened? Why did the king send you all away?" Ivy asked.

"The king had just sealed the Doorway. To Pimcaux."

"Sealed? But why?"

The children were stunned. If everything they'd heard about Pimcaux was true, it was most certainly a place they wanted to visit. But now, to hear that the door was closed?

"But why was he—King Verdigris—so morose?" Rowan wondered.

"He had, at his side, a sinister counselor, among other things," Axle replied. "He was in mourning, remember."

"In mourning? For who?" asked Ivy.

"All this history is in my book, children."

"Begging you pardon," Rowan said after a pause, "it isn't." Rowan was indeed sure that the *Field Guide* contained little if any reference to the old king—certainly not a detailed history, which might be found treasonous.

"Oh, I think you'll find otherwise." The trestleman's eyes twinkled. "You just need to look harder."

Rowan thought he couldn't wait to do so.

"Once the Good King went into mourning," Axle continued on, "he never recovered. He stopped performing great feats of wonder. He had the Doorway to Pimcaux sealed and wiped all memory of it from his thoughts. He allowed no one to see him, except his trusted advisor, the man you saw there just now. Vidal Verjouce.

"But realize this: up until Verjouce, poison was unknown in Caux. Plants were used to heal! They were respected and rejoiced—not used angrily and carelessly. What a different place it was to live! Caux was a land of apotheopaths, who respected the art of healing."

Rowan was still shaken from the experience of seeing the Guild's Director so close, so young. The image of Verjouce's eyes searching him out would stay with him for many nights.

"With Verjouce at the Guild's helm, Caux became what it is now. Healers became poisoners—and Verjouce installed himself in the seat of power at Rocamadour. The dark forests were breached, and the more potent herbs were harvested for ill use."

They sat silently. Rowan was conflicted. Everything he thought he knew—being a taster in the realm of King Nightshade and the years of schooling at Verjouce's esteemed Guild—was now all muddled.

The trestleman was at his favorite place by the window, with a pair of opera glasses being held to his eyes by one of his pincers.

"The Crown has taken over the Bettle. Nightshade works quickly when it comes to taxes."

Indeed, reinforcements had arrived and were busy flying the Belladonna—King Nightshade's purple flag—from Cecil's rusty old flagpole.

Ivy realized heavily that there was no going home. She suddenly felt quite drained.

Removing the spyglass and replacing his pince-nez a bit askew, Axle turned back to the pair.

"The time has come. Perhaps," he said, wrapping his small body in his substantial greatcoat, "I might ask you both to meet me in the parlor?"

Chapter Fourteen

The Return of Shoo

The trestleman had left the pair in the company of mugs of steamed milk and a plate of meringues, which did much to better only the first few minutes of their wait. They were both quiet, the mood a thoughtful one after their experience in Axle's study. Ivy watched as Rowan stood and fidgeted uncomfortably from foot to foot, and they both separately wondered at Axle's whereabouts. Rowan found himself drawn to the brightest thing in the room—the cracked red bettle in the old brandy bottle. It still rested upon the window ledge and, for the taster, imparted upon all the proceedings a sense of legitimacy.

When finally the trestleman returned to the parlor, he seemed to bring in a bit of the cold with him, and he held beneath his small arm a tight package of some sort.

"Pardon my delay," Axle began. "I had to wait until it was safe." He set down his package on the table with bright eyes. He began unwrapping the shroud that covered his parcel.

"Pass me that, please," the trestleman ordered.

Rowan looked helplessly around.

"That," Axle said, looking up. "Ivy's bottle! Quickly!"

Rowan did as ordered, watching Axle remove the cover of the balsa box he held. At first in the low light the box appeared empty, but peering in closer, both Ivy and Rowan gasped. It was, in fact, quite full, containing a knot of the deepest black feathers in the shape of a motionless crow.

"Oh, Shoo!" Ivy reached to touch.

"Is he . . . ?" Rowan couldn't finish his sad thought.

"He's alive. But just barely."

Axle busied himself with the delicate wire that laced the cork securely in the bottle, and once it was freed, he pulled the stopper deftly, resulting in a satisfying *pop*. Retrieving a small glass the size of a thimble, Axle poured a mere token of a drop into it and, finding the crow's beak, transferred it again ever so carefully into the animal's mouth.

"That should do it," the trestleman muttered.

"Axle, what in the world are you doing?" Ivy demanded.

Rowan's eyes widened at the cloying scent that filled the room. "That smell!" the taster whispered.

"Appalling, isn't it? Stopper it up, why don't you?" Axle ordered.

"No—I mean, I think I recognize it," said Rowan.

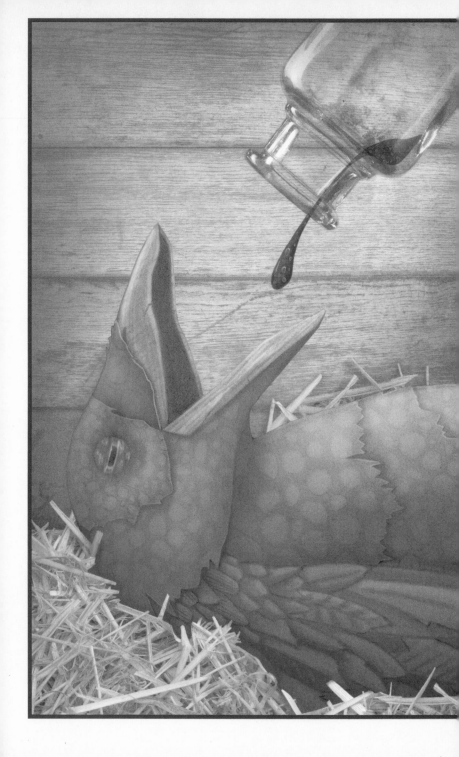

Axle waved his small hand dismissively.

"It's not what you think. It's Ivy's attempt at Aqua Artilla."

"My *last* attempt."

"I'm sure Rowan would agree the scent of the queen's perfume lacks all subtlety. Your uncle, when he interrupted you, saw you pour the infusion back into the bottle—but he need only have used his nose."

"The queen's poison! That's the worst kind!" Rowan's voice was shrill.

"Hardly. It doesn't do a thing," Ivy answered glumly.

"In fact"—the trestleman looked at Ivy—"just the opposite."

The children watched Shoo closely for signs of distress.

The crow had slowly come to look as if it had been placed in the sun—the ruffled and dust-coated feathers unified again into a lustrous ordered pattern, gleaming with a light of their own. A ripple of life swept up and through them, like a wind blowing against the grain, and tiny dust motes spun crazily in the draft. As the two watched, a small black eye opened like a shiny button, blinked once, and then again. The old crow let out a small caw.

Rowan whistled. "What's *in* that?" he asked, turning to Ivy.

Ivy's face was quite pale. Stunned as she was at Shoo's miraculous recovery, she was even more surprised at the part her elixir played in it.

"Nothing that should do that!" she croaked.

Axle turned his attention to Shoo and whispered softly, and Ivy held out her arm. Soon the crow was perched upon it unsteadily.

"Remarkable," Rowan muttered.

The three were silent as Shoo began the job of preening himself. Rowan stared darkly at the amber bottle.

"Did Cecil know what my elixir could do?" Ivy suddenly wondered.

Axle nodded.

"So that must be why he left his medicines behind," she figured. "I found them when I was running from Flux and the Outrider."

"He had all he needed," Axle replied.

While Ivy busied herself with the reunion with Shoo, Rowan stepped closer to Axle.

"Mr. D. Roux—"

"You can call me Axle."

"Um, Axle. Something's been bothering me. I was wondering just what exactly an Outrider was doing chasing us in the first place."

"Yes, yes. A good question. Any ideas of your own?"

"I don't know." Rowan was thoughtful. "Because I poisoned all those sentries . . . ?"

"An Outrider? He hunts bigger game than uncollared tasters."

"Yes, I suppose." Rowan was relieved.

"Outriders are first and foremost servants of the Guild. They do only Verjouce's bidding."

"Well, what did he want, then?"

Axle paused and seemed to consider his words carefully. He stared fondly across the room at Ivy's back, her light hair a fine contrast beside the crow. She brushed her knuckles on the underside of Shoo's beak, talking softly to the bird. The trestleman wanted so very badly not to alarm the girl, and leaned in to the taster.

"I assume you are familiar with the Prophecy?" Axle asked after some inner debate.

Rowan thought hard.

"The Prophecy of the Noble Child?" Axle prompted impatiently.

"No." Rowan shook his head, quite sure. Nothing of the sort appeared in the *Field Guide,* and as he was readying himself to make just this point, Axle interrupted.

"No? I don't supposed they'd teach you that at the Guild. The Prophecy was written long ago, but the ancient pages have gone missing from their binding." Axle paused. "It is said that a child of noble birth—a child of extraordinary circumstance—will banish the darkness from the forests, evil from where it dwells, and restore Caux to truth and light." Axle peered at the taster intently.

"How will this happen?" Rowan was wide-eyed.

"The child must cure the king."

"Oh." Rowan frowned. This seemed entirely unlikely, but he held his tongue.

"The Outrider was not searching for you, Rowan Truax. Look to the Estate of Turner Taxus, if you fear being followed. You abandoned your charge, your Oath. The Taxus family are an . . . *interesting* clan—and they will surely search for you. And it's their right. They are many in number, as I'm sure you know."

Rowan nodded glumly.

"No, the Outrider was here performing Verjouce's bidding"—Axle's voice soured at the Director's name—"and in search of the Noble Child."

Chapter Fifteen

Repose

The trestleman left Rowan to squeeze into a small daybed in the parlor while he walked Ivy down the narrow hall, Shoo perched comfortably on her shoulder. It was agreed they should leave for Templar posthaste, since it was there that Axle thought Ivy's uncle to be found, but he insisted that the children rest before they departed. Stopping at the entrance to a little guest room, Axle opened the door.

Although unaccustomed to guests, he was impeccably prepared for them. The room was a vision of hospitality, but it was a delicious little bed that Ivy saw first, and although it was trestleman-sized, it was wonderfully suited to the proportions of an eleven-year-old girl.

The room had a small window, and Axle reached to discreetly close the curtains against the hive of Nightshade activity at the tavern. Shoo flew to a side table, where the little yellow cinquefoil now rested. Axle placed a pile of seeds from his waistcoat pocket beside the crow.

"There. That should do it. Are you sure there isn't anything I can get you—some warm milk? Sweet tea?"

"Oh, Axle, I'm just fine." She stifled a yawn. "I think I'll just rest now, for a moment."

Ivy sat back on the softest, fluffiest bed she'd ever felt. It seemed to be made entirely of eiderdown, and the second she settled upon it, she nearly disappeared within it. Her eyes were having trouble remaining open. The small man sighed deeply.

"Now, with the arrival of the sentries, I must say it confirms my fear that your uncle's errand has failed. He is, at best, waylaid."

Ivy was of the same opinion and managed to mumble so. The day's events had caught up to her.

"He went in your stead, you know. To Templar. He hoped to cure the king with your elixir and thereby have you avoid the destiny that now calls you."

"What destiny?"

Shoo let out a low, throaty grumble.

"Cecil was always very hopeful of your abilities. He saw in them an opportunity for greatness. But he was worried you weren't prepared." Ivy thought that sounded a lot like Cecil. She thought of the tavern, her workshop and secret experiments. Her accidental elixir—it had healed Shoo! It seemed to her that Cecil, once she found him, would have less right to be so demanding about her studies.

But for now her destiny would have to wait while she rested. Her eyes were closing despite themselves, and Axle covered her gently.

"I've always wanted to go to Templar," she announced dreamily. "But the Deadly Nightshades . . ."

"There is nothing to worry about—not now. Trust this old man when he says things are not often as dreadful as they seem. Haven't I always told you that you are meant for even brighter prospects than you can imagine or dream? Sleep now, so that you will awaken closer to them."

It was in these dreams that Ivy finally got her first look at Cecil's apotheopathic remedies. She unwrapped the soft leather that enclosed the clinking ampoules and, heart beating, ran her fingers along them. And, in the way that dreams have, Cecil was there, too, smiling at her thoughtfully, and she knew what he was about to say. That only with time and practice would she be able to master them.

Chapter Sixteen

Flight

Working with Turner Taxus had involved a lot of travel, but the taster never got used to the disconcerting feeling of waking up and not knowing where he was. The tiny bed hadn't been a restful match—he'd curled up on it anyway, yet somehow his eyes would not shut. Rather, they were drawn to Ivy's elixir in the brandy bottle, and the red bettle inside it, sitting on the small table. His dreams finally did come, anxious and fleeting. In the morning, he staggered from the parlor.

Ivy was already up and, judging from appearances, had been for some time. Her face was alive with excitement at her reunion with Shoo, and the old bird shifted back and forth on his spindly legs. Axle had hot cocoa ready for Rowan, and Ivy was already holding hers, blowing on it impatiently.

"Morning," Rowan offered, but then wondered just exactly what time it was. It was a bright day; the morning's subtle tones were gone.

"Did you sleep well?" Axle asked the young taster. "I am sorry if the train disturbed you. I must say I was quite surprised to hear one come through—highly irregular. Back in the day, trains kept to schedules."

"Train? What train?" Rowan was bleary-eyed—it seemed he'd dozed off after all.

"Ah—you're a good sleeper, then! Ivy was less fortunate."

Axle was putting the finishing touches on an enormous picnic basket. "I've taken the liberty to pack some provisions for the trip."

It was handmade by tiny fingers, woven of delicate river fronds, lightweight and indestructible. Rowan couldn't help but picture Axle out for an afternoon's scavenge, harvesting the reeds that pleased him. As he stared happily at the basket, Axle retrieved the bettle bottle from the parlor.

"You must hurry to Templar. But you'll have to be ever mindful of the Estate of Turner Taxus, of course. Mindful, really, of *everything*." He looked pointedly at Rowan. "The tongue is your lone guardian."

Ivy smiled at him. "He means, watch what you eat."

"Won't you come, too?" Rowan cried.

"Me?!" Axle was taken aback. He looked from Ivy to the taster and back again.

"Axle doesn't get out much," Ivy offered. "Trestlemen don't like leaving their trestle. They get, well, *nervous*."

"Trestlemen get nothing of the sort. It's just—it's highly

unnatural, that's all. Besides, I am hard at work on the thir-teenth edition—with a strict deadline." Axle adjusted his pince-nez and looked at Rowan uncomfortably, clearing his throat. "I did, however, inscribe you something inside your *Guide.* You'll have to be content with that, until the next time we meet."

Rowan jumped to his feet, nearly hitting his head again, and clutched his beloved book as the trestleman returned it to him. Indeed, within the front cover was a flourish of thick ink in small and neat handwriting, followed with a valiant autograph.

Taste and Inform.

"The Tasters' Credo." Rowan looked up from the page.

"Good instructions." Axle nodded. To Ivy, the trestleman said, "You carry that bettle, remember, inside the bottle. People are attracted to it—and never the right people. And above all, guard the elixir. Your success depends upon it."

She stowed the small bottle in her waistband carefully.

"Start through the Wood," Axle continued, referring to Southern Wood—the dark expanse of ancient trees to the south of the mill house. "It is still the only way to avoid Roca-madour. If you get lost or are ever in danger, know that you have safe passage wherever you might find a trestle or bridge.

"But I offer this piece of advice: make haste! Head to Templar before the Winds hit. There is a bridge there—a truly spectacular bridge, quite an old one. The Knox. It leads you into the city of Templar. There are shops and restaurants built right upon it, and many generations of trestlemen call it their home. The Knox is an ancient place for honest trade and exchange of conventional ideas. A gathering place. And my brother lives there."

At this, Ivy was surprised. "You never told me you had a brother, Axle!"

"Yes. Ask for Peps. Peps D. Roux. If there's any news of Cecil Manx, I'll have it waiting there with him. I shall write him to expect you."

Without much more delay, the children were to leave their friend's house, with a renewed spirit of adventure upon them. Shoo was to stay behind, ostensibly to complete his recovery, but Rowan thought perhaps Ivy worried the trestleman might suffer from loneliness at her departure. And since Ivy had much to learn before she might employ Cecil's medicine kit, it, too, would stay with Axle and await its rightful owner.

In his home below the tracks, with the olive-colored water flowing softly beneath the floorboards, Axle retreated quietly to his study and his desk.

From the window he watched the scarlet birds as they dipped in flight, sipping up small bugs on the water's surface. A fine mist rolled about, hitting the caked mud walls and tumbling against itself. The fog cleared, a sheer glass revealed beneath—the water only disturbed in small circles where fish were feeding. The reflection was perfect—the trees overhanging mirrored in the water, the large waterfowl flying upstream in the distance. The trestle's belly reflected back at itself.

He found the beauty of the river could still send a wave of emotion through his old bones.

It is of some note that the train that had earlier roused Ivy from her sleep was destined for Templar.

It was a lush train for this day and age, still with a good polish and kept up quite well. It was filled with every amenity

that the Guild's Director desired. The lettering on its side, in a rich gold script, proclaimed its name to be Ambrosia. And aboard it was Ivy's previous taster, Mr. Sorrel Flux, who after wrestling with the wind on the little footbridge was now treating himself to a spiked cup of hot marigold tea.

Part 11

Elixir

Oh, lady, what could it be in your pretty potion, please,
Tell me, what do you put in there?
A pinch of the sun, a slice of the moon,
With great care I prepare the despair.

—an etching upon a Cauvian gravestone

Chapter Seventeen
The Director

idal Verjouce was a terrible man—that, no one could dispute. But in the way of the day, where there was no shortage of terrible ladies or gentlemen, no one would dare speak directly to the Guild's Director of his terribleness. Not even as a compliment, the way King Nightshade might be flattered when reminded of his own somewhat lesser brand of awfulness. Verjouce was the kind of terrible that even frightened King Nightshade, although he was loath to admit such.

Even if Verjouce weren't such a frightening apparition, his glowering countenance and vicious tongue were enough to give children nightmares. He stood head and shoulders above his cowering subrectors, with a mane of long hair parted severely down the center of his scalp—its shade one that was hard to pinpoint, almost devoid of color, as if all the pigment were somehow leached out of it.

Yet it was Verjouce's eyes that were by far his most frightening feature—not because where his eyes once were now rested only hollow pits and discolored knots of scar tissue. The frightening thing about his eyes was that *he was the source of his own disfigurement*—having blinded himself with his own hands to devote himself more fully to the sense of taste.

So it was that Vidal Verjouce was in need of an assistant who could help him negotiate the daily obstacles of the temporal world—the stairs, the curbs, the cobblestones. A glorified guide dog. This assistant must be discreet, since the Guild's Director was indisputably the most powerful

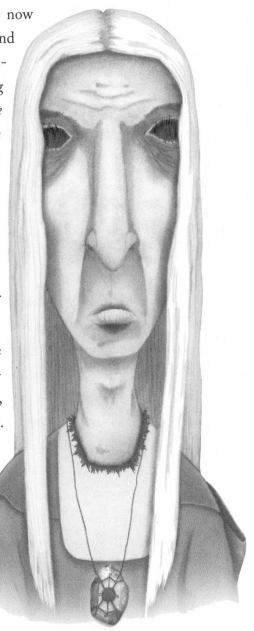

man in Caux (a fact known to everyone, except, perhaps, the Nightshades). He must be loyal and reliable and detail-oriented. Luckily for Sorrel Flux, appearances did not matter.

Sorrel Flux had been Vidal Verjouce's trusted assistant for many years. He had come to know the Guild's Director in ways that no one should. Because, arguably, one of the best talents Flux possessed was the ability to recognize and coddle a meal ticket, Sorrel Flux tried never, ever to disappoint his master.

"Clearly you have failed me." Verjouce's voice was cold and severe and, to Sorrel Flux's horror, directed at him. "There is no girl with you?" The blind man turned his unseeing face this way and that, searching.

They were being lulled by the train's steady passage along the tracks.

"Director," Flux heard his voice whimper, "*please*. There was an unexpected group of Nightshade sentries—"

"Your laziness is exceed only by your fallibility."

The Guild's most frightening Director was tapping his cane—a cane he used not to negotiate his way around the world of the seeing, but rather to intimidate and torture.

"Something about unpaid taxes—" Flux yelped.

"You were to see to the affairs of the tavern during your stay—were you not?"

Flux looked suddenly sheepish.

"On second thought, *nothing* surpasses your laziness," Verjouce hissed.

"They took over the tavern—"

"So you've managed to involve the Crown."

Sorrel Flux swallowed nervously—his turkey neck bobbing with the effort. The Guild's Director had been very explicit on this point—do not under any circumstances involve the Nightshades in this little adventure.

"Answer me. Have you brought me the girl?" Verjouce once more asked, the pits of his eyes burning into Sorrel Flux's own.

"No." Flux barely spoke the word, he was so horrified. "The girl escaped."

The Director just stared at him, almost seeing, with those awful sightless eyes, for the remainder of the trip to Templar. By the time the Ambrosia—the Guild's private train—pulled into the glass and iron arches of the Templar terminal, Flux was a complete, wilted mess.

Chapter Eighteen
Arsenious

In the ancient walled city of Templar, Arsenious Nightshade was suffering badly from a cramp in his royal foot. The king shifted his weight clumsily. In an evil twist of fate, he was made twice discomforted, first by his tragic disfigurement and then by the absence of his favorite royal throne. In the chaos of the move, it had been waylaid. So he suffered standing upright, although he would much prefer to be sitting, making the afternoon a tormented one for the rest of the palace. Occasionally, he mopped his royal brow as he stared unenthusiastically out the window to the royal balcony, and the square below.

It had been over a year since he'd drawn the country's attention to his embarrassing disfigurement—against his better judgment. Still, no cure had been found for his hideous clubfoot. The embarrassment of going public was hardly worth it—except to the queen, who happily tortured all the failures.

He'd endured smelly ointments and mustard poultices, bitter teas and mud baths. Still, he suffered so, enduring shooting pains and muscle spasms. As he agonized, he tried not to remind himself of just how old the city was—he hated anything old, creaky, or dusty, and this sack of stones his wife called a castle was just that. The only reason they came here at all was because his wife *insisted*. She preferred to celebrate the Festival of the Winds here—she thought the acoustics were impeccable, and acoustics were important to her because it amplified the suffering she planned to cause.

The King of Caux cast a quick glance at a hulking monstrosity of an armchair masquerading as a throne upon the dais. His *spare* throne, his footmen had called it, but he knew it for what it was: a filthy antique. He longed for the one he sat on for most of the year in Kruxt, to the south, where he had moved Caux's capital in a stroke of genius after assuming power. The sun, the beach, the palms—the climate was much more agreeable down there, with nothing to remind him of the ticklish subject of, well, his subjects. Templar was decidedly gloomy, and this was coming from a man who liked gloom—even invited it into as many lives as he could. The whole city was filled with antiques. He shuddered, sneaking another look at the old Verdigris throne.

The king was in a hard place. He liked all the pomp and trappings of royalty—what Nightshade wouldn't?—but anything with a pedigree older than his own reign caused him enormous anxiety, guaranteeing a cold sweat and occasionally even welts and boils.

Arsenious limped around so his back faced the window.

The King of Caux, the notorious King Nightshade, was a small man and painfully thin to look at. The dull light of the gray morning added nothing to his dreary complexion from the front and almost gave up entirely as he turned away. His long sparse beard was trimmed in the fashion of the times, and as he picked at it absentmindedly, he was joined by perhaps the more infamous of the pair—the queen.

In she walked, briskly, and the king's mood lifted momentarily. She looked around like she meant business—always exciting for the king. Queen Artilla, pale and dark-haired, was ever so wicked. King Nightshade was wicked, too, but even he would freely admit that his wife's wickedness trumped his own quite handsomely. It was for this reason that he loved her.

"Ohhh," the king groaned. "Artilla! I am most miserable. Please, dear, lift my spirits, won't you?"

"The king decrees he is most miserable!" loudly cried the Royal Diarist, writing in a parchment roll from the corner of the room.

The king, at the queen's urging, had thoroughly begun to document his royal life for the history books. Caux was, after all, still a literary land—even though King Nightshade had most of the ancient books burned—and the king, fancying himself a bit of a poet, wanted history to favor him.

"What else is new?" asked the queen, rolling her eyes. She had little patience for people's suffering unless she'd caused it.

Not sufficiently comforted by the queen, King Nightshade turned to his right, where in an enormous overstuffed wheelchair sat his twin brother, although, to look at the two, one would hardly know of their relation. This gluttonous lump was Prince Francis. The prince was stone-deaf, and when he wasn't sleeping, he was eating. (As with most people who are missing one of the five senses, he compensated with one of the other four.)

The king gave his brother a withering look, and knowing his audience, he turned instead to complain to the general room, containing the usual assortment of indentured servants, led by the dim-witted Lowly Boskoop.

"Perhaps it was the long journey, my king?" suggested Lowly Boskoop, whose duties required him to endure not only the trip from Kruxt with the royal family each year, but the indignity of his name.

"The journey? The journey, you say? The journey I make every blasted Windy Season to this damp and dismal castle?"

"Perhaps a touch of indigestion?" tried another helpful aide. The room was filled with helpful aides, each hoping to make it through the day.

"A touch of something, that's for sure." The queen sighed.

"You are not helping, Artilla. A little sympathy is in order. If you were feeling poorly, I assure you I'd turn the kingdom upside down for something to make you better."

"Yes, but I *never* feel poorly," quipped the queen.

"Perhaps the bicarbonate you liked so much last time?" offered Lowly Boskoop. Bicarbonate was Lowly Boskoop's failsafe cure for all ills—he used it often and for anything, but primarily because he frequently ate too much treacle.

"Oh, let me see if I follow you, *Lowly* Boskoop. You're suggesting bicarbonate will help my foot cramp?"

"You might try it, Arsenious—" the queen attempted.

"What kind of thoughtless buffoon do I have in my service? Are you even qualified to dispense this advice? Perhaps you have a diploma, then? From the school of *Quackery*? Who even authorized you to speak, you vulgarian?!" The king looked around the room, fuming. He paused theatrically.

He felt a poem coming on—and instinctively, everyone in the room cringed. When intelligible, his poems featured awful acts of unkindness and injury, and often the listener was reminded of his previous meal. But to the great relief of his captive audience, the king, after a creative pause, continued with his lecture.

"What if this is the work of a treacherous poisoner? Has anyone thought about that? What if I, the king, have been poisoned cruelly? Would you feel foolish offering him a *bicarbonate of soda*?!" The king's tone was now high-pitched.

"Woe be it to the fool who offers the King of Caux a cure, for he prefers to suffer!" cried the Royal Diarist.

The king sagged, deflated.

"You have not been poisoned, Arsenious." The queen sighed again. "You have a foot cramp. Besides, you barely eat! Your brother sees to that—" The queen pointed a jeweled finger at the prince, who indeed served as King Nightshade's trusted taster. Beside the king, the prince stirred, but seeing no food before him, he settled back into sleep.

"If a king can't trust his own brother, who can he trust?" said King Nightshade defensively. He had become quite reliant on his twin—he liked the fact that he wasn't forced into idle chitchat with someone from the Guild. Thinking of the Guild, the king looked around the room.

"Any sign of the Director?"

"Ugh. That man. Don't you see enough of him in Kruxt?"

"Artilla. Please."

"He'd better be bringing me someone good this time," the queen said. "You did remember to ask him, Arsenious, didn't you?"

The queen, as usual, was in need of a new taster. The king had forgotten to ask.

"Of course, my dear," he said.

"They keep sending me amateurs."

"Artilla. The reason you are in need, yet again, of a taster is that you keep finishing them off. No one, my dear, stands a chance against you."

"You compliment me so."

She took a moment to admire her bejeweled hands,

whereupon one finger sat an especially large and dangerous-looking green ring.

When she looked up, the tall and imposing figure of the Guild's Director stood silently before her, a slightly evil smirk playing about his lips.

The king sat up as if stung by a bee.

"Everyone," he ordered, "OUT!"

Chapter Nineteen
The Terrible Tonic

One of the things Sorrel Flux liked most about his job was the effect his master had upon other people. Generally, as with most people who are drawn to power, Flux felt a little surge of his own worth when his master was so feared and respected. But Sorrel Flux had never had the pleasure of the company of the king or queen—most of his duties kept him in Rocamadour shuffling papers and overseeing the petulant subrectors, which he did with a giddy authority. And until today, Vidal Verjouce had always preferred to see Arsenious Nightshade on his own, enacting some sort of private ritual with the King of Caux.

So it was that Flux made his courtly debut, slinking in the Director's shadow, a place where he was unlikely to be noticed with the Director towering over him. To anyone in the room, he would have appeared completely unremarkable—except for the odd yellowish cast of his waxen skin.

The Director wore his dress robes, a stiff boiled wool, which fell to the floor in precise pleats. Tied neatly around his neck was the taster's collar, and in startling contrast to his drab wool, a substantially large and beautiful bettle dangled from his long neck—a splash of brilliant orange. This was suspended in a cage of gold filigree, and immediately King Nightshade's eyes were drawn to it hungrily. It was simply enormous, even with all the ostentation of their current surroundings—and rarer still, it matched in both color and brilliance the one that gripped the Director's cane.

Sorrel Flux was not a subrector and did not wear a bettle. In fact, he never really took much pains with his appearance— a fact that bothered him at present. He could not disguise that he was completely consumed by nervousness at his proximity to royalty. Specifically, the queen—who struck fear in the hearts of every taster. Flux arranged himself as much behind Verjouce as he could, attempting to dodge the deadly looks Her Highness now directed at his master.

"It's time for my tour of the grounds," she announced, eyes lowered into slits. Each year, the Nightshades' seasonal arrival meant a great deal of work for the servants—Queen Nightshade would have it no other way. Artilla personally insisted on examining the royal silver and china, and cross-checking the inventories for thievery, and being generally difficult. It was time for her surprise inspections.

The queen exited in a cloud of perfume, and although

Verjouce made no effort to step aside as she passed, Sorrel Flux found himself falling into a bow so deep it surprised his stiff back—allowing him an eyeful of the pitted stone floor and leaving him wondering how he would rise.

"I think I'll start with the head butler. He really should have announced our visitor," Artilla called.

Verjouce stood silently for a moment, taking in the room that for him held many memories.

"You are well?" he finally asked the king after the queen's departure.

"Hardly," he scoffed. The subject of his health was one on which the king felt confident in his own expertise, even when addressing the Director. "You're late. I was expecting you over an hour ago."

The king kept his eyes even with the Director's bettle, which was a fine place, he decided, since the alternative was the Director's frightening face.

If there was one person to make the wicked King Nightshade cringe, it was Vidal Verjouce. For one thing, the Director was very old, and that reminded the king of his innate fear of antiques. His age—anyone's old age, including his own impending—made the king uneasy. Old people are in the way most of the time was the king's thought. And like antiques, they have a funny smell.

Vidal Verjouce's association with the old king Verdigris,

too, made him uneasy. Verjouce at one time held the honor of being the old king's most trusted confidant before traitorously conducting the coup that brought him, King Nightshade, to power. Reasonably, this made the king uncomfortable.

But most of all, the fact that the king needed Vidal Verjouce for a very private and secret reason made King Nightshade very, very uneasy.

"I am *decidedly* not well," sniffed the king morosely.

"Foot cramps again?"

The king gave the Director a nasty look. To Sorrel Flux's surprise, he watched as the king's face graduated into a full grimace and was joined by his hands waving ridiculously atop his head. It took Flux a moment to realize what he was seeing: King Nightshade was making faces at the blind Director. He watched, completely aghast, as the king tried on several childish contortions involving tongue-waggling and ear-pulling, finally interrupting himself when he noticed Flux.

"Who goes there? Is there someone *hiding* behind you?"

"It's merely Flux, my trusted assistant."

"I see," said the king, as if he really didn't, uninterested.

Sorrel Flux prepared for the introduction of his life, to the wicked ruler of all of Caux, but it did not come.

Instead, King Nightshade limped back to the window, drawing Sorrel Flux's attention—against his better judgment—to the king's monstrous left foot, the sight of which provided Flux with his first great shock of the day. He forced himself to look elsewhere—anywhere—and found his gaze upon a series of family portraits hanging showily on the wall.

"Did you bring them?" The king's tone was attempting to be casual.

"Yes."

"Ah. Good."

The Guild's Director took from a hidden pocket in his robes a plain muslin bag and handed it to Flux. When Sorrel realized it was his duty to cross the parlor with the king's delivery, he felt slightly faint. The air in the castle was stale and damp, and his sinuses were already acting up. He couldn't leave soon enough. But he did as he was bid and handed the clinking sack into the outstretched damp palm of the king, falling immediately into another backbreaking bow. Somehow he remembered to walk backward, shuffling away in a slightly less-impressive bow but without breaking protocol and turning his face from the king. Not that King Nightshade would have noticed—he was almost giddy with the delivery and skipped, to the best of a clubfooted man's ability, across the room.

Opening the bag, he inspected its contents—drawing in a sharp breath.

"Amazing, Verjouce, you've outdone yourself."

The king seemed emboldened with new life and confidence. He slipped, unthinking, into the padded seat of the offending old throne. No sooner was he seated than he jumped to his feet shrieking—the insult of finding himself in Verdigris's throne too much for his nerves.

He quickly settled into the queen's more delicate and feminine throne—it was softer than he'd expected and just the place to rest his weary bones. Although the picture this created was decidedly unkingly, he was far from caring. Verjouce was helping the king untie the straps that secured the plain sack, and just then Sorrel Flux got the second shock of his already stimulating day.

King Nightshade produced from the small bag a collection of priceless bettles and selected one—a translucent rose—and, with shaking hands, dropped it with a clink into a marble receptacle on the tabletop. He felt around the embroidered tablecloth for his pestle, the tip of which seemed to catch the light.

With a quick stab, he splintered the priceless bettle and began grinding the shards into a fine rosy powder. Sorrel Flux nearly dropped to the ground with astonishment at such decadence. King Nightshade was humming a little excited tune.

The powder was now transferred to a heavy chalice reserved for this purpose, and the contents of a gleaming pitcher were poured on top. King Nightshade stirred the concoction with a golden spoon.

"Drink it, before it thickens," he muttered to himself.

And he soon thought no more about the unfortunate encounter with the antique throne or his menacing company.

After a moment of anticipation, the king reclined, awaiting the mellowing results of his terrible tonic.

"Oh, Artilla needs another taster," the king remembered.

"Of course. She can take Flux here."

The Director had said it so casually, Sorrel almost didn't understand he'd just been handed his third awful surprise of the day.

Chapter Twenty

Southern Wood

The thing about Southern Wood, the thing that both her uncle and Axle had always told Ivy, was that it was to be avoided at all costs.

Growing up with it looming darkly right across the Marcel, she never once had any desire to disagree. The edge of the Wood ran right to the riverbank, where it formed an uneasy truce with the water. In the summer, when the sun set over the enormous trees, there was hardly any deciphering of the forest floor—Southern Wood seemed intent on keeping its secrets.

It was an unlikely place to find herself, Ivy thought. But it was the best way to go—other than by train—if Ivy was to get word of her uncle.

It was hard to tell just what time of day it was. The Wood existed in a sort of permanent twilight; the enormous canopy of treetops was interwoven into a vast veil, allowing hardly any true sunlight through. Everything floated in an amber light—dust motes and a preponderance of wasps and bees, flying fretfully with the end of their year.

The trees of the forest were ancient things, enormous in girth and height, and now that Ivy was right up next to one, she could really marvel at it. The bark grew in huge shaggy strips, and occasionally it would flake away from the tree and float lazily down to the ground, landing in a muffled thud. These unpredictable noises did much to enhance Ivy's nervousness—the Wood made her uncomfortable, and she couldn't help but feel they were not alone. They had slipped silently from Axle's trestle earlier, but she couldn't shake the sensation that the eyes of the awful Outrider were turned toward her. The forest floor was soft and springy, and she found herself searching for any signs that they were being followed.

The Wood was also host to a vast array of lush plant life. It was filled with a veritable delight of many interesting specimens—undisturbed and ancient. Rowan was thrilled to pull out his newly autographed copy of the *Field Guide* and research his findings, but it soon started slowing them down. Ivy wanted to make some progress—after all, there was an uncle to find, and she knew that Templar was no easy journey. There was something else, though—something in the air that made her want to hurry.

"Look at this!" Rowan called ahead to where Ivy was.

"This species of vine. I'm almost certain it's shadow phlox; I'd know it anywhere! A complete rarity, it blooms only in the deep of night."

"That?" Ivy turned for a quick look. "Common bindweed. *Convolvulus scammonia.*"

"Bindweed?" Rowan scoffed. "Please. I've studied this, remember, for *years* at the seminary. It can't be bindweed. Look, its woody parts are simply way too thick."

He leaned in for a closer look.

Ivy shrugged. "It's just a particularly old vine. No one's come along to disturb it. If I were you, I'd be careful—"

She squinted ahead, trying to decipher the slight path as it wound through the undergrowth.

"—Bindweed moves fast."

"Thank you," Rowan replied stiffly. "But since it's shadow phlox, and since I'd like a cutting to compare with the *Guide,* I hardly think—"

But it was too late. From behind her, Ivy heard Rowan gasp.

"Rowan!" Ivy shouted, turning back just in time. "Step away—quick!"

But before he could do so—his nose was just emerging from Axle's book—his ankles were immobilized by the quick-moving vine, and the plant was rapidly snaking up his leg. His balance was thrown to one side, and, as bindweed does, the vine was swiftly making its way up to his chest, immobilizing his arms. Axle's *Field Guide* dropped to the ground, where soon after, Rowan joined it in an unceremonious lump.

Ivy dashed back and stomped on the advancing weed, putting all her weight into it as it struggled beneath her foot, lashing about. Prying open Axle's picnic basket, she felt around desperately—her hand finally landing on the neatly organized bundles of eating utensils. She grabbed the first thing she could and poked and speared the ancient thing with one of Axle's salad forks. Rowan was frozen with fear at the weed's assault as the tendrils whipped across the path and pulled tightly on his chest. After much effort, the vine finally let go, leaving him stunned and rubbing his wrists and legs. It left welts.

"I told you it was bindweed," Ivy admonished breathlessly.

The taster sniffed, gingerly recovering the *Guide* from the brush. To his great embarrassment, he found his face hot and knew it to be a vivid shade of crimson.

"But bindweed can look a lot like phlox," Ivy conceded, seeing his discomfort. "I might have made the same mistake."

Rowan smiled weakly. He somehow doubted this, but he felt better. Still, he found he was far less curious after this encounter. He satisfied himself by pointing with a long walking stick each time he saw something of interest and prodding it, with one hand ready to ward off any assault.

After arm's-length encounters with stinging nettles and crampbark—Rowan knew not to get too close—he grew tired of his lesson. He bravely poked at a fine specimen of the unfortunately named pukeweed while prudently sidestepping bladderwrack, but all the while his mind was on the picnic basket that he carried.

The earth rose in slight mounds to meet the massive trees, creating tempting little inlets of soft mossy bedding here and there—great places for a rest and a picnic lunch. But the last time he'd suggested sitting for a spell, Ivy coldly reminded him that she wasn't one to sit and dawdle when her uncle was missing. Rowan could smell something remarkably savory wafting up from the basket—ham and cheese on Axle's thick pillow-soft bread? Whatever it was, it was time to eat it, he decided. He'd insist—just after they rounded this dark tree.

As they did so, the forest retreated from view.

"Look!"

The pair had come to a stop before the strangest sight.

It was a tree like any other. But impossibly, where the old and gnarled trunk met the forest floor, there bulged a squat and very inviting little cottage, growing—inconceivably— from the living wood. The massive tree and the bungalow had formed some sort of agreement many, many years ago.

"How completely and utterly peculiar!" said Ivy.

"I wonder who lives here," Rowan replied somewhat nervously. He had a particular dislike for strangers lately, especially ones without tongues or descendants of the Taxus clan.

There it sat, a small wooden structure, snugly in the

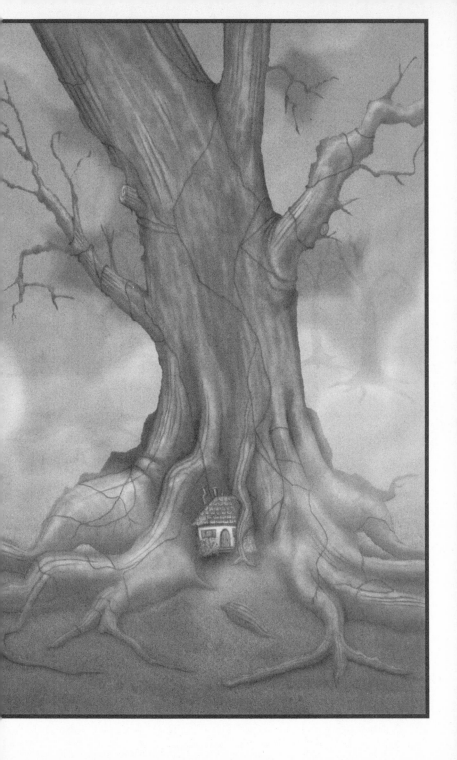

middle of the tree. In between massive tree roots, the chimney, an old stone stack, jutted lopsidedly. Green honeysuckle vines with broad pink florets covered most of the cottage's front view, a picture of coziness. The shutters were open, and even from where they stood, they could see there was another window on the back side, and through it the forest continued on normally.

"What a great place for our lunch!" Rowan suggested, his stomach winning the battle between hunger and trepidation.

Ivy was at the door already and, shaking her head, said it was locked.

"Well, we'll just have to sit on the front stoop," Rowan said firmly. His stomach was rumbling uncomfortably. As he set about clearing the moss and dirt from the stone, she looked through the little window into the single room beyond.

"There's a table! It's set for two." Indeed, a small rustic table awaited unknown occupants beside the vast hearth, which took up most of one side of the cottage. Everything was covered in a fine dust, undisturbed. After trying the door once more, she pulled herself away—and caught sight of something else.

"Look at this stone!" She was referring to the stoop that Rowan was preparing as their table. Rowan had cleared most of the debris.

"It says something!"

The pair peered at it, Ivy using her hands to pull off one persistent clump of lichen.

"It's a marker of some sort," Rowan decided.

" '506 knarls'—what's a knarl?"

"Got me."

"506 knarls, and then there's this arrow."

"A knarl must be a unit of measurement." Rowan hoped that this sounded educated. The Tasters' Guild was especially strict with its many courses on weights and measurements—and Rowan excelled at none of them.

Ivy was still clearing the last of the moss, which came free finally, leaving a puff of fine dirt floating in the air.

The two stared wide-eyed at what remained.

506 knarls to Pimcaux

Rowan forgot all thoughts of Axle's fine food.

"Wow! Maybe a knarl is just a few paces!" He started walking enthusiastically around looking for something that might resemble a lost and forgotten land.

"Somehow I doubt it," Ivy decided.

But whatever a knarl was would have to wait for the time being.

His path had taken him to a clearing behind the cottage, and it was here that Rowan saw evidence that they were not alone. Before him rippled a span of seamless white, startling his eyes, which had grown accustomed to the dimness of the forest. For a moment, he just blinked. Then, as he squinted, Rowan found himself staring at a remarkable-looking gossamer tent—a dramatic enclosure with roof peaks and streamers and generous front flaps tied closed with white ribbons.

"What is that doing here?" Ivy asked as she joined him. The tent was billowing in the softest wind.

"Hello?" she called. Ivy didn't really think anyone was inside, seeing as the fabric had a sheerness about it, but she thought it polite to try. After calling again, louder, she approached the tent and tried the flaps.

"I can't get hold of them!"

It seemed simple enough to untie the loose knots, but there was something unusually slippery about the ribbons, and Ivy found them uncooperative. Shifting the precious bottle in her waistband, she bent down. Rowan tried, too, and together they hardly managed to loosen one.

"I don't suppose it would be okay to just cut them?" Rowan thought of the cutlery in the basket.

Ivy thought that under the circumstances, a little vandalism was in order.

But Ivy had been right, it turned out, about her worry that they might be followed. The forest floor was too soft. With their backs to the path, neither one knew what hit them—and before they could gather themselves properly, they were separated.

The last thing Rowan remembered seeing before Ivy disappeared into—and somehow down below—the tent was a snuffling and snorting mass of white bristle.

Chapter Twenty-one

The Bettle Boar

There was for a minute a confused whirlwind of brilliant white—the tent, the light, the fur of the snarling animal that seemed to be everywhere at once. Ivy had little time to register what was happening as she was swept away from the tent's opening and down, seemingly underground.

The thing about it, Rowan later thought, was that he never asked himself how he knew Ivy was being charged—and potentially mauled—by a large wild boar. He hadn't seen the animal go by, except in a flash. He only knew that in one second, he was attempting to break into a strange tent, and the next, he was staring at the distant treetops up above from the not uncomfortable vantage point of his back. He would have, in fact, stayed on in that restful position if he didn't know the indisputable fact that pigs can be dangerous, if not downright deadly.

In all of three seconds, he was following the beast and his new friend through the tent's entrance, where he found only one thing inside. A small hole was excavated into the loam, and having nowhere else to go, Rowan followed them down into the earth below.

There he found Ivy, rolled in a ball as the animal snorted and snuffled excitedly.

"He wants the bottle!" Rowan called to her, hoping that she might give it up and save herself. He was right—the pig was distinctly drawn to Ivy's elixir, which she clutched desperately. The creature exhibited an amazing tenacity, a single-mindedness and fierce intent that worried Ivy immensely—even more than catching her breath.

"Well, he can't have it!"

"Actually, *she* wants your bottle," a voice corrected. It was clear and captivating, with a slight unrecognizable accent, and the words seemed to float in the air long after they were spoken.

As Ivy lay pinned against the underground floor, they were joined in the shallow room by a woman of such height and presence that Rowan, too, felt a short supply of air.

She was so tall, much taller than Rowan, that she stooped beneath the modest ceiling, but even in this indelicate stance she radiated a thrilling confidence, a self-possession that Ivy instantly admired. She had one hand on her hip, below which flowed in crisp angles her long and beautifully tailored stark white skirts. The gown proceeded to the floor and appeared to be made of the same fabric as the tent. From her neck draped a similarly exotic scarf, and although both the dress and scarf brushed the earth, neither displayed any sign of dust.

She was immaculate.

Her other hand held a lantern with a reservoir of clear oil, and the added light gave them a better look at the animal.

It was a wild-looking boar, of a much more impressive height than Ivy, hackles that arched with fe-rocious quills meet-ing her at eye level. The boar was white as snow from tusk to tail, except for its pale blue eyes, and equally untouched by Cauvian dirt. And Ivy noticed its smell: crisp and cold, the smell of the mountaintops.

"Well, Poppy," said the woman in a voice that filled the room with a light melody. "What have you here?"

Ivy's calls for help had ceased, but her discomfort had not. Being the object of a boar's complete attention was unnerving, and she steeled herself for a showdown. The animal's viscous snout quivered with anticipation.

The woman advanced toward Ivy, reached decisively into the fray, and plucked the small bottle from Ivy's embrace.

"Hey—that's mine! You leave it alone!"

Rowan couldn't understand why Ivy wouldn't want to give it to her. Certainly, if this strange vision asked him for anything—his robes, his *Field Guide*—he would be honored to give it up. He had to stop himself from offering her the picnic from Axle there in his hands.

Ivy's prized possession rose from the lady's open palm.

And then, oddly, she laughed. (And what a laugh it was—one full of melody and birdsong.)

"Poppy! I should have known. You've found yourself a bettle!"

It was then that Rowan, being

somewhat of an expert in pigs, realized what he was looking at.

"A bettle boar!" he cried.

Poppy was indeed a bettle boar, a boar used exclusively for the mining of bettles in the Craggy Burls. They possess an uncanny ability to smell the jewels beneath the earth of the mines. Rowan had never seen a bettle boar before—he thought they were only found on the tops of snowy mountains—and this was a real treat for the son of a pig farmer.

The woman reached into a side pocket of her white skirts and pulled out what was to be only the second bettle Ivy had ever seen. A brilliant orange. She waved it around, and when she'd caught the attention of the boar, she tossed the priceless jewel back the way that she'd come. The boar was gone in a flash, bounding after her toy.

"That should occupy her for the time being. Now to the business of introductions."

Poppy, in the distance, could be plainly heard joyfully snorting. Occasionally, the bettle clinked against the pig's teeth.

"My name is Rowan Truax. Guild-accredited taster, at your service."

Ivy rolled her eyes. She was still smarting from her introduction to Poppy and considered not speaking at all.

"Where are we?" she asked instead. The question was a

reasonable one, since they seemed to be in a small underground chamber.

"This is Poison Ivy," Rowan volunteered. He was happy to say anything at the moment, and the words were tumbling out of his mouth. "Ivy Manx. That's her uncle's bettle there, inside that bottle you have. It's hollow, they say. Come to think of it, that's probably why he named it the Hollow Bettle. . . ."

"Rowan!" Ivy hollered, ending his blather.

"Poison Ivy?" Their host looked amused. "My name is Clothilde." Her smile—a slight crescent with two upward ends—made its way slowly across her face.

Ivy glared in return. "May I please have my bottle back? *Clothilde?*"

"I don't see why not," the woman said merrily. "It's of no use to me."

The children found this highly irregular, but as Clothilde seemed about to return the bottle, Ivy wisely said nothing.

"A *hollow* bettle, you say?" Clothilde seemed to reconsider. "Surely not."

Ivy scowled at the taster.

In the clear light of the oil lamp, the bettle blazed—catching the light in its central flaw and for a moment shining as bright as any mirror. The woman held the lantern up to her face—her skin glowed remarkably white in the clear light—and with her other hand she carefully held up the bottle to examine the captive bettle. Her face took on a new expression, a slight softening around her eyes, and she turned the bottle to better see the stone. Suddenly a light, as clear and bright as any, drew a jagged line from her forehead to her chin. It shone eerily from the bottle in a shadow play upon her white face—at first quite indistinct, but soon falling crisply into focus.

Upon Clothilde's face, and seemingly shining from the bettle, was an ancient-looking and quite curious insignia, one not entirely unknown to either of the children. A flower with five petals.

A cinquefoil.

"Yes," Clothilde exhaled. "I remember this bettle." She looked over to Ivy.

"No, you don't!" Ivy reached for her bottle. The strange vision—and the cinquefoil—vanished, leaving Ivy shaken. "I mean, that's impossible. It's my uncle's bettle." She examined it gently swaying in the amber liquid for any damage.

"Amazing," Rowan managed, quite bewitched.

Clothilde blinked once, and Ivy had the impression she was about to say something. She noticed the woman's eyes now: a translucent, bleached-out center, like water, while the outer part of the iris faded into a russet red-brown rim.

"As you like." Clothilde turned away. In the silence that followed, Poppy could be heard gnawing on her own bettle.

"Well, Ivy Manx and Rowan Truax, graduate of the Guild. Allow me, since you're here, to show you around."

Chapter Twenty-two

Underwood

W hen you grow up on a pig farm, and the Truax family farm was one of the biggest in the region, you develop what Rowan's father came to call pig sense. As everyone knows, pigs are highly intelligent animals. What Rowan's dad meant by pig sense was simple: if you get to thinking like a pig, the pigs get to thinking like you. It makes for a happy pig and a happy farmer. And one of the things anyone with pig sense knows is that pigs like to have fun. Rowan's father was pleased to possess a son with an awful lot of pig sense.

Poppy was at a large set of doors on the far wall, snorting with excitement. The boar seemed especially thrilled with Rowan—and bounded immediately to take up position by his side, carrying the orange bettle in her mouth.

"Oh, don't worry about her," Clothilde said, seeing Ivy hesitate. "She's fine now that she has her favorite toy. It was necessary to take it away so she could guard the entrance. All the same, she forgot her duties." A distinct note in her voice made it quite clear to the children that they should avoid disappointing her.

Poppy was—to Ivy's relief—quite content to walk beside Rowan. Clothilde marched ahead and threw open the great set of arched doors made from what seemed to be densely woven wooden branches darned with many years of ancient patina. The wood seemed to pulse as if each strand were alive, giving the impression that it was only by the greatest of efforts that it maintained its doorlike shape. It opened easily, but not on hinges. It was as if the wood moved itself on its own accord at her touch.

But that was just the beginning. For what Ivy and Rowan walked into was a room—if one might call something so vast and intricate a mere room—like no other.

"Welcome, children, to Underwood."

The walls, the pillars, the distant ceiling stretched out wondrously ahead. And they were all constructed of various widths of twisting, squirming wood—roots and sprigs—some the thickness of ten men, some as slender and delicate as a splinter. And all remarkably fashioned into the most impressive cavernous grand hall the two had ever seen.

Underwood existed in a soft, pleasing glow, a type of diffused light that seemed at once both perfectly natural and unearthly in its green tinge. From where this special light emanated was unclear—it felt weighty, as if it could be captured and held in one's pocket for a darker moment. The smell, like the forest above it, was pure and woodsy.

"Wow," they both chorused together.

But even with the vague lighting, there was no end in sight to the Great Room of Underwood. Ivy's impression that the walls were alive grew as she ran her hands over an ornate column to her side, the knots together forming an intricate gnarled braid, and she felt the ancient strength of its components.

"I've never seen anything like it," she whispered.

"What . . . what . . . *is* this place?" Rowan asked.

"At one time—in its heyday—Underwood was King Verdigris's retreat, a place of magic and meditation for him."

"King Verdigris . . . came here?" Rowan was incredulous. He remembered his vision in Axle's study and the shadowy face of the pained king in his final days.

"King Verdigris *built* it," she corrected, and Ivy caught Rowan's eye, impressed.

They walked along, the massive corridor seemingly endless.

"He fashioned it from the ancient roots of the trees above—in Southern Wood."

"Underwood is alive!" Ivy realized now why the walls seemed to be pulsating.

"Yes," Clothilde said. "For now. But Underwood is dying.

At one time, these roots were green with youth, and new shoots and tendrils would break free at their own whim. At its height of life, it was constantly twisting and reinventing itself into new rooms. You could easily get lost or turn the corner and find an entirely new place to explore. But no more. Perhaps the great trees above have outgrown themselves. Or perhaps they need their creator to nourish them in other ways. And Verdigris, as the forest knows, is gone."

"Who comes here now?" Rowan asked. The place looked empty except for themselves, and he hoped this was true. He thought how Poppy had been stationed above, and suddenly wondered from what danger Clothilde wanted guarding.

"Underwood became the sanctuary of renegades after Verdigris left it. A place of outlaws."

This was not the news Rowan was hoping for. It would be nice to relax for a little bit without thinking about the Estate of Turner Taxus or that Outrider. He began to look more closely into the darker corners of the cavern.

"What are *you* doing here?" Ivy asked suspiciously.

"Me? I came here hoping to find someone."

"Who?"

"An apotheopath."

"An apotheopath! Why would you think you'd find one here?"

"This became their stronghold after they were forced underground."

"Underground! That's clever." Rowan looked around. "Hey—Ivy's uncle is an apotheopath! Maybe he's here, too."

This was just what Ivy was thinking but had hoped to keep to herself. Rowan's desire to share everything with this strange lady was beginning to annoy her. But Clothilde seemed elsewhere.

"No. There's no one here."

For the first time, Ivy noticed a note of melancholia in their host.

"Are you sure? The place seems so big," Ivy said. Her uncle might be hiding anywhere down here, and the thought did occur to her that she might call out to him.

"Yes, I'm sure."

"What do you need an apotheopath for? You're not sick, are you?" A crease of worry lined Rowan's young forehead.

"Hardly," she scoffed. "Do I look sick to you?"

Rowan admitted she was the picture of health indeed.

They now came upon a little hallway with a vaulted woody ceiling, into which Clothilde turned, ducking. The unearthly lighting continued down the path, the galloping roof reminding Ivy very much of the inside of a barrel. Stopping along the haphazard path, their host turned to them, and framed against the knotty caverns of the low ceiling, she looked even grander. Clothilde spied Rowan's prized picnic basket in his arms, and her eyes narrowed.

"This way." She gestured. And then to Ivy, "I don't think your taster can wait any longer for his lunch."

Rowan, flushing a beet red, wondered if Clothilde had heard his stomach groan.

"I'll tell you everything once we've properly dined in the king's chambers."

King Verdigris's chambers? Ivy and Rowan were appropriately quiet as they walked the length of the hall, with Poppy taking up the rear, nipping playfully at the taster's heels.

Chapter Twenty-three

The Amber Room

Ivy's normally excellent sense of direction was rendered negligible by the time they arrived at the tunnel's end, and she had the distinct impression that they had several times doubled back on themselves. Together they now faced a door fashioned like the others they'd passed but with one notable addition: little panels of stained glass twinkled at them welcomingly, lit from what could only be a fireplace inside. The glass was old, and in the way that old glass tends to drape and sag, the surface had become quite uneven. It was all variations of one color, many lights and darks and warm mid-tones of amber.

Time, or vandals, had broken a small pane through which Clothilde now inserted her long white-clad arm, and finding the knob on the inside, opened the door.

The room that lay beyond, this room that King Verdigris called his inner chambers, was small and welcoming—and yet one of complete and astounding beauty. Immediately Ivy and Rowan felt the warmth of the fire and saw it reflected a thousandfold in the glass tiles that lined the walls and ceiling. It was as if each glossy square held its own miniature flame. The fireplace was straight ahead of them, and on either side were grand wingback chairs, stuffed to the point that the golden velvet that kept the insides tucked away threatened to part at the seams. Rowan was accustomed to the Guild's stiff and polished luxury, a secretive sort reserved for the subrectors, and the inviting comfort of the Good King's inner chambers was a welcome relief.

Ivy, closest to the wall, inspected a row of tiles at eye level and discovered what made them twinkle so.

"There's a golden key inside every one of them!" she gasped.

It was true—each tile held in it a key, each different from the next, as Ivy was determined to prove by examining every one she could see. The keys glittered in the firelight.

"Where do they all go?"

"Nowhere," Clothilde replied.

In a swift and awful moment, she was at the wall, prying off one of the tiles. As she held it up, Ivy and Rowan gathered around. It was transparent amber, like the door, and the key—a long graceful skeleton key with a bettle-shaped head—looked ancient and mysterious. With barely any effort, Clothilde caused the entire thing to crumble in her long pale hand—Ivy gasped as a fine sifting of gold dust trickled to the earthen floor.

"The keys are an illusion—they vanish, turn to dust, when the amber is broken."

Ivy despaired, looking around at all the untouchable keys, and hoped their host wouldn't break another one.

"These tiles were fashioned from the sap of the great trees above, in Southern Wood, many, many years ago. The locks to these keys are long gone, if they ever existed in the first place. The whole entire room, this room of amber, was moved, in fact. It once resided in the spire of the Library at Rocamadour. It was moved piece by piece shortly before the Good King's . . . illness."

Rowan thought of the intimidating Library at his former Guild. He knew the spire only too well—it pierced the dark clouds above it, and in the center, there was an odd diamond-shaped window from which he always felt watched. It wasn't a place of beauty at all—it was cold and austere, frightening, in fact, having appeared to him many times in his anxious dreams.

Poppy had made her way to the fireplace and was curled up in a comfortable ball, snorting softly with delight at her clever position. She was soon fast asleep, dreaming, as bettle boars do, of icicles and snowflakes.

"Rowan, come join us." Clothilde smiled brightly. "After all, we need a taster for our meal!"

He inspected the table studiously as Ivy and Clothilde unloaded the food. Axle's picnic was extensive.

Clothilde arranged on a little tin plate a selection of miniature tea sandwiches—thick with sugar and cinnamon, savory bacon and cucumber, and sweet nut butter and thick jam. A stack of silver olives and simple sliced apple beside crisp, salted crackers. For each, a cup of strong, steaming tea, with a plate of Axle's famous honey cakes beside the teapot.

"What fortunate diners are we to have at our table a Guild-accredited taster!" Clothilde raised her teacup to Rowan, who flushed with pride.

When Clothilde cast her eyes upon you, like a bright lighthouse, the world seemed clear and purposeful. Rowan began chatting happily with their host about his taster duties. But a lighthouse is able to shine in only one direction at a time, and while Rowan found comfort in Clothilde's company, Ivy now felt acutely uncomforted—disagreeable, even. She was left with little to do but roll her eyes as he related various

Guild-related capers to the table. Rowan made a showy point of tasting Clothilde's plate first, followed by Ivy's.

"Fit to eat." He flashed a wide smile at Clothilde.

"Thank you, Rowan." Their host smiled her peculiar smile in return. And then, turning, "Tasters. Such a noble profession, don't you agree, Ivy? To fine-tune one's sense to the point where one lives by one's tongue. Lives or dies."

"Rowan," Ivy reminded him. "Didn't you abandon your charge?"

Rowan merely ignored her.

"Do try these; they look simply marvelous." Clothilde offered the taster a plump package of Axle's rosewater taffies. Each lump was dusted with a thick layer of powdered sugar and looked the picture of perfection.

"Don't mind if I do." Rowan bowed his head as he placed one carefully in his mouth.

"Here." She reached across. "Have another." Clothilde's long delicate fingers fed the taster several more. Her hand seemed to linger beside his lips, withdrawing only once she was satisfied his mouth was quite full of the candy. Then their host poured another helping of the fragrant tea into Axle's flowered tin cup.

"You know." Clothilde turned after reaching over to dust Rowan's sugared mouth with her own napkin. "I just came from the Hollow Bettle. And it was much changed. Dark."

She talked in smooth, soft tones—that slight accent of

hers was bewitching, and at first Ivy wasn't sure if she had heard her. She sat up, electrified.

"You what?"

"Poppy and I, we came from the Bettle—you do call it that, don't you? But the front door was missing, the inside curiously abandoned. Not a person to be found—just an old, disagreeable crow. Naturally, I came straight here."

The lady smiled. Clothilde's charm now turned to shine its bright light upon Ivy, and quite quickly did the young girl's temper change. Ivy suddenly found that she could look upon this lady without issue, that she was growing quite fond of her—even against her will. In a mere moment, she now struggled to remember her dislike for Clothilde and wondered what she had found so objectionable about her in the first place.

"Whatever for?" Rowan's jaw hung open in a very un-taster-like fashion.

"But I've already told you!" Clothilde reminded him. "I was looking for an apotheopath. We had a long-standing meeting arranged, actually."

"An apotheopath? You were meeting an apotheopath at the Bettle? You must mean Ivy's uncle!" Rowan gasped.

"Rowan—" Ivy warned, glowering at her companion. The first chance she got, she planned on taking the taster aside and lecturing him on discretion—but for now Ivy was desperate to hear more.

"What long-standing meeting?"

Rowan grabbed a handful of the rosewater taffies and, disregarding his extensive training, shoved them into his mouth at once, chewing noisily. They tasted deliciously of faint perfume and melted on his tongue.

"Oh, something agreed upon years ago. He was keeping something safe for me, you see."

"Something of yours? What do you mean?" Ivy's mind thrashed through the memory of her uncle's hodgepodge of possessions and couldn't think of a thing to which she'd assign this regal lady ownership.

"Something of great value."

"The bettle?" Rowan wondered aloud. He was horrified to receive a cold look from Clothilde.

"Hardly." She turned to Ivy, who was biting her lip anxiously. "He was keeping you."

"Me?"

"Ivy?" Rowan gasped.

"Yes, Ivy. You."

Chapter Twenty-four

Poisonry

I t was Poppy who broke the spell the room seemed to have fallen under. The bettle boar clattered suddenly to her feet, hackles raised and teeth bared. Ivy was reminded of the boar's true wild identity.

"Trying to redeem yourself?" Clothilde asked the boar. To the children, rising, she excused herself calmly. "Poppy's heard something."

She left the room quite quickly, and Ivy wondered uncertainly whether the elegant lady's white slippers ever really touched the floor. For a stunned moment, they sat in the ensuing silence. Poppy's alarm was contagious, and each wondered at the potential danger—anyone could have easily tracked them into Underwood, and Ivy was appalled that they'd let their guard down. The pair was frozen before their meal, with ears perked and appetites damaged.

Yet as soon as their host had departed, the strange bewitchment ceased and their annoyance with each other vanished.

"You don't suppose the Outrider's found us, do you?" Ivy asked nervously.

Rowan looked around uncomfortably.

"I hope not. All the same, I bet he'd be no match for her," he added.

"I suppose." She paused. "Rowan, what do you think Clothilde means, that Cecil was keeping me safe for her?"

"I don't know. And safe from what?" Rising, the taster pulled from his robes the thick *Guide*. "I've been wondering about something since Axle's." He inspected the thick volume in the firelight.

Ivy was trying unsuccessfully to imagine her uncle and their host conducting business. What had Cecil not told her?

"Here—look." Rowan pointed to an innocuous page that detailed the various swamp grasses to be found beside Caux's rivers and streams. At first Ivy noticed nothing.

"Look, see what happens when you hold it to the light?"

The thin parchment glowed with the firelight, becoming nearly transparent. For a minute there was nothing, and Ivy, exasperated, was about to look away. But it was then that she noticed an odd effect—the print on each side of the page combined into one darker, cohesive scrawl, and together now became a new text. A secret text.

"I think this is what Axle meant!" Rowan exclaimed. The fire was dancing behind the thin paper, and Rowan began excitedly tracing his finger over it. "Right here he's embedded the history of Verdigris!"

"What does it say?" Ivy's eyes were tiring at the effort. Rowan read, haltingly:

Once—not so very long ago—there was a king who had but one daughter. This was the Good King Verdigris of Caux, a man of much wisdom and power. When his daughter, Princess Violet, was of marrying age, she fell in love with a prince from Caux's sisterland, the neighboring land of Pimcaux. No one had ever seen a couple more deeply in love. The princess and prince were wed, and the celebration lasted an entire month, at the end of which she departed from Caux to reside with the prince in his kingdom—a land of majestic beauty.

Husband and wife lived happily at first. But then tragedy struck. A year to the date of their vows, Princess Violet died a tragic death, poisoned by her meal. When the news reached her father, he was deeply saddened and fiercely angry at the prince—holding him solely responsible for his daughter's death. How is it that the prince lived, it was whispered, and the princess died, when they ate from the same plate?

The King of Caux ordered the Doorway to the land of Pimcaux closed forever and the one key destroyed. He abdicated control to his treacherous advisor, Vidal Verjouce. But when the Good King Verdigris closed up the entrance into Pimcaux, he unknowingly closed his people off from their true natures and doomed them all to a life of mischief and suspicion. Grief brought about the king's own sad defeat and the appearance of the new, terrible King Nightshade in his stead.

Ivy had been so involved in the story, she hadn't noticed Rowan's voice becoming progressively weaker as he read. Finally, after a feeble cough and an odd gargle, he drifted off to silence.

"Rowan?" She stole a concerned look at her companion and was horrified to see that he looked unwell—he was pale, and his forehead was dotted with sweat.

The taster, for his part, was aware of Ivy's scrutiny, which did little to make him feel better. It was a bit too warm, perhaps from the fire or the effort of reading the hidden passage. He found it hard to think, and he hoped that standing might clear his head. With effort he pushed against the plush chair, weakly trying to disengage from its soft grasp. What Rowan got instead was a sudden sense of dizziness, and dizziness coupled with fatigue is a heady mix.

"I . . . I don't feel so good," Rowan managed, clutching his stomach.

"You don't look so good, either!"

A terrible thought occurred to him.

"I think . . . I think it's something I ate." Rowan looked at his friend helplessly. He knew how highly irregular it was for a graduate of the Guild to find himself in such a compromising position.

"What? You don't mean—"

"Ivy, I think I've been poisoned!"

"That's impossible!" Ivy looked around at the table, desperately. "Axle made everything here!"

And then Ivy froze.

"She didn't eat a thing," she noticed. "Clothilde. She didn't eat the food!" She turned back to Rowan.

"Rowan! Didn't you *taste* anything?"

He shook his head miserably. He had been too entranced by their host. His heart was pounding, and he felt both flushed and weak.

"I am such a wretched taster!" he cried as the amber tones of the room spun about maddeningly and then faded to black.

He tried to call out for Ivy but abruptly found he could not move, and as the darkness closed in around him, his thoughts turned to Turner Taxus—his first and only charge. He had failed him! The Taxus Estate—they would petition for his Epistle, and . . . His mind lurched. Pages from the *Field Guide*

swam in front of his eyes: the small and familiar typeset twisting and curling and somehow transforming itself into a curious, incomprehensible script, the pages growing monstrously,
swirling and suddenly becoming an enormous tower of inky
print. The black spire of the Library now rose above him perilously, and he quailed in its shadow. The Tasters' Guild! Their
dark henchmen would surely find him and punish him stiffly.
The terrible Director's blind and disfigured eyes swam across
his vision—searching, *seeing* him. Verjouce's blindness, his terrible, all-seeing blindness.

As Ivy leaned over the taster and shook him, she realized
Poppy was suddenly at her side and Clothilde behind her.
Clothilde was agitated and seemed unaware of any plight the
taster might be experiencing. Instead, she abruptly announced
they would need to depart.

"We've been followed. I was tracked from the tavern."

"But Rowan is sick!" Ivy indicated, panicked.

Clothilde looked momentarily like she'd tasted something
bitter. Her crystal eyes narrowed and blinked.

"Hmm. So he is." Her tone was unconcerned.

The tall woman dragged the taster to his feet and draped
him carelessly over the large boar, motioning Ivy to follow. She
crossed the room in two great strides and knelt beside the fireplace. Ignoring the flames, Clothilde reached into the hearth,
feeling about on the sooty wall, searching for something. To

Ivy's great amazement, a small stone door swung open to the side of the massive chimney. But even before she could marvel at this new and exciting development, Ivy was distracted by a noise behind her.

Where the great lady had been standing, in front of the amber-tiled door, something even more miraculous was occurring. The opening was swiftly growing over with new green shoots and tendrils, winding together in a maze of vegetation. Underwood was sealing the door behind them, covering over the amber tiles with a bramble-like blanket.

"Come!" Clothilde called from the fireplace. "There's no time to lose. The Outrider will be here shortly."

Running for the small new doorway, Ivy suddenly stopped. Turning behind her, she scrambled for the table and managed to retrieve her bottle, the bettle inside, just as the forest was reclaiming their picnic.

Chapter Twenty-five

The Dungeon

As the king dozed dreamlessly from the effects of his tonic, the queen was busying herself with her tour of the grounds.

Queen Artilla was on her way to the Gray Gardens—no small feat in the Templar castle, with its winding corridors and twisting halls. It was almost as if the castle's architect had confusion in mind when he drew up the design. Each year she arrived and attempted this very same excursion, and each year she found herself hopelessly lost—as if the castle had sprouted new halls and vast wings in their absence.

The Gray Gardens were spectacularly disobedient. Queen Artilla could get nothing of color to bloom there. Even the enormous roses, hanging heavy from their thorny canes, were a neutral shade of gray. Gray ivy and thick ground cover were overrunning the place. Spongy gray moss grew over the stone benches and statuary. It was as if the color had drained from all life—leaving only the magnified scent to enjoy.

The olive grove produced gray olives from its silvery leaves and dull leathery trunks. Clear water collected in a hollow beside a series of stepping-stones, reflecting only storm clouds. Anything the queen planted here grew intently, but devoid of all color, leaving Her Majesty a vision of vividness against the drab backdrop.

It was, above all, pleasing to her.

The queen stood now in the corner tower, confusion rising with an equal jolt of annoyance. She looked out at the view from a thin barred window. A flanking tower rose up along the fortified curtain wall, and there she found an entrance into a postern, a long footbridge leading over the swampy sod beside the moat. The moat was her husband's inspiration and the only improvement that the Nightshades had bothered with. She had no idea how the previous monarch kept the commoners at bay without one.

Before the arched doorway stood a royal guard, and it was from him that the queen demanded directions.

"The gardens?"

He nodded and, moving aside, let her through and onto the outdoor passage that linked one colossal side of the castle to another. In the moat below a sort of oily film glistened on the surface of the water, which bubbled wickedly, releasing its poisonous gases. From up here the queen had a view of the majority of the city, its twisting streets and hidden storefronts.

She quickly reached the end of the walkway and called for entry through the thick timber door.

"The gardens?" she asked this sentry stationed at the entrance.

After thinking a moment with a furrowed brow, the guard directed her to a staircase directly across from them, and the queen slipped down it, resuming her impressive pace. Soon she had arrived through a low door in a part of the castle she had never before been. Before her sat a large squat table upon the earthen floor. A small fire was burning against the far wall, a steaming kettle over it, and she realized with great annoyance she'd stumbled into the servants' kitchen.

Taking a moment to make the best out of a bad situation, the queen looked around for Lowly Boskoop, or any of his minions, with the idea of a surprise inspection, yet there was no one to intimidate. (They were all receiving another shipment of royal baggage somewhere far above her.) Lifting the lid on the large cauldron over the crackling fire, she took a half-interested peek.

Setting out again through a set of doors, the queen emerged into a wide hallway that seemed to double as a depository for old junk. It was filled with forgotten odds and ends—filthy old armor and rusty weapons, stacks of mildewed paintings, a shield bearing the old Verdigris coat of arms, everything with that sickly inferior flower upon it.

Antiques!

With a start, Queen Nightshade realized the insolence to which she was witness. Her husband had outlawed it all, yet there it sat—apparently for some time—defying the king's orders of destruction. She quickly cataloged several of the more recent and offending pieces, including a set of footstools whose only crime was to remind her husband of his loathsome defect.

She would take care of this impertinence. Smiling wickedly, she knew of just the thing.

Picking up her extensive skirts, Queen Nightshade made a beeline back to the bubbling cauldron and, with a quick flick of her hand, opened her fine emerald ring—revealing a hidden chamber within. A misty white vapor poured out and into the servants' stew. Queen Artilla stirred it with a weathered-looking wooden spoon hanging from a hook on the mantel and finished with an approving nod. Turning, she resumed her pace with a renewed sense of enthusiasm for her tour.

The confusing hall finally leveled out for a jaunt and let out, to her great relief, into one of her favorite places. The castle's dungeon. She was directly under the garden, she knew, since the cryptlike cells were built—by Vidal Verjouce—beneath it. It was the last stop for infidels, enemies of the monarchy, and anyone that might simply displease Their Highnesses. And it was empty, uncharacteristically, since the royal family had just arrived.

Empty, except for the very last cell.

The queen could hear heavy snoring at the end of the vaulted corridor, and approaching the iron grating, clearing a layer of cobwebs as she did, she demanded to know who was the trespasser.

"You. Wake up. What are you doing in my dungeon?"

With a large snort, the man, dressed only in rags and wrapped in a threadbare blanket, jumped awake.

"Um—Your Highness put me here," the man said.

"Nonsense. We've only just arrived."

"I beg your pardon, but you did, Your Majesty."

"Are you disagreeing with your queen?"

"If I may—I was put down here last year."

"Last year?" the queen asked incredulously.

"Yes. Your Highness."

"Under what charge?"

"Let's see. Quacksalvery, I believe."

"Quacksalvery? You are an apotheopath?!" She eyed him with a mixture of repugnance and disdain and, although she hid it well, a touch of intrigue—a look she normally reserved for her novice tasters.

"Yes, Your Highness."

"I don't remember you."

"I answered the general call to cure the king's foot."

"I see."

"I was arrested before I was given the chance."

"Of course you were. Apotheopaths are outlaws."

"So it seems."

"Punishable by death."

"So I hear."

The queen looked around his neat cell.

"How have you survived?"

"I manage."

"Hmm. So you do."

She regarded the prisoner thoughtfully. There was a part of her evilness that would have enjoyed discussing in grand fashion all the wonders of his craft with this apotheopath. A meeting of the minds. The dungeon did always bring out the best in her.

"What's that there behind you, prisoner?"

The queen had spotted something in the cell's dank corner, growing in defiance of the lack of sun.

"Yes, isn't that wonderful?" he replied.

"What is it?"

"It appeared this very morning. A cinquefoil!"

Queen Artilla reacted very much as if she'd seen a rat.

"But how is that possible?"

The dirt floor was packed and unnourishing with the years of prisoners sleeping on it. Nothing could grow there.

Her voice turned icy.

"Destroy it at once."

"Oh, I couldn't do that."

"You must, and you will."

The prisoner shrugged, leaned down, and plucked the tiny yellow flower from its stem. As soon as he did, the petals dropped to the floor, where they instantly sprouted each another cinquefoil. The queen gasped.

"Very well, apotheopath."

She paused, evilly.

"I do so apologize for making you wait like this; it's quite irregular. Quacksalvery is, of course, a serious crime indeed. And I'll see to it that your sentence is carried out swiftly. I shall take great pleasure in addressing the issue personally. And sorry for any inconvenience this might have caused."

"Don't mind at all."

The queen looked back down the way she came.

"This the way out?"

"I believe so."

"Goodbye."

"Goodbye, Your Highness."

Queen Artilla walked toward the guard's booth.

"That prisoner there, he overwintered here?"

"Yes, Your Highness."

"Do you have a name for him?"

"Yes, Your Highness."

"Well, what is it, then?"

"He calls himself Manx. Cecil Manx."

Chapter Twenty-six

The Royal Cobbler

"ArrRRrrggggg!" King Nightshade screamed.

He sat upon a small, bleak stool, but the source of his discomfort lay at his feet. He was receiving a visit from the Royal Prosthetic Cobbler, a shoemaker of great talent who outfitted both the king's good foot and bad foot in a remarkable variety of clever footwear.

Gudgeon, for that was his name, made the king one fine right shoe, but the true artistry was on the left foot. Gudgeon transformed King Nightshade's enormous clawlike appendage—warty and clenched in a permanent contortion—into something of a matching set. True, there were several inches of elevation to the sole, and no one could hide the disparity of size, but really, the job for all intents and purposes was expert.

The only problem for both the king and his staff was each

new pair required a fitting, a painful fitting, which the king was enduring at present.

"Gudgeon—please, if you value your life, make this fitting end. This is worse than the mustard plaster and leeches!" The king was referring to a notorious experiment he underwent at the hands of one of the early contestants.

"I'm sorry, Your Highness, I'm nearly finished."

Gudgeon was the pinnacle of professionalism as he measured the king's bulbous big toe with a calibrated set of pincers.

A slight snoring came from the corner where someone had wheeled Prince Francis. But Lowly Boskoop was awake, very awake, and trying hard to find any place to rest his eyes besides his king's monstrous foot. A film of sweat beaded his forehead—he was feeling awful, truly awful, but not from the fitting unfolding before him. Although the king's bare foot was enough to give anyone pause, he had stopped into the staff's dining area for a quick lunch and ever since then his gut rumbled in a furious way.

"Might I recommend the green leather this time, Your Highness?"

"Is it soft?"

"The most supple."

"Yes, then."

Gudgeon was strapping and unstrapping what appeared to be a very uncomfortable set of belts on the king's foot, making minor adjustments as he went. The king groaned and distracted himself from the tortures with thoughts of bettles. He would just have time to take his tonic before the queen was due for lunch.

Almost as if she knew of his thoughts, Queen Artilla sailed into the room.

"Darling—I can't seem to find anyone in this wretched castle to help me." She stopped and looked at her husband's choice of seating.

"Nice throne."

The king sighed, visions of his tonic evaporating. He decided to ignore her—anything was better than an antique.

"Help you with what, my dear?" he asked.

"Ah—I want to draft a royal invitation to the reclusive author of my favorite book."

"What book?"

"My *favorite* book." She eyed her husband dangerously. *"The Field Guide to the Poisons of Caux."*

"Hmm." King Nightshade was uninterested. Whatever Gudgeon was doing was slightly tickly now, and that made concentration somewhat difficult.

"I'll need some help finding out just where he lives, though." The queen was picturing many of her evil ways of interrogation. "He is, after all, reclusive."

"A most excellent project, Artilla," King Nightshade agreed, thinking any project that would distract her from disrupting his own plans was a good one.

"But I can't find any of the help."

"Have you rung for them?"

"Of course."

"Have you shouted, then?"

"I thought I'd pop in here before I started screaming. Lowly"—she turned to the footman—"where is everyone? What is this insolence?"

Lowly Boskoop was caught in the midst of a violent wave of nausea and was speechless before the queen.

The king, finally noticing his servant's pallor, turned to his wife.

"Artilla. Lowly isn't looking so well. Lowly, have you *eaten* anything recently?" This he asked casually, never leaving his wife's eyes.

The question had an immediate effect on the queen, as the king intended.

"Just a spot of soup, Your Highness, nothing that might take me away from your side for too long."

"Oh. Then." The queen's tone was suddenly clipped, and she looked about the room, purposefully avoiding her husband's eyes. In her excitement, she'd forgotten the little incident with her ring in the servants' kitchen. "Perhaps, Lowly, since you are right here, you can take down this note for me— I'll dictate—and see that it gets into the right hands."

"But first, Lowly," said the king, "why not tell the rest of the staff to avoid the soup. Seems like a good idea, no?"

The king softened his tone, leaning toward his wife. "I know it's just your nature, darling. But I'm sure you'd agree we really need everybody to help with the preparations for the Feast."

"Oh—that reminds me! I was in the dungeon, darling, and you'll never guess what I found!"

"Do tell."

Gudgeon, for his part, was carefully replacing his strange tools into a leather bag and rolling up his leather samples. It was his aim to leave as soon as reasonably possible, both to get started on the king's Feast shoes and to depart the queen's company hastily. He turned now to redress the king's clubfoot in its enormous stocking and large velvet slipper.

"A prisoner!"

"A prisoner? How is that possible? We've only just arrived."

"Yes—I said the same thing. Apparently, he's been there all winter!"

"Oh. That's exciting!"

"Yes, I thought you'd find that amusing. And, Arsenious—he's an *apotheopath*! He came to try his hand at your foot."

The mention of the outlawed and disgraced profession caused Gudgeon to scatter his armful of rolled skins.

"An apotheopath! I don't remember seeing an apotheopath last year. I would most certainly remember that."

"I think he was immediately arrested. It is, after all, one of your outlawed professions. . . . Should we summon Verjouce?" she asked casually.

It was at Vidal Verjouce's insistence that the king outlawed this onetime very popular branch of medicine, and it was known that should any of these outlaws be captured, the Director was to be summoned at once.

"Noooo," said the king thoughtfully. "Have this . . . this apotheopath—"

"Cecil something, I think."

"Have him brought here before me, and let's give him his chance. He did come all this way. . . ." Here the king was thinking not only of his own well-being, but of just how much this would infuriate the Guild's Director.

"And if he can't cure your foot?"

"Then, Artilla, I leave him in your capable hands, as always."

This was just what the queen had hoped.

Chapter Twenty-seven

Prisoner No. 11,802

Sorrel Flux knew that to survive in the castle through his next meal, he needed to draw upon all of his inner resources. It had been many years since he'd performed as a taster in any real way and then only for the least demanding of clients in the halls of the Guild—visiting dignitaries and guests of the Director. Anyone of these sorts was usually an accomplished taster in his own right or used a taster provided by the host—this behavior, for obvious reasons, was only among the closest of friends and associates and only in the most exclusive halls of the rich and powerful. There was a casualness that Sorrel noted among the very elite, one that Verjouce at times had him use to his advantage.

Verjouce had encouraged Flux to pursue other talents, illicit activities that made the dark Director more powerful and feared. He was just the man to perform the secret midnight deliveries, or worse: the occasional dispatching of enemies of the Guild with a few drops of something deadly. In a strange twist of fate, Flux turned out to be much more adept at hiding poison in a dish than detecting its presence.

Now here he was, in Templar, tasting for the queen. He was very rusty. And this would never do.

Before his departure, Verjouce had assured him that he was needed here, that his presence would distract the royal family while Verjouce succeeded where Flux had failed—in capturing the unpleasant child. But Sorrel Flux was not entirely convinced—an alarm inside his conniving head was ringing. He couldn't escape the feeling that he was being punished for his apparent missteps at the Hollow Bettle.

He needed to keep his head down. He quickly realized that if he was to survive, he needed to create a distraction, whatever necessary, so that the queen had no time to turn her attention to him. Sorrel was, after all, capable of creating much mischief. He decided to quickly befriend the servant whose job it was to oversee the king's kitchen. And since Boskoop was feeling poorly, it was a golden opportunity.

"Prisoner eleven thousand eight hundred and two, Your Highness," said the sentry standing at attention in the enormous double doors.

Prisoner eleven thousand eight hundred and two was very delighted to be free from confinement, even for the moment, and bowed deeply to the assembled royal family. He was encumbered even in this small act of movement by an enormous knot of rope confining his hands before him, ostensibly to keep the apotheopath from any surprise medicinal tricks. Should the rope fail in this preventive measure, an excessive grouping of guards was there to protect the royal family from the dangerous quack with their pointy staffs.

Sorrel Flux, standing in position against the wall behind the queen, had met Cecil only once and was hard-pressed to recognize this man as one and the same. He was dirty and pale; his clothes were in tatters. But there was an appalling quiet dignity with which the apotheopath presented himself, and it was that quality alone—a self-possession that so eluded Sorrel Flux's own character—that roiled the taster into a smugness at the unfortunate man's straits.

When Sorrel had recovered from his surprise—after all, this was the man in whose bed he'd slept for an entire miserable year—he shifted ever so slightly so that the queen was directly in front of him.

"Hmm," said the king. And then again, "Hmm."

The Royal Diarist broke the silence that followed. "The king contemplates!" he clarified.

The thing was, the king had never before seen an apotheopath in person, nor had the queen—except for their first encounter in the nether regions of the dank basement of the castle.

Apotheopaths were rare creatures indeed after the coup that brought the Deadly Nightshades to power. Even before the takeover, Verjouce had seen to it that the entire profession was persecuted while he still had the ear of the old king Verdigris. They were said to be at best charlatans and at worst, well, King Nightshade wasn't quite sure what Verjouce had said the worst of them were. Only that their brand of healing was never to be trusted, and they were capable of much Verdigris mischief.

And here one was, in person.

Not much to look at, either.

"Do you have a name, apotheopath?" asked the king.

"Yes, Your Highness. Cecil Manx, Your Highness."

"You say you can cure the king?" asked Lowly Boskoop, who looked like he should be in bed, recovering with a hot water bottle and a good book.

"I was hoping to." Cecil nodded.

"Is it painful?" asked King Nightshade, with the memories of Gudgeon's last fitting fresh in his mind.

"No, I shouldn't think so, Your Highness. Just a few drops of a brandied tincture in your mouth."

"Well, then." The king looked around the room, and remembering his cobbler and the painful next fitting, he made a quick decision. "I'll give it a try. Providing, of course, you try it on yourself first. Can't be too careful, you know." The king patted his wife's hand affectionately.

"Well, Your Highness, the thing is . . . they took my medicine when they arrested me. If I just might get it back . . ."

Lowly Boskoop cleared his throat and consulted a long scroll of parchment.

"Yes. When he was jailed, they would have most certainly confiscated his medicines."

"Can they be brought up from wherever they are being held?"

"Um. They would have been destroyed, Your Highness."

The king sighed. Another disappointment.

"But perhaps the apotheopath can make his tincture again?" Boskoop suggested. The king perked up.

"Why, yes—there's an idea! You could just dash off another bottle! My wife would be more than happy to loan you her workshop."

"I would?" the queen asked.

"All hail the generosity of the king!" the Royal Diarist piped in.

"Perhaps Mawn might even be of some assistance, Artilla?"

But before the queen could find a reason why her trusted perfumer could not help cure her husband's deformity, the prisoner spoke.

"Well, Your Highness. The thing of it is, I don't really know what the ingredients are."

"You don't know what's in your own bottle of medicine?!"

The Royal Diarist scribbled, trying to keep up.

"You see, my niece made it."

"Your niece?"

"Yes, my niece—she's very clever with these sorts of things."

"Your niece . . ." The king drummed his fingers. In truth, this was beginning to bore him. He had the thought that this niece sounded a lot like she, too, was an outlaw.

Sorrel Flux thought of the little brat, how she was always busy doing something to annoy him. He was insulted by his master's attention to the girl and suspicious of it, too. It was because of her that he was here—in this dreadful castle! His master would be incensed if the king turned his attention her way. The Guild wanted to keep her away at all costs from the king. But for what reason? He saw no value in the child's company—only tediousness. In fact, he harbored a slight notion, although this was tempered with vanity, that the brat might have been poisoning him while he stayed with her.

So naturally, it was appealing to him that Verjouce's hard-laid plans might run amiss, but he thought it prudent—for now—to just watch and listen.

"But I'm certain she could do it again," Cecil tried hopefully. "We could just pop over and get her. . . ."

Lowly Boskoop cleared his throat again and consulted his paperwork.

"The Crown was at this man's residence—a tavern

apparently called the Blemished Bettle—and reported no one there. No girl. No one except a score of dead sentries."

At this news, Sorrel prudently ducked deeper behind the queen's throne.

"Really? How odd," said the king, referring not, it turned out, to the dead men. "Everyone knows bettles can't be blemished! What a curious name!" The king smiled at the thought. "A bit of the old poet in you, eh, apotheopath?"

Boskoop busily thumbed through another stack nearby.

"Um. Your Highness. Something else. There's no record of prisoner eleven thousand eight hundred and two even having a niece."

"What's this? No niece?!" cried the king. The whole thing was making his head hurt. Niece or not, this apotheopath/poet was not living up to expectations. Weren't they supposed to harness the forest and use it at their will? Did they not reveal the true, secret nature of plants with their increased powers of perception? It was high time that he cast this prisoner off to his wife.

Cecil Manx paused. He was about to break a promise to a trestleman—not something advisable under any circumstance—but he saw this interview was not going in his favor.

"Your Majesty, if I may. She's not *technically* my niece. She was found as a baby, floating in the river in the middle of the Windy Season. I named the child Ivy and raised her as my own."

At this confession, Sorrel Flux's many suspicions were, if not entirely confirmed, then at least validated. He was one of only a few who had access to the remaining ancient dusty books in Rocamadour's Library, where the many scholars deciphered the incomprehensible works night and day without halting. He knew now why his master had been so disappointed with him. Sorrel Flux put two and two together and arrived at a new and completely fascinating twist.

He knew the child in the great and ancient Prophecy to be a foundling.

Part III

The Winds of Caux

Neither the feeble heart nor the feeble mind will find refuge

from the harrowing Winds of Caux.

—The Field Guide to the Poisons of Caux

Chapter Twenty-eight

The Potion

Ivy was realizing a tender heart was needed to find beauty in a wild, bristly boar. Poppy was enormous by anyone's standards, especially an eleven-year-old girl's. At the boar's highest point, she was heads taller than Ivy. The muscled ridge between her shoulders crested with large spiky bristles, like an amusing drunken crown. And she was wide, half as wide as she was tall, making her quite stocky in overall appearance—and rarely, if ever, is stoutness confused with beauty.

And then there were the tusks. Long and bowed, they jutted from her pink gums, accenting her incredibly long snout and giving her a permanent snarl. But her eyes—light blue buttons—were deep and kind, and it was in these eyes that Ivy found hope.

This long snout was what the bettle miners so prized: it

was capable of sniffing out a vein of the raw stones through ancient impenetrable rock. But another of the bettle boars' jobs high atop the Craggy Burls was transport. Not of human cargo, as she carried now, but of an equally priceless burden: freshly mined bettles.

Poppy carried the taster with care through the doorway of their secret exit. The passage stretched upward, endless in the dim light. Ivy bounded after her. The way was quite narrow at times and steep, but since Poppy was born and bred to navigate steep mountain passes, this translated quite well to carrying a taster up the uneven stone steps.

Clothilde was last. She had stayed just long enough to extinguish the fire in the fireplace, and with a last look at the wondrous Amber Room—the inner sanctum of Caux's most magical king—she shut the door to Underwood, sealing it to its fate.

At last, the stair let out into a small room, and with a surge of affection Ivy breathed the air of the early morning—a surprise indeed to see they had somehow passed the entire night beneath the forest.

They had emerged from the fireside passage, up through a door cut in stone. The room held little more than the hearth, several open windows, and a rustic table, and it almost seemed—at first glance—they had left Underwood by way of the little forest cottage. A small cozy fire was burning in a fireplace beside them, and to this Poppy brought the sick taster,

ever so gently depositing his limp form on the stone hearth. She sat down beside him, hind legs jutting out from under her plump belly.

Rowan was very pale when Ivy turned to him. His breathing was shallow, and his eyes, although open, were glazed and unfocused. He muttered to himself in a worrying way, and Ivy heard him say the word *Estate* several times.

"He needs help," Clothilde said matter-of-factly. "He needs an apotheopath."

She looked at the taster, leaning in for a better view of Rowan's dilated pupils. "Hasn't Cecil been preparing you for just this? Are you not meant to follow in his footsteps? You must have years of study under your belt."

Her uncle. Cecil would know what to do. If only she had better attended to her studies rather than being so disobedient! She tried to collect her thoughts and assess his symptoms as she had been taught to do, but she found it impossible to recall her lessons.

"He thinks the Estate has come for him," Ivy found herself stating helplessly. The poor taster was moaning lowly now. Poppy looked concerned as she nosed his face with her wet snout.

"What," Clothilde demanded pointedly, "*has* he been teaching you?"

"Even if I knew what to give him, I left all of the

medicines with Axle," Ivy lamented, a jittery panic rising to her throat.

"Think," urged the lady. "Something less . . . traditional? Surely you can improvise."

There was one thing.

There was the elixir she carried.

But opening it would break a promise to a trestleman—something no one should ever do. At the trestle, Axle had taken her aside while Rowan still slept and made her pledge not to waste a drop, saying it would be clear to her when the time had come to use it. Surely, though, Axle wouldn't wish her to let Rowan die?

Ivy also didn't want to open the bottle for fear that Poppy would tackle her again if she smelled the bettle. She suddenly felt crowded by both the boar and Clothilde. And she didn't care for the look in Clothilde's eyes—one of distant amusement. Odd and unsettling, considering the current circumstances.

But Ivy saw that she really had no choice, and when she produced the brandywine bottle, Poppy merely looked up, nose sniffling slightly—and returned her gaze to the ailing taster. Ivy opened the delicate cut-glass top to the elixir, unwinding the thread of golden wire. Within, the bettle blazed against the fire. The stopper untwisted easily. Prying open Rowan's mouth, she carefully took several drops of the golden liquid and placed them on his tongue.

The effect was remarkably instantaneous.

The young taster's complexion went from gravely ashen, as the tonic touched his tongue, to a slow golden spread of health beginning from his mouth and seeping across and up his face, down his neck, to the tips of his fingers and toes. He seemed to sparkle. An unseen breath tickled his hair, passing down his dark robes and over the soles of his boots. Little swirls of golden sparks graced his cheeks, leaving a summer's flush behind, twinkling as they blew away. A great sigh—one of pure contentment—passed from his mouth, and he looked the picture of peace.

His eyes fluttered open, and in his face rose a healthy blush when he realized everyone was staring down at him.

"Well," Clothilde said softly. "Well."

"Wh-what happened?" Rowan managed. He felt himself reddening, but for the first time in memory, he didn't seem to mind.

The room was silent.

"What have you been hiding there, my dear?" Clothilde's eyes were narrow with interest.

"It's nothing," Ivy said as she wound the thin wire back into place. She was determined to forget the whole thing.

"That's some brandywine," Clothilde pressed.

"I'll say," Rowan agreed.

"May I see it, please?" Clothilde asked.

"No, I don't think so." Ivy was not feeling the spirit of co-operation.

"Give it here," Clothilde ordered in a voice quite unused to refusal.

"No," Ivy said, stronger. She put the entire thing behind her back and glared at the white lady.

"Ivy Manx," Clothilde began carefully, menacingly. Her arm tensed by her side, and Ivy wondered if she was going to take the bottle from her all the same. But her tone changed suddenly.

"As you wish," she said, this time sweetly, with complete composure. "Let's just keep that bottle safe. I'm not sure you realize what you have."

"I think I do," Ivy muttered.

"May I have some more, please?" Rowan asked eagerly. He was feeling better than he ever could remember feeling. His heart beat a pleasing rhythm in his chest, and the world seemed somehow more colorful. He stretched his legs, which still tingled pleasantly.

"I wouldn't have had to use it at all if you hadn't poisoned him!" Ivy glared at Clothilde.

Rowan's eyes widened indeed as he recalled this trespass.

"It was remarkably easy." Clothilde shrugged, and everyone was once again reminded of his failures as a taster.

"Well, it was a rotten thing to do," Ivy said bitterly. "He could have died! And for what? What did he ever do to you?"

"Rowan was never in any mortal peril. It was a small dose of baneberry—"

At this, Rowan groaned. It was an elementary poison at best, one any first year would have known.

"—and if you couldn't have cured him, I had the antidote." Clothilde produced a small vial from her pocket. "Ivy, it was the only way I could be sure that you were who they said you were."

"What does that mean?" Ivy failed to see how poisoning her friend was a necessary step in their introduction and said so.

"Cecil was supposed to have explained everything to you—it's quite tedious to have to do so myself. It was careless that he left it so long."

"Well, my uncle never mentioned you. And I don't know anything about a meeting." Ivy scowled.

At this, Clothilde softened.

"No, I don't suppose you would. It was arranged quite some time ago. You were a small child."

She paused.

"Ivy, I poisoned Rowan so that you might cure him."

She turned to the taster, intently. "My apologies, Rowan."

Rowan nodded, dazed.

"I needed to know if you were the one." Clothilde's crystal eyes didn't blink.

"One? What one?"

The sun chose this moment to break through the night, declaring morning officially begun. The soft light shimmered against the plank floor, reaching across to touch the wall. It ended the standoff completely, as sunshine sometimes can.

"The Noble Child. The one who has come to save Caux."

Chapter Twenty-nine

Bearing Stones

It is a strange sort of occasion to be one person one day and someone completely different the next. Imagine it yourself—to fall asleep one thing and wake something completely other, separated only by the peace and restfulness of your dreams. For eleven years, Ivy Manx played quietly on the limestone banks of the river Marcel and experimented in her garden and her workshop. To think, as she was forced to do of late, that her uncle—and Axle—for all those years was keeping something from her, something monumental, was a startling thought indeed.

And then to think, as it was reasonable of Ivy to do, that if she was someone quite different than she thought, then perhaps, too, her uncle needed a fresh perspective, another look.

Clothilde was providing this occasion. "Cecil Manx was— is—an apotheopath, yes. But not an ordinary apotheopath.

He is a Master Apotheopath, the last of a long line. Your uncle—as you know him—was at one time quite a fixture in Templar."

"Cecil?!"

"Yes. He was an intimate advisor to the Good King."

It was quite a task to picture this.

"King Verdigris? Are you sure?"

"Yes. He was the king's own apotheopath."

For a brief interval, the children were privileged to hear of the old king, his extensive and magical collections—particularly medicinal books and charts, which he stored in the Library in Rocamadour. They heard of Cecil there and his involvement in this gentle part of history, his personal discoveries (he was persistent in his learning, patient in demeanor, and responsible for many advancements in the arts—an entire wing in one of the most prestigious colleges was named for him!). His capacity for discovery was limitless; his abilities with healing plants were legendary.

Ivy's vivid imagination had no trouble bringing to life a mysterious scene of adult discourse between her uncle and the Good King Verdigris, but it was still tinged with an air of incredulity. After Clothilde was done, Ivy was even more perplexed than when she'd begun. She wondered just how this regal lady might have come to know her uncle—and what in particular this had to do with her.

"Were you at Templar, too, then?" Ivy asked, a bit timidly.

"Of course," came the answer as Clothilde smoothed a nonexistent wrinkle from her dress. "But I came to know Cecil only later. And, I should add, his disappearance has inconvenienced me greatly."

Ivy blinked, expressionless.

"And when the king departed?" Rowan asked.

"Ivy's uncle went quietly away. And, like many people of the old ways, waited."

"Waited for what?" Ivy wondered.

"Waited for the coming of the Prophecy. For you, apparently."

The three sat in silence.

"This Prophecy. You're certain it has to do with me?"

"Certain?" she scoffed, turning from the window, where Ivy had the impression she had been examining her own reflection.

"Regretfully, I am." Her head was held high, jaw clenched. Her profile, in the morning light, blazed at Ivy like a golden coin.

"Before that elixir, I would have said no. But it is as it is written."

The children could not help but notice bitter disappointment heavy in her voice.

In the silence that followed, Rowan moved to stretch his legs and, with Poppy bounding beside him, turned to the hearth where he had lain as an invalid.

"Uh, Ivy?" Rowan whispered. "Could you come here a minute?"

The taster had been convalescing upon a very interesting stone.

"479 knarls . . . to *Pimcaux*," they both read together.

A quick look behind them confirmed Clothilde was back at the window.

"We seem to be getting closer," Rowan pointed out.

"Yes!" Ivy agreed, reaching out to touch it.

The stone was smooth and carved with a fine hand, in intricate script, just like the one they'd seen in Southern Wood.

"It's warm. Here, feel it!"

Their hands—Ivy's small and delicate one, Rowan's sturdier example—rested beside each other on the ancient slab.

"A bearing stone," came Clothilde's proud voice, suddenly behind them.

The children jumped.

"Bearing stones were once everywhere—at every crossroad or smallest winding path—when Verdigris was here. If you were lost, they seemed to sprout up from the earth right when you needed them. But bearing stones are quite rare now—your new king had them all impounded. It is their magical nature that when they're moved, their information changes, too."

"What does it mean?" Rowan asked, recovering from his fright.

"Well, it's pretty straightforward, I'd say. Let's see—this one says 479 knarls—"

"What's a knarl?" he interrupted.

Her look told him never to interrupt her again.

"An old way of measuring distance."

The pair waited for her to continue.

"Roughly, it should take a good man one hour to walk a knarl. But I've done it much quicker," she added, smiling to herself.

"Are we near Pimcaux, then?" Ivy asked hopefully.

"Hardly."

"Have you been?" Ivy wondered.

"Of course. It's where I'm from."

Clothilde examined the two stunned faces and suddenly burst out in a refreshing peal of laughter.

"And if I'm going to get there—or anywhere, for that matter—I need to see a trestleman. The one under that little bridge just there, the nearest trestle. We will need something from him if we're to get off this island."

"Island?" Ivy ran to the window—and sure enough, they were in the middle of a vast, calm lake. How could she not have noticed? The whole place was dotted with tiny islands, as far as her eyes could see, each like a round green bubble in the still water. White mist clung to the lake's surface as the sun gained strength.

"Where are we?" she asked.

"The Lake District."

"The Lake District?" Ivy couldn't imagine how they'd traveled so far underground. Somehow, they'd emerged from beneath the entire Southern Wood and arrived at these splendid waters, once reputed to have healing powers.

"You're in a King's Cottage," Clothilde explained. "There are several around the kingdom, all alike, all set and ready for the king's return."

Ivy realized now that the cottage in Southern Wood was one, too.

"Somehow I don't think you're talking about King Nightshade," Rowan said.

"I'm talking about my grandfather. King Verdigris."

"Princess Violet had a daughter?" Ivy thought of the history Rowan had discovered in the *Guide*. The cinquefoil crest, the one that appeared on Clothilde's face in Underwood. She was indeed highborn.

The tall lady nodded and tightened the knot in her hair. She eyed the enormous lake in a way one might if one owned it.

The children sat in stunned silence.

"But how will you get there?" Ivy asked finally, peering out the window at the beautiful scene. "The trestle connects those islands over there. There's nothing but water between us!"

"Why, swim, of course!" And with that, Clothilde opened

the cottage door and walked two long strides, diving gracefully into the morning light.

While her departure left the pair wide-eyed, it had little
effect on the pig, who was chewing on her tail with great enthusiasm.

Chapter Thirty

Windwhippers

gain, as the tall lady's lively spirit left the room, the pair experienced a shift in mood. This time, a dark impatience settled in, and the shadows that were kept at bay by Clothilde's brightness quite soon resumed their dim shade. Ivy found herself fixated on the darker side of waiting.

"This Prophecy," Ivy began. "There's nothing about it in the *Guide*?"

"Nothing." Rowan shook his head.

"On the trestle, Axle told me that Uncle Cecil went to Templar in my stead."

"Why? To protect you? Maybe that's why he didn't tell you about *her*." He nodded in the direction of the door, contemplating. "Ivy, she frightens me."

Ivy nodded in complete agreement. She knew they needed

her, though—to get off the island—so she tried hard to forget that Clothilde had poisoned her friend with baneberry.

The pair moved to a huddle on the bearing stone, which now seemed a little too close for comfort to the small door and the bleak stairs down to Underwood.

"You don't suppose the Outrider could follow us here, do you?" Ivy glanced back at the stone chimney.

Rowan shuddered, the darkness further intruding.

"I doubt it. Either way, we're stuck here. Look at all this water!"

A gentle yet persistent lapping of the water's edge encompassed them as it nudged the island and the old cottage. Rowan, although sufficiently athletic, was not a confident swimmer even when outfitted with the proper attire. The water made the taster nervous, and rather than confide this in his new friend, he allowed his mind to turn to his grim brush with death. The visage of Vidal Verjouce returned to him and with it the recollection of some of what he was taught at the Guild. His heart sank.

"The thing about Outriders is their persistence. They never fail. He won't return to Rocamadour empty-handed. He's not allowed."

Ivy frowned. This didn't fit into her plan of finding her uncle.

"I wonder if the same goes for Mr. Flux," she whispered. He seemed, in the way of a tick, to be small but persistent.

The lady in white was back in record time, accompanied by a *clickity-clack*-like noise that heralded her arrival—and with her came the sun. The door opened, and Clothilde stepped inside holding what seemed, to Ivy, to be the remainder of an old umbrella. The contraption folded neatly, as an umbrella would, but had no repellent fabric—making it utterly useless in a rainstorm. It had strapping that crisscrossed the chest and shoulders, and a little pull cord dangled off the handle.

"One for you and you."

Clothilde distributed a rickety device to each of them.

"What . . . ?" Ivy began.

"Windwhippers." Clothilde smiled radiantly.

"Wind-whats?" Rowan asked, jaw dropping.

"Windwhippers—for flying. From the trestleman. They're such an inventive race, wouldn't you say? Quite useful at times. Odd fellows, though—every one of them."

True, the little thing seemed well made, albeit incredible. It was heavier than Ivy imagined it to be, something that did not lend itself well to flight. There were four paddles that unfolded from the central leader and presumably spun hard enough to carry her weight from one point to another.

"Is it safe?" Rowan asked.

"Of course." Clothilde gave him a sharp look. "Really. You should loosen up a bit."

"But what about Poppy?" Ivy asked. There were only three windwhippers.

"Poppy? How ridiculous! Pigs can't fly!" She laughed, amused.

Clothilde snapped her fingers and Poppy bounded over, leaving Rowan. She leaned down and whispered into the white boar's pointed ear for what seemed like an extraordinarily long time to converse with an animal. Ivy and Rowan exchanged concerned looks. Clothilde then rose and stepped back, revealing the new morning through the open door.

"Poppy's going home, you see."

"Home?" Ivy cried. She had grown to enjoy the boar's company.

"No!" Rowan echoed Ivy's sentiment. Poppy had helped save him, after all, and Rowan was easily endeared to pigs of any variety.

"What? Don't be silly, the two of you. We need her to get help. And fast. Poppy knows the way—it's not far from here. At least, as the crow flies."

Ivy threw her arms around the white boar's tall and muscular neck. She smelled like a surprise frost, cold and clean.

"Bye, Poppy, you be safe," Ivy whispered as Rowan rubbed the animal behind a bristly ear.

"Go now, quickly," Clothilde commanded.

And with that, the enormous white boar turned and trotted on cloven hooves across the cottage floor and—with less grace than her mistress but still quite eagerly—belly-flopped into the waters of the Lake District. Ivy watched from the door as the boar made surprising progress, soon fading away altogether into the mist.

The windwhippers—true to trestleman form—proved to be in good working order. The pull cords clicked pleasingly when exercised, and the paddles unfolded and extended into position, beginning slowly to rotate. After a minute or two, the things actually began to pull their wearers upward, an exhilarating sensation after they overcame the initial wobbliness.

Ivy, being the smallest of the three, had the least problem staying sufficiently airborne, although try as she might, the thing would not fly higher than a couple feet off the water's surface. It seemed designed to skim the rider along, like a leisurely Sunday drive, where one might be less buffeted by atmospheric conditions.

Rowan's contraption, however, proved to be more idiosyncratic. His robes immediately threatened to drag in the water, and he was forced to gather them in his spare hand and hold them aloft lest they become too wet, and too heavy, to fly. This immediately put him at a disadvantage, because steering was easier with two hands. He had to contend, too, with the added liability of his numerous pockets, which were full with the regulation paraphernalia that accompanies a boy in his position—one more accustomed to tasting than flying.

Clothilde, needless to say, was expert in the finer subtleties of flight. She bobbed sometimes less than patiently over the smooth surface—in the manner of one unaccustomed to imperfection—giving curt advice to the struggling taster.

"Straighten your arm. Loosen your shoulder. Keep the windwhipper perfectly vertical; otherwise, you'll be taking a bath."

It was maddening, but Rowan finally mastered flight—not exactly gracefully, but with enough utility, he hoped, to get him where they needed to go. Which, the lady assured the children, was a short trip across the waters to the biggest of the islands and then—should all go as planned—on to Templar.

There was not a more beautiful place, they all would have agreed, for a morning fly-about. The Lake District was one of Caux's natural jewels, vast and deep at the foothills of the Craggy Burls. The waters were freckled with satisfying little islands—little green humps parting the small waves on their backs. Clothilde's skirts billowed primly beneath her, refusing to be buffeted by the breeze—she was somehow dry and pristine, even from her earlier swim. She led the way, followed by Rowan, then Ivy.

The sun was nearly up above the mountains to the east, and Rowan, who had spent most of his youth waiting to see the Craggy Burls in person, felt a surge of expectation rising within him—the sort of feeling one can only get from vast, snow-topped peaks. These were the very mountains of which he'd so often dreamt! Ivy, too, felt at once humbled and thrilled; the contrast of cliff and its watery reflection was breathtaking. Somewhere up there Poppy had to make her precarious way—the peaks rose from the earth to jagged points high in the blue sky. As they clacked along, the brandy bottle tightly stowed in her waistband, Ivy wondered if the trip ahead for the boar was impossible.

And then, as they rounded a particularly large island, there was finally some sign of life. A sturdy pair of towers rose spectacularly in front of them, their caps pointing in opposing directions, and Rowan and Ivy scanned the waters eagerly. The stout towers, connected centrally by a covered transom, were mysterious and thrilling, but to Ivy's great regret, they were not the group's destination. In fact, Clothilde picked up the pace.

There was also something new to contend with— something atmospheric. The water, as calm as glass in the early morning, was forming little whipping waves, some even crested with froth, beneath them as they flew. Ivy had noticed it, too. Flight, as a general rule, is safer and easier when there aren't unruly winds with which to contend. Fortunately, the winds seemed to be pushing them toward their destination rather than away, but in a cruel trick they also seemed to be pushing them lower and lower—when the gusts blew down from the mountains, there was a very real possibility of being buffeted and slapped against the waves.

Rowan, who lagged behind, was taking the brunt of these damaging winds. His windwhipper had not been cooperating since it took him airborne, but it was now undeniably losing steam. He noticed with growing alarm that it was flying lower, forcing him even at times to pick up his heels. He had considered stopping briefly on the nearby island, but a rational fear of not being able to restart the contraption overtook him. That, and he was mildly sure he saw a pair of eyes watching them from a thin dark window in one of the towers—a set of eyes that vanished just as quickly as they appeared.

"The weather's changing," Ivy called ahead to Clothilde, but the wind never delivered her message.

Ivy turned to look back at her friend and saw his feet dipping in and out of the water. He was losing altitude quickly, and soon there'd be nothing he could do but swim. She urged her windwhipper ahead and finally caught Clothilde's attention.

"Should we land on that island with the towers?" Ivy asked, hoping they might turn back.

"Not a good idea."

"But I don't think his windwhipper will make it much farther!"

Indeed, Rowan's propellers had sputtered and stopped—and gasped back to life.

"Tower Island is a Nightshade outpost," Clothilde yelled over her shoulder.

Ahead, Ivy was happy to see they were approaching the largest of the lake's islands, an island called the Eath. Clothilde had turned back and was swooping in just in time to catch the taster by his collar and drag him, dripping, behind her.

It was in that undistinguished way that Rowan made his arrival, drenched and bedraggled, to the shores of an ancient retreat.

Here, on the biggest island by far, the lake met the Burls in a dramatic contrast between water and stone. Here, also, was one of the more dangerous places, due to the architecture of the mountains and the origin of the winds above, to wait out the Windy Season. It was notoriously unsafe. The collection of vast wooden structures before them was not fit for such an assault—in normal times a caretaker was responsible for closing down the property sufficiently to withstand the Winds, his main duty being the shuttering and boarding up of all the windows. But the windows were overgrown, and the caretaker was long ago poisoned by the island's new inhabitants.

Chapter Thirty-one

The Mildew Sisters

Ivy folded her windwhipper into a satisfyingly small bundle and immediately checked her cargo. To her relief, the bottle was quite safe and snug. She turned to help Rowan, who was battling his own contraption even on the ground; it was refusing to retract, and enraged, the taster had resorted to kicking it about the rocky beach where Clothilde had deposited him in an ungraceful heap. Clothilde stood fierce in the oncoming wind, beside several bracken-covered boulders made to guard a structure seemingly of shadow-brick and weed-mortar.

"Who could possibly live *here*?" Ivy wondered.

The taster stopped, with an anxious look upon his face, and pawed at his robes. Finally, with a sigh of relief, he pulled Axle's *Field Guide* from an inside pocket, swollen and damp from his swim.

The children huddled around it, Ivy happy to see the familiar cover on such unfamiliar turf.

"It's soaked," Rowan despaired.

"It'll dry. What're you looking up?"

Rowan had begun busily combing through pages clumped together with lake water, coming finally to a section detailing the Eath.

" 'A visit to the Eath was once a visit of privilege for Caux's few. Now, however, you will notice that the retreat has seen better days,' " Rowan read, pages flapping in the wind.

"No kidding," Ivy agreed.

" 'Those who remain await the day when the forests return to their true nature. Their attempts to summon plant spirits have merely resulted in the castle's overgrowth and decay.' " Rowan scanned the remainder of the entry silently for word on their hosts.

"Great," he began morosely. "Listen to this. 'Should you find yourself upon the Eath, you would be well advised to wear the cloak of neither a taster nor a taxman—for it is hard to tell which is more unwelcome.' "

"But we've nowhere else to go," Ivy reminded him.

Rowan thought of the set of menacing eyes he had glimpsed from the air as they'd rounded the island with the old towers.

"We've got to get inside, and away from the Winds," Ivy added.

The Winds of Caux—they blow from the north and funnel through the Craggy Burls, where they pick up speed and force as they have always done each year, at the same time. Strange and harrowing, the Winds will blow a chill into the bones and, it is written, an evil purpose into those of feeble hearts.

Above the weed-strewn shore, in the distance, Clothilde's white dress shone against a series of battered buildings. She greeted their hosts, indifferent to the children's whereabouts, and—without a backward glance—disappeared inside.

"Yes, I suppose so," Rowan replied dully. His trip had been exhausting, and he was cold and wet and unaccustomed to what he felt were such poor manners. He was overcome with regret. Were he still under the employ of Turner Taxus, he would be taking precious refuge against the notorious Winds in Templar—like *civilized* people. He knew his place, and this was not it.

Slowly, against the wind, the two trudged toward the retreat.

The Eath, once a desired destination, was now in ruins and shadow. Its great wooden turrets and fine arbored pathways were rotted and crumbling. Inside the main entrance, weed and dusk were taking over. A substantial dogwood tree grew through a hole in the floor, and scrappy saplings sprouted from between the wooden planks and ruined carpet. Dark water dripped from the ceiling and sky—the room could barely be considered indoors. This was no refuge, Ivy realized: the Winds could find it quite easy to sneak in through the floorboards, the wall joints—anyplace, really, that conspired to have in itself some sort of opening.

They found Clothilde quietly conversing with an odd threesome. If there was any beauty about these landladies, it had long ago been lost to the damp. They stood beside a tall pile of moss-covered bones and a small fire, which fizzled dispiritedly, threatening to extinguish at any moment. Upon the face of the first sprouted small pale mushrooms, so much so that her skin was entirely lumpish with the fungus. The next was wrapped in a cloak of moss and bracken, which grew about her in a manner that indicated it was unlikely she might ever remove it. A family of snails had taken up home upon her shoulders. The last of the Mildew Sisters, for this was their name, had about her pale skin a marbled pattern of blue mold, and her flesh threatened to crumble away—very much like a well-aged cheese. They shared between them a large fetid cup of tea, dark and vicious, which they passed from one to the other intently.

With Ivy's appearance, all conversation stopped. The taller, more treelike of the three poked a bony elbow into the gut of her neighbor and nodded at the doorway where the children stood. It had been her turn with the teacup, and she suddenly flung the dark brew out before her upon the ruined

carpet, and the sisters hurried to decipher the mess. They
peered down at the soaked leaves and scratched their chins.

"The forests will awaken," croaked the ivy-cloaked one.

"Ah, but dark plants stir along with those from the light,"
warned the mushroomed sister.

216

"A king," divined the moldy-veined sister, "will be cured by a child." The Mildew Sisters looked up.

"That's the one." She pointed. "Beside the taster."

Ivy's mouth opened in astonishment but quickly snapped shut when she heard the following words.

"The girl is welcome. But he is not." They continued in a chorus of protest at the presence of a member of the Guild for several minutes, at which point Clothilde, very much annoyed, interrupted.

"Ladies," Clothilde explained, somewhat less than patiently, "Rowan Truax is a guest of mine and therefore yours. Although indeed he is a scholar of the Guild, he's to be treated justly. And," she added after a moment's reflection, "he has renounced his official position by his own failure to perform his required duties."

It was an impressive accomplishment that when the conversation was over, Clothilde had indeed secured an invitation for the taster, but upon viewing his ruined room, Rowan found himself wondering if he would not be safer outside in the elements. He picked his way across an outcropping of what he was sure was ryegrass, in between broken gaps in the floorboards, and found eventually a small weedy bed and nightstand.

He ran a tepid bath of cloudy water, and after a disappointing time of emptying his damp pockets, he lined up his various instruments and utensils with care and set his beloved *Guide* out, open, so that it might dry. The robes would need to be cleaned and tended to, in the fashion that was instilled in the taster by his years of training, and Rowan happily found his small sewing kit still in working order in one of the tinier pockets.

Yet when he emerged from his bath, his heart sank as he looked about the room for his taster's attire. It was nowhere to be found. Instead, in its place upon the bed was a slightly musty green robe. The thought of someone else handling his taster's robes was a terrible one to him, and he set out in search of Ivy to complain.

Her room was just down the creaky hall, and as he navigated the rotting carpet, from somewhere he heard a lonesome piano—apparently their hosts had other interests besides tea leaves. The peeling walls, the sagging ceilings, everywhere was splashed with the dark stains and disintegrating plant matter of their thick brews. Apparently, the Mildew Sisters, in their attempts at divination, flung their tea about with great disregard.

Rowan was surprised to find the door ajar. It creaked in protest, the hinges heavy with rust. Clearing his throat to announce his visit and peering into the room, he could hardly imagine what awaited him. There, beside Ivy's sleeping figure, was Clothilde. In her hand, the delicate bottle.

"Hey—" he cried, all thoughts of his missing robes gone for now. "That's Ivy's!"

Clothilde turned to him, swirling the bottle, the amber liquid a vortex inside. "What did it taste like, taster?" she whispered. "Or could you not say?"

Rowan noticed, unhappily, that Ivy had not woken up—and a dark thought passed through his mind. What if Clothilde had poisoned her, too?

"What have you done to Ivy?" He glared. A pounding rhythm distracted him, and he recognized it as his own heartbeat. *"Ivy?"* Rowan called loudly. He stole a glance at her, but she was not moving.

At first he was unsure as to whether it was a trick of the small lantern in the room, for an unusual brightness was issuing forth steadily from the bottle in Clothilde's pale hand. The bottle light flared eerily. It exaggerated Clothilde's arched brows, making her appear at once old and greedy, while Rowan swiftly became peevish and spiteful. Ivy, however, shone with the peaceful glow of a child. (She even let out a small, sleepy sigh.)

Rowan was relieved to see that Ivy seemed to be simply asleep—in breath, in color, she had all the appearance of one enjoying a hard-earned slumber. Still, she hadn't woken up. He called to her again.

"All these years!" Clothilde was saying. "For this! From a mere child!"

As if powered by the force of her passion, the brightness grew steadily as she talked. "Such responsibility for one so young!"

The light issuing forth from Clothilde's hand had become almost unbearably bright. Still, Rowan was forced to look. The bettle glinted brilliantly, the amber liquid rolling about thick and viscously. He felt almost as if he were aboard a ship, rocking and swaying along with the elixir; his stomach lurched violently. With a crash, the window blew open; the winds beat against Clothilde's skirts, which billowed about like sails.

"Do you know, could you *fathom*, the value of such a thing? If it was to fall into the wrong hands . . ."

Rowan wondered horribly if it just had.

He took a deep breath and tried desperately to remember his disarming classes from the Guild.

There was a moment in time where it seemed almost possible to procure the bottle. But the taster moved too slowly, just as the bettle flashed with its own potent power—a swift and sharp glinting light. Clothilde's long fingers, once so delicate, now displayed a clawlike grip, and the white brilliance flared from between them. Suddenly she shrieked as if burned, and her hand withdrew in pain—leaving the bottle there, suspended in the air for a split second, impossibly hovering.

And then, as it must do, the small bottle crashed to the floor.

A familiar cloying scent overpowered the room, and to Rowan's great relief, it finally awoke young Ivy.

"What have you done?!" Ivy's voice was hoarse.

With horror, Rowan found Ivy staring at him. Looking

down, he was surprised to find he was cradling her uncle's bottle. All around him, the amber liquid of her panacea was departing quickly through the thirsty dry floor.

"I never did like the smell of that perfume," Clothilde sniffed.

Now, although Rowan had renounced the Guild, he was still, after all, a product of its making, and deep within him he held a great deal of respect for the priceless bottle—the ultimate charm against poison and atrocities of all sorts. But he had never held one until this very moment. In his palm it felt surprisingly heavy, and the grooves of its natural shaping, as he ran his thumb over them, lent to the stone a character of being carved by someone's own hand, carved as if to represent the vague shape of a winged creature, the wings folded flightlessly around its body. Somehow cocoonish. And it was warmer than he thought it might be. In short, Rowan quickly decided that it felt quite good in the palm of his hand, that it added a natural suggestion of another appendage.

"The bottle! You've broken it—and *the elixir's lost!*" Ivy was staring fiercely at him, mad with rage.

"No! She was trying to steal it!" Rowan remembered. "I came in and caught her red-handed."

"Nonsense." Clothilde dismissed his accusations with a wave. "I came in to check on Ivy. And what, may I ask, were you doing here, taster?"

Rowan was nearly shaking with anger.

"I came to find my robes." He glared. "Someone took them."

He held up the bettle, with the intent of returning it to its owner right away—but something caught his eye. The stone's central flaw was even more pronounced since its release from the bottle. Inside, the bettle was nearly cracked in half, the hollow within now much more evident. It seemed to flash like fire.

Ivy grabbed it back at once, and Rowan had a sharp pang of sadness at both the bettle's departure from his possession and the look directed at him by his friend. He wasn't sure if Ivy believed him at all.

Chapter Thirty-two
The Lien

Rowan could no longer disguise his distaste for his current hosts and the creaky lodging they occupied. He stormed out when Clothilde suggested to Ivy that he had desired the bettle enough to steal it—furious, too, that Ivy seemed to consider this a real possibility. His heart sank to his shoes and his stomach was knotted up in tangles from the withering look his friend had delivered. He intended to see that his missing robes were returned. He would brave the Mildew Sisters to file a complaint.

The Mildew Sisters' style of housekeeping was one that overlooked neatness and timely repairs and embraced chaos and decay. The old retreat existed as a collection of many smaller structures linked by old garden walks and trellised paths—once a spectacular way to spend a summer. Through the dark, he could just detect a light—from the looks of it, a chandelier straining to stay still. He found an old door leading to an outdoor pathway and unfastened it, but the wind caught it—and it rammed open with great force. It took all his strength to pull it closed again; as he did so, his borrowed robe pressed against his back in an unfamiliar way—a further annoying reminder of his errand at hand.

He paused outside, with nothing but his imagination to provide the setting to either side of him—it was a pitch-black brought on by both storm and night. Ignoring the impenetrable darkness, he focused on the amber light ahead. He could see long tentacles of vines, set free from their trellis in the wind. They batted about the archway like sharp whips and stung at Rowan's face. He covered his eyes with his forearm just in time to prevent a blinding blow—he was bleeding now from his brow. As he shuddered at the close call, the image of the sightless Director came to mind. Verjouce and the knotted scars that once were his eyes—what would drive a man to snuff out his own sight?

Through a small windowpane, Rowan peered into what was once a fine dining area but under the Mildew Sisters had settled into something of a repository for old tables and chairs. It was at that moment that he realized his own hunger, but his hand froze on its way to the doorknob. Inside, he heard the recognizable sounds of tea service: the clinks of spoons and tinkles of refills, the occasional splash.

"They will burden us for just one night—" came a hoarse voice he recognized as the mushroomed one's.

There was a grunt in response, a sigh.

"A member of the Guild—here! Nothing good can come of it!" grumbled the bracken-clothed one.

"Yes, well, we can always lash him to the raft and set him off for Tower Island," suggested the last sister. "Her plans are only with the girl."

At that, Rowan's hunger vanished.

"She said he's a wanted one, you know. There's a lien on him. A handsome reward's being offered."

At that, Rowan recoiled.

"It could be ours for the taking."

And at that, Rowan turned on his heels and set out for the shore.

He was outside immediately, once again fighting the whipping tangle of vines. He shielded his face the best he could as he dashed blindly through the underbrush and ran toward the shore. The rain had set in, and he was quickly drenched, and although normally this condition would have caused him pause, not so now. He was becoming hardened to the indignities of travel.

His ears still stung from the conversation he'd overheard.

They can't turn me over to the Taxus Estate if they can't find me, he thought bitterly. The whole day had been truly his most awful: he had been poisoned by the very hands of their host, issued a faulty windwhipper, and then made a mockery of upon arrival to this wretched place. To top it off, his robes had been waylaid!

He'd soon be done with the painful memories here.

At the pebble beach there was an inlet he'd spied upon arrival, where he remembered seeing some rickety watercraft. Anything would do, so long as it could float. He found his way there against the wind's assault, but he groaned at the state of the boats. On the short walk his mind had been imagining himself setting sail, and gracefully harnessing the wind to do his will with skill and bravery. It was a heroic picture, a heroic departure.

But he soon saw, as he wiped the streamlets of rain from his eyes, that he was offered two choices. Neither a dignified one. He could cling helplessly to a raft and hope to make it across the vast waters without any means of steering, or he could trouble himself in a small and battered paddleboat, the kind made very much for leisure and not at all for quick escape. With each, if he didn't sink to the bottom of the lake, there was the very real chance of alighting upon Tower Island and becoming prisoner to the Nightshades.

The paddleboat seemed the safer of the two, and in he went.

He went about the bone-chilling business of untying the old and frayed rope, and finally settled upon simply loosening it sufficiently to cast off. As he rubbed his hands together to warm them and sat, readying his legs to paddle against the breaking waves, he felt his first regret.

It was not his biggest of regrets—for they seemed to come not in order of importance, but instead in small, manageable packages. But it caused him to remain in the boat, unmoving, while he contemplated it. For he had thought of his favorite book, still in his room where he had left it. He thought of Axle's *Field Guide,* with its personalized—yet cryptic— inscription. *Taste and Inform.* Why had the trestleman auto- graphed it that way, with such a revered Guild credo? Didn't Axle mistrust the Tasters' Guild more than practically anyone? And as thoughts can do, this one small reminder ballooned into his next regret.

From Axle's guidebook, he thought more of Axle himself. And the promise the trestleman had extracted from him be- fore they'd left—his promise to stay by Ivy's side. Was he really about to break a promise to a trestleman? As he contemplated this awful thought, and the storm and the dock were conspir- ing to batter his small paddleboat, he had no powers of per- ception to spare. This deficiency caused him to miss the arrival of another individual upon the rickety dock. A grand individ- ual, one who seemed to possess in her a subtle light for which to mark the treacherous way, dressed immaculately in white.

"You'll not get far in that contraption," came Clothilde's strong voice over the wind. "Come ashore."

Rowan shook off his plaguing regrets at the sound of her voice, and with a look over his shoulder, he started paddling.

"I'll take my chance on the water, thank you," he called.

"Nonsense."

Clothilde was outfitted with a white umbrella of remarkable size, and it was no effort for her to lean it out slightly and cover both herself and the captain of the paddleboat. The effect of the umbrella was remarkable. It brought with it not only a shield from the weather, but the warmth of a summer day, and soon Rowan was unwilling to leave its comforts. Suddenly quite overwhelmed with fatigue, he took Clothilde's outstretched hand and joined her on the relative safety of the dock.

"You're quite foolish, you know," she began.

Clothilde's white umbrella possessed a separate and distinct weather pattern of its own, Rowan was now discovering. He looked about him and saw to his amazement that they were in an oasis from the slashing rain and wind, as one might reasonably expect from an umbrella of any design. But beneath its white boundaries was cast not a shadow, but a sunny day, or afternoon, or perhaps the glowing of a particularly nice summer sunset—which of these Rowan was unclear because the evening was so dark and the umbrella so welcoming. He began to dry.

"Someone told the Mildew Sisters about the Estate, and I'd rather not wait around for them to turn me in," Rowan began.

"Someone?"

Rowan nodded.

"And you think I encouraged them, naturally."

"Uh . . ."

"Well, Rowan Truax. Do you realize that the Taxus Estate is the least of your worries? If you're caught by the Nightshades—or anyone, for that matter, who will deliver you into the hands of the Guild—do you realize what your destiny will be?"

Clothilde leaned in, examining the young taster's face in the summer light of the umbrella. A moth had found its way under its protection—guided by the warm light—and Rowan watched it flit around.

"It's grim. You will face the Director, and as punishment for breaking your Oath, you will be degulleted. The ultimate penalty for a disgraced taster. They will remove your tongue, and what will you be then, taster?"

Rowan hardly needed to answer.

"An Outrider," he whispered.

Chapter Thirty-three

Departure

The next morning brought with it very little of a dawn. In fact, most of the night just stayed on, uninvited, and Ivy had a hard time making out much of the view from her bedroom window. The dark gray of the Eath's piqued waters distinguished itself from the dim storm clouds only by sheer will.

As Ivy leaned on the windowsill, she contemplated the gloomy scene. She was desperate to leave the Eath at any cost. The uninviting landscape did little to buoy her spirits as she thought morosely of the lost potion. Axle had said to keep it safe—and now look what had happened. There was no way to re-create it—she hadn't kept proper notes and by the end was impulsively experimenting with every possible ingredient she could find. She considered Shoo, his nervous hovering, and sighed. If she could just somehow convince the ornery bird to talk, she was certain he would know the recipe.

Elixir or not, she needed to get to Templar to find her uncle.

Just *how* was the question. The Mildew Sisters' lodge at one time offered its guests a pleasant variety of summer pastimes, but with the demise of the off-season caretaker, the few remaining watercraft were abandoned, tethered to themselves haphazardly. It was these that Ivy could barely spy below her—waterlogged and in need of great repair. A floating raft, at one time a swimmer's destination, bobbed lopsidedly in the distance. She watched as the wind picked the waves up by their scruff and sheared their tops off—sending them hurling at the shore.

With the worst of the weather still to come, this was no place to stay—but from what she saw out her window, they'd never make it to shore. Even if Rowan somehow agreed, the windwhippers were out of the question in this weather.

With a knock at the door, she found herself happy to see Rowan.

"Rowan! Your robes!"

Indeed, the taster was back in his somber vestments, which looked clean and pressed and none too worse for the wear.

"Yes," he answered somewhat haltingly. "Clothilde gave them to me just this morning. When she brought me breakfast."

"She brought you breakfast?" Ivy hadn't eaten.

Rowan flushed and looked uneasily around the room.

"Listen," he began quickly. "I wanted to tell you something. I'm sorry for last night, Ivy. Axle asked me to watch over you, and I should never have stormed out like that."

"Rowan—" Ivy wanted to apologize to him for thinking that he'd tried to steal her bottle, but he didn't give her the chance.

"And also, I wanted to thank you for saving my life, Ivy. Before, in the cottage."

It was Ivy's turn to flush.

"I think I know what Shoo felt like after Axle gave him your potion."

It was true: after his swift and astonishing recovery, his heart beat a pleasing rhythm in his chest, and his thoughts were surprisingly unmuddled. Rowan thought himself lucky to have sampled it.

Ivy's face clouded over again at the thought of her lost elixir. The bottle would be safe if Clothilde hadn't touched it—and she mentioned this now to her friend, miserably.

"And you know what else? She's never going to take us to Templar," Ivy concluded.

"She is! She said so." Rowan was certain. He was even sure that the grand lady would take them further on, to Pimcaux, but thought better of mentioning it. In fact, after his encounter with Clothilde under the umbrella, his feelings for the woman were sunny and tempered.

Ivy was casting him a dark look, arms crossed.

"What else did she say?"

He took a breath.

"That you can make more of that potion."

"No, I can't."

"I could help, Ivy!"

She shook her head, despairingly.

"Besides, I don't want to." She waited to see if Rowan might object, but a confused frown flitted across the taster's face. "I just want to find Uncle Cecil and go home again. I don't care about Axle's Prophecy!"

"Wait!" He produced the trestleman's wondrous volume from an inner pocket. "I wanted to show you something."

Rowan pointed out the page where Axle had written his personalized greeting to the young taster.

" 'Taste and Inform,' " Ivy read. "So what?"

"The Tasters' Credo," Rowan explained. "I was thinking that it's not just an inscription. It's *instructions*."

He stole a glance at her, but she was still pouting. She extended her hand.

"Do you mind if I take a look?"

He eagerly handed the *Guide* over, but Ivy flipped to the midsection and began folding out a map.

"I need to get to Templar. Even if I have to go by myself," she sniffed.

Given time, Ivy was certain her powers of persuasion would have easily won Rowan over. But the interval for this or any other private conversation ended abruptly as the pair was joined by Clothilde. Ivy watched Rowan's eyes shine as he gazed upon her, and she set her jaw defiantly.

"Time to depart," Clothilde announced. Rowan nodded in appreciation, and flashed Ivy a superior look.

"Quickly, though, if you will. I'm afraid those foolish Sisters have indeed notified the Nightshade outpost, and they are here, downstairs, to collect you."

Judging by the noise outside the door, the sentries weren't waiting.

Chapter Thirty-four

Skytop Glory

eep beneath the Eath, beneath even the waters that lapped its shore, there was a masterful piece of ancient know-how. It was a tunnel, and it snaked its way to the foothills of the mountains, where it opened into a steep climb. But like the Mildew Sisters' lodge above it, it was perilously in need of repair. Tiles, depicting lavish bettles of all shapes and colors, were cracked and missing in places. Damp was taking over.

It was only accessed by a small, rickety elevator, through which Ivy, Rowan, and Clothilde had made a swift escape, nearly taking a small battalion of Nightshade soldiers with them. As the heavy iron doors finally closed, Ivy's stomach was filled with butterflies, and Clothilde had looked pale and annoyed. The thing seemed to take a full minute to grind into action—all the while the sentries were shouting at each other and prying at the door.

Finally, after an excruciatingly slow ride down, the accordion doors folded open, revealing a secondary set—emblazoned with a familiar seal that sent Ivy's spirits soaring. The Royal Cauvian Rail.

It was an underground station.

A dull, flickery glow seemed to be coming from everywhere at once, accompanied by a low buzz. On the wide platform, the tiles were slick with puddles and resembled more a bathhouse than a once-fine train terminus. Yet even with the decay and neglect, the luxury of their surroundings was impossible to ignore.

Rowan, Ivy, and Clothilde were waiting in the dank terminal, excavated many years ago beneath the island. They stared into the darkness, the sound of dripping water insistent in their ears. In front of them, an empty set of tracks. While the group waited anxiously, a large square loosened from the arched ceiling and nearly hit Rowan on the head. The tile missed him, but the stream of water that followed it did not.

It was Ivy to first hear the train approach.

"It's coming!" she shouted, leaving all thoughts of the elevator behind.

And at long last, the buzz of the light became a separate low rumbling and the travelers suddenly snapped into action. There were several enormous leather chests awaiting them— Clothilde had scavenged the contents of the cook's larder— and it was a task to keep them dry. A whistle called to them from the depths of the tunnel. And although it would be some time before even the single glowing headlamp would be clear—the architecture of the tunnel, and its distinctive slope, prevented light from shining until the train was almost upon them—everyone relaxed in an almost cheerful way.

Once the headlamp made itself known—it shone brilliantly on all three expectant faces and illuminated the dazzling colors of the tiles throughout the terminal—the roar and echo became intolerable. Clothilde's dress was reduced to a white glare against the train's advance. Ivy held her ears as it pulled in beside them and exhaled a sharp burst of steam.

In the quiet that followed, a single door opened outward. It was a small door, of wood, and meant for a polite single file of passengers.

Ivy could no longer help herself. She had little idea where the train was bound (*up* was all she knew), but it was enough to be leaving the Eath behind. Not even a clatter of ceiling tiles hitting the floor directly in her path—and a perilously wide stream of water to follow—could stop her. And that was because she knew, as anyone can tell you, there is but one way to really travel. And that is by train—simply the very best way to see anything and everything at all.

She ran to be the first aboard.

This train, the Skytop Glory, was unlike most in Caux. It was of a sort with cogwheels, and these produced the rumble that everyone had heard. The cogs, combined with their mates on the tracks they sat on, enabled the train very specifically to mount slopes normally reserved for mountain goats or bettle boars. The cogwheels, like the inner workings of a clock, did not allow the train to slip.

And as soon as Clothilde had explained just this to her two travel companions, the train sputtered again to life—and they were off, reversing the path upon which it came.

They were traveling now beneath the Eath, a fact that made Rowan quite uncomfortable. He couldn't help but picture all that water overhead and remember the crumbling state of the underground station. Even worse, once they had departed, the lights on board dimmed noticeably.

After some time, they felt the ascent begin. And just then the tunnel beneath the lakes ended, and the bright day flashed its blinding light through the windows. Both Ivy and Rowan were left blinking at the brilliant foothills of the immense Craggy Burls.

Chapter Thirty-five

The End of the Line

"Well, thank goodness that's over," Clothilde said briskly as she smoothed her skirt in her plush seat.

The two assumed she had been referring to the excruciating wait for the train, but her next sentence would show them to be wrong.

"And not a minute too soon. Those Mildew Sisters. They are so immensely tedious."

Ivy, for her part, couldn't agree more but was annoyed that Rowan was staring raptly at Clothilde as she talked.

"They are bitter and unhappy and look to others for the promise of a better day. How does that make them any different from anyone in Caux? I hardly wanted to take you there. But it was a necessity. There was no other way to catch the train—and we've now done that successfully. Which, to my great satisfaction, means Poppy got the message through. So my advice to you is to sit back and enjoy the ride—you are in for a spectacular view."

"But where are you taking us? This can't be the way to Templar," Ivy blurted. She was greeted with a cold stare from Rowan, which she ignored.

"Really." Clothilde's voice was chilly. "We can hardly get to Templar by road or regular rail, can we? This is the only safe way. It's a forgotten route on an ancient train that I've arranged at great personal expense. You two are enemies of the realm, and I—well, as special as I am, I hardly blend in around here, do I? And, ignoring the Outrider for the moment, were we to set out in any normal fashion, we'd have to pass by Rocamadour—something none of us is eager to do, are we?" Clothilde looked from Ivy to Rowan. "So. We're going to Templar the easiest way we can—as the crow flies. Directly over the Craggy Burls to the other side."

Rowan frowned. "Um, Clothilde, I'm sure you have a plan, but if we're enemies of the realm, as you say, how are we going to move around the most heavily guarded city in Caux? The place is teeming with Nightshade sentries. Not to mention the king is there for the season . . . the king . . . *and* the queen." He shivered. Rowan, having been stationed at Templar with Turner Taxus, knew it quite well. It was a fortress of a city, re-markable in that it was sturdy enough to survive impassively any of the Winds of Caux.

Clothilde made it clear she was done conversing by simply

ignoring his question. And Rowan, not wanting to appear as tedious as the Mildew Sisters, thought it best to let it go unanswered.

"I told you she was taking us to Templar," Rowan whispered to Ivy, who scowled.

But it was only a moment later, as the sun cut a ray through a blanket of clouds, that she found her optimism getting the better of her. She leaned over and reminded the taster, "In Templar, Axle said to find his brother, Peps. He'll know what to do."

Rowan, for the moment, felt much better.

When the Skytop Glory thumped up and over a ridge, the world below opened up to them for the first time since leaving Underwood. And it was a magnificent vista. The earth laid out in patchwork, a view Rowan's imagination had tried, but failed, to compose in his childhood dreams of mountains. The land rolled away from the Burls and met the sky in a gray mist somewhere far away, above the distant sea.

But what Rowan saw next—albeit a speck in the distance— made his heart heavy and his knees tremble. The old mountains hosted many inlets in their rocky foothills. On the other side of the ridge that met the Lake District, surrounded by the poisoned barbs of hawthorns, was the place he dreaded most of all.

Rocamadour.

It was the great vultures he saw first—straining against the wind but always managing to hold their position, flying as

they always did, day after day, around the piercing black spire of the Library.

The Tasters' Guild. His old seminary struck a fear in him like he'd never known before. The dark, remote, needle-like spire seethed from the black hamlet below.

"Ivy," Rowan whispered hoarsely. His voiced seemed far away.

"Is that what I think it is?" she whispered.

Rowan nodded mutely. Ivy was particularly interested in seeing the infamous Guild from the relative safety of the distance. She pressed her face to the glass, but just as she did so, the train pitched into a tunnel.

As they clattered along in the darkness, the taster was thrown into a panic.

"What—what's happening?" he cried, abandoning all attempts at sounding calm.

"A tunnel," Clothilde called. "One of many. After all, we have a mountain to climb!"

The old train had some tricks left in it yet, and finally managed to produce for its passengers some decent light. Little reading lamps beside each chair flickered alive, thankfully, and the car was once again a hospitable and gratifying place to be.

"Rowan." Ivy turned to her friend, hoping to bolster his courage. "The mountains! Haven't you always wanted to climb the Burls?"

But with the lights, Ivy discovered that Rowan was no longer beside her. He had moved in the dark to Clothilde's side, and from the looks of it, he was enjoying her current lecture. Alone, Ivy took advantage of her reading lamp and turned to Rowan's *Field Guide*.

As she paged through the familiar text (the Craggy Burls, its lowlands and geology), she felt better. While in the past she might have found this very passage tedious and wordy, now it was a vehicle to bring her closer to Axle—and she was happy to read it. Happy, too, to be on her way to Templar.

On they rode, sometimes with a view and sometimes without, but steadily up the steep mountain. Leaving behind Rocamadour, they were soon gliding past enormous craggy rocks in massive, severe formations. Hoarfrost glazed the desolate landscape. Then ice and snow. Then an icefall—the water frozen in long, intricate gray threads. Hugging the worn book to her chest and catching only snippets of the conversation between the taster and Clothilde, Ivy swallowed frequently against her popping ears.

They passed the tree line—not a leaf or a needle would be seen from this point on. Then they passed the scrub line. Still, they traveled on. Crystals of frozen water sliced the sunlight into neat packages of color that danced on the train's interior.

Then up, up, up, ears popping—and once again into a tunnel, this one the darkest, it seemed to the young girl. Now there were twists and rises and finally, oddly, the Skytop Glory started going down. Slowly down into the mountain itself. And then, after a good long ride to satisfy the biggest train enthusiast, the journey ended abruptly on a thin platform.

"End of the line," Clothilde called after the immense noise of the termination ceased. "Everybody out!"

Peering through the old glass after her eyes adjusted to the dark, Ivy blinked at what she saw.

They were to disembark on an impossibly old and particularly rickety trestle.

Chapter Thirty-six

The Mines

Ivy was the first on the Skytop Glory and the last off.

Clothilde had enlisted Rowan already to help unload the cargo, a favor that he was more than willing to perform. Ivy was forgotten, which was fine. She wanted a moment with the trestle, which inhabited the cavernous tunnel end in a permanent twilight. Hulking and rusty, it spanned an impossible gorge.

Although decrepit and abandoned, it reminded her of home. It was of the same basic construction as Axle's, and she was suddenly thrown into a vivid recollection of the trestleman's sturdy and welcoming residence, its tangles of vines and roosting mourning doves.

The wooden platform, Ivy noticed, was barely presentable—a high contrast to the luxury of the train. It was rotted through here and there, and entire planks were missing in places where planks would be most useful. She didn't think she was imagining the sway of the old bridge, either—and she wondered whether it was wise to park such a heavy train here.

Ahead, the tracks were blocked with rubble cast off from the living mountain wall and, by the looks of it, had been for some time. Large gaps opened to a view of the bridge's lower framework and tangles of rusted barbed wire. Creeping along, Ivy noticed the old wood had an unlikely sound to it—light and airy, like chalk. Beneath her, the chasm rolled out in a dark carpet of rocks and echo.

"Hello?" she called. She realized she'd been hoping to find some evidence that the trestle was occupied. Clutching Axle's book to her still, she missed him fiercely.

"Hello? Hello? Hello?" Her voice sounded small and afraid coming back at her.

An unlikely flock of birds—crows, perhaps, but tatty and unkempt—was startled at her arrival. They squawked all at once, quite unpleasantly, and reminded Ivy nothing of her old friend Shoo.

"Oh, stop your complaining," she called out, waving away the confetti of dust and feathers floating about her. She watched as the birds descended into the black chasm, disappearing. Heavy in her other hand was Rowan's copy of the *Field Guide,* and, curious, she opened it.

The first page, with Axle's round writing, caught her eye.
Taste and Inform.
Hadn't Rowan said something to her at the Eath—that

perhaps Axle had meant it as more than an inscription? She ran her thumb along the dark lines. The ink had dried, making a noticeable ridge in the paper's texture. Shrugging, she brought her thumb to her mouth to taste.

Suddenly a large crack sounded—very much like lightning. The noise dislodged the remaining unpleasant birds from their shabby roosts, and Ivy ducked as they darted around her head in terror. The bang reverberated throughout the gorge, awfully.

Looking down, she realized the source of the noise was in her hands. To her dismay, the binding of Rowan's *Field Guide to the Poisons of Caux* lay broken. The emancipated pages were littering the old trestle, falling like leaves at her feet. Recipes for mulled cider, directions for various useful knots, instructions for setting a table and making toadstool tea—all now hopelessly muddled and made even more incomprehensible by Ivy's frantic gathering. Clear over the edge of the trestle went chapters and maps, floating in the twilight as on a lake, down to the murk below. Several pieces of the parchment were hopelessly snagged in the tangle of barbed wire beneath the bridge and fluttered helplessly.

Ivy was faint with dizziness. What would Rowan say? His beloved book!

There, flitting beside her in the thin air, a pressed flower.

Axle's cinquefoil.

She slapped her hands together, capturing it. The frantic

squawking of the birds began to fade, and through it, a voice. Albeit thin and distant, it was undeniably that of her friend Axle.

Ivy Manx, he began as the black of the gorge closed in around her and, inexplicably, the winds picked up.

Rowan, for his part, was in high spirits. Even the unfriendly comment from Clothilde, concerning his relative strength to his size when he was unable to move a single chest on his own, had little effect on his mood. His youthful wish for adventure—to climb the tallest mountain in Caux—had been realized. He could taste the thinness of the air and feel the coldness of the mountain on his back.

Clothilde had marched off in long strides, and he was forced to trot to keep up with her. He quickly found himself in a smaller tunnel, lit with simple strands of clinking bulbs. Ahead, Clothilde's whiteness glowed luminous within the mountain.

The path headed down, further into the mountain's belly.

Soon they came to a widening, and Rowan saw in the vast room an outcropping of white structures perched willy-nilly. Each had a circle for an entranceway and a high, peaked roof—an odd scattering of giant birdhouses, he hazarded a guess. But he needn't have troubled himself further, for his debate was interrupted by the form of a familiar flash of white bristle. From one of the dwellings rushed Poppy—they were apparently the perfect size for pigs, he realized—and Rowan now found himself on the rocky floor happily reunited with the bettle boar.

"Oh, Poppy! We missed you, girl!" he cried over her endearing grunts and snorts. "I'm so glad to see you!"

"Really, Poppy," Clothilde scolded. "Such a display."

Poppy pulled back but remained by the taster's side.

When Rowan rose, sufficiently rumpled, he found a crowd had gathered. In the mines it was rare to have visitors. The miners—and each of their own bettle boars—had gathered to greet them. They wore prickly beards, and their hearty mustaches were trained out to either side with wax, not unlike a pair of tusks. In their arms, long staffs of lit torches pointed at the visitors.

"Boxelder," Clothilde addressed the head miner. "I see Poppy made it in time to deliver my message." She tossed Poppy's prized orange bettle at her, and the pig caught it eagerly. "The old train was a welcome sight."

"We said anytime, and we meant it," replied the burly man, his boar sniffing the air by his side.

"Well, I can't say enough how grateful I am. As a small token, I've managed to bring you a few supplies." The miners appeared to have endured no shortage of supplies, Rowan thought, if their waistlines were any measure, but all the same they seemed quite delighted with this information. "The burden was too much for the taster, and I've left them beside the train."

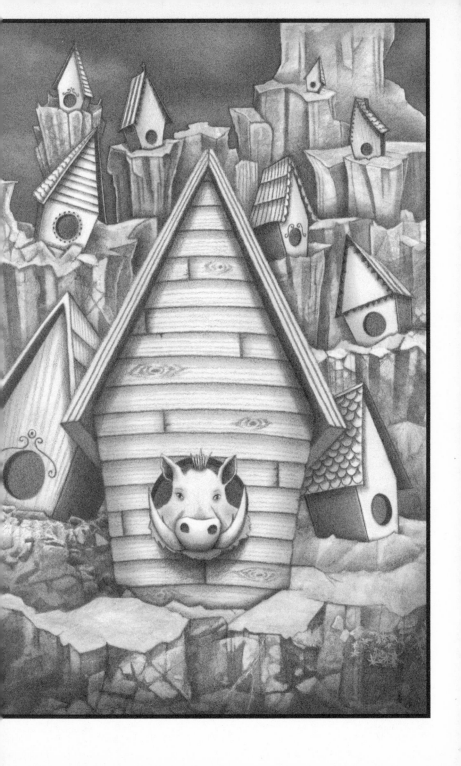

"Taster?" The miner named Boxelder redirected his flame at Rowan.

"He is on an errand with me," Clothilde responded, and this seemed sufficient.

It was dawning on Rowan that he was in a mine. Miners and bettle boars really could mean only one thing—but was it possible he was deep inside a bettle mine, where the priceless jewels of the kingdom were carefully extracted from the living rock wall? The very origin of Caux's privileged indulgence? He looked around with a keener eye along the dark corridors of the mine, but there was little to indicate what magic existed within the Craggy Burls.

Beside them was a small widening in the cave. The miners finished conversing with Clothilde, and several of them had opened dented flasks, filling the room with the smell of something hot and bitter. Boxelder directed their attention to a corner, pointing with a tool that normally hung by his side from a thick leather belt.

The miner's boar trotted on ahead to the corner. There was a break in the hard rock, a vein of loam. Now that Rowan had noticed it, he became aware that this crumbly soil was everywhere in the walls of the mountain. It was layered with stripes of it, and as it turned out, these layers were where the bettles were mined.

The beast, excited to burrow in the loam, eagerly began sniffing the entire work area, sticking the length of her snout into the rich earth. She bounded around from point to point enthusiastically, snorting—sneezing once. Soon enough she found what she was looking for, and her whole body tensed. She began digging feverishly.

Boxelder took his pitchfork and ordered his boar back by his side—no easy task for the excited animal. He began carefully digging in the loam, separating the thick clumps by hand at times. The dark earth smelled rich and satisfying in the sterile rock of the mine, and Rowan was reminded of his father digging carefully for potatoes in the back garden. From his years of study Rowan knew the miner needed to be careful here—bettles come out of the earth soft and gummy and are easily damaged. When exposed to air, they instantly harden, becoming virtually unbreakable—the only known substance that can break a bettle is another bettle.

But Boxelder worked intently and not long after was rewarded by a find. He turned around to the group to display the bettle—a small green one, still with clumps of earth clinging to it.

"A souvenir," said the head miner, and casually tossed it to Rowan. A current of desire moved through the boars. He caught it and looked about the dimly lit cavernous space, incredulous.

"For me?"

"A gift. From your host, Vidal Verjouce," he said soberly.

Rowan nearly dropped the jewel, which was still warm and

slightly slippery. Of course the mines were controlled by Verjouce; his mighty grip on the precious commodity was to be expected. In his excitement Rowan had forgotten this, and now, hearing the Director's name, he began to feel claustrophobic. Clothilde, however, seemed indifferent and had resumed her hushed tones with another miner. It was a good thing, he realized, he had found his robes.

"If you don't like it, you can always give it to the boar," Boxelder advised, misinterpreting the taster's look. Poppy, by Rowan's side, was watching the bettle with an intensity saved only for prey.

But there was no giving it away. Rowan stammered his appreciation. He was a product of Caux, after all, and had just been given something few could afford on their own. A clever dark sea green—wonderful.

His wonder turned to surprise, however, when he realized that Ivy was nowhere to be seen. He had assumed her to be right behind him. Figuring she was back by the trestle, he volunteered to accompany Clothilde and the clan of miners on the errand of retrieving the chests, where he hoped to show her his new acquisition.

Chapter Thirty-seven
The Hollow Bettle

It was not black at all, Ivy was realizing, but a very dark storm she was witnessing as the vision unfolded before her. The familiar Winds of Caux blew about her relentlessly. Ahead, the Marcel. It was nearly impossible to discern the edge of the raging waters she was seeing against the blackness of the sky, the snap of the branches as they whipped against the shore. Somehow, she could just make out the hulking steel skeleton of a familiar trestle.

As she listened to her old friend's reedy voice, the vision became clearer. In the deep gray, she saw the small form of the trestleman as he struggled against the wind (how unlike Axle to be out in this weather!), making his way down the embankment. There, with the help of his outstretched walking stick, he was attempting to dislodge a small crate that bobbed in the waves in a tangle of driftwood.

It was extremely precarious, and he lost his footing more than once, grasping at river reeds to save his fall. Drenched and exhausted, he was successful in the end. Bringing the crate to shore and from there up to his warm apartments, he finally opened the box as Ivy watched.

Beside the fire, she saw what lay inside. A bundle, wrapped in gossamer—a familiar white fabric seemingly impervious to dirt and damp. And within, completely warm and safe, slept a miraculous baby girl. And Ivy knew at once what she was seeing: this sleeping child in the trestleman's nervous arms was herself. And if that were not enough, she saw, as the trestleman's shaking hands unwound the stark white gauze that swaddled her, that nestled with her was a red bettle. The very bettle of the Hollow Bettle's namesake.

A child of special birth, of extraordinary circumstance, Axle was saying.

The vision was dissipating and with it again the feeling of electricity.

Although I wanted nothing more than to keep you safe . . . Axle's voice trailed off. *I am, after all, a trestleman (and a particular one at that), and I knew you should be with your own kind. So Cecil raised you as his own, and together we swore to keep the secret of your arrival safe, safe from even you, until the time was right.*

Ivy could no longer make out Axle's voice, and she realized she was once again beside the cogwheel train, high above the dark chasm. At her feet, curiously intact, was Axle's book.

Clothilde was her mother? The Good King Verdigris was her great-grandfather? Ivy was reeling.

She knew that white fabric; it was unmistakable. *Child of special birth.* Remembering that in her breast pocket was the red bettle, Ivy clasped her hand to her heart.

But any further contemplation was to be impossible for now, for a roar like no other filled her ears. Snarling, snuffling, and the clattering of hooves filled the vast chamber, and Ivy's next thought was a surprising one: apparently not all bettle boars come in white. For before Ivy, and nearly filling the entire cavern, was an army of boars. And they were racing her way. In fact, although many were indeed white like Poppy, many more were not—some were spotted and dappled, some were shaggy and brindled—but all were breathing steam as they pounded toward her in the cold mountainous air. Ivy caught a momentary glimpse of Rowan, in among the beasts, an exuberant look upon his face—but he was lost in the pack of animals almost as quickly.

For as far as Ivy could see, there was nothing but tusk and fur.

And then, through the sea of boars, Rowan was suddenly by her side.

Panic was rising in her chest, but her friend's arrival calmed her somewhat. Still, she did the only thing she could: she held the bettle above her head in a desperate attempt to ward off the onslaught of snorting and huffing animals all bent on seizing it.

A fierce chorus of whistles filled the air, obviously meant for the bettle boars, and to Ivy's great relief, the animals froze—their eyes on her upstretched fist, their noses quivering in anticipation. A few of the stout miners pushed their way into the bundle—a most peculiar group, thought Ivy. Rowan's eyes—in fact, *all* eyes—were upon her upstretched arm.

The cavernous chamber was suddenly achingly quiet, and Ivy noticed it had taken on a new, strange illumination. The entire audience, too, was bathed in a subdued light, and beast and man alike stared unblinkingly at its source.

It was coming from above her.

In her clenched fist high above her head, Ivy's bettle was glowing with an intensity unlike any flame before it. Her entire hand blazed a crimson red, and where her small fingers met, the light poured forth as if she'd scooped up a star.

Ivy slowly lowered her shaking hand and, cradling it in her other palm, opened it.

For a moment, before her eyes adjusted, she was overcome with a brilliant, hot light, but that quite quickly faded to a dull glow, and as the room looked on, the bettle's inner light dimmed slightly and pulsed in her open palm.

A cry rose from the gallery. "The mark of the Good King!"

Beside her, Rowan could see Ivy's face and, upon it, the blazing outline of a cinquefoil.

"Verdigris's crest," he heard Boxelder utter from somewhere nearby, his voice hoarse and unsteady.

And then, in a final surprise, the bettle, warm in her outstretched hand, gave a little jump. A small pulse, or flutter. There was no mistaking it, and Ivy was so surprised she nearly dropped it to the ground.

"So you see," Clothilde said sharply as she looked around the gloomy cavern, finding Boxelder's eye, "why I need to get the children to Templar. We'll go by way of Skytop."

The miners gathered around her in a quiet huddle and proceeded to talk in low tones.

Rowan and Ivy peered into her cupped hands, heads together, bathed in a rosy light.

"The crest! Ivy, it was on your face—just like Clothilde's!" Rowan whispered. With the mark of the king making an appearance on his friend, he found himself feeling timid and slightly foolish beside her.

"We have to get away," Ivy said urgently. "Just the two of us. I'll explain later."

"But what do you suppose this Skytop is?" Rowan asked.

Ivy cast him a look that plainly showed her annoyance. "What does it matter? I'm sure you'd follow *her* there—anywhere, for that matter."

"What do you mean?" Rowan looked down at his feet, knowing perfectly well what she meant.

"All I'm saying is, you've been awfully cozy with someone who poisoned you." She snapped her fingers shut over the soothing light in her hand and stood straight.

"There's a path over there," Ivy challenged. "Let's go now, while we have the chance."

Rowan looked about the room and made a quick decision.

"Okay, but we take Poppy, too." He couldn't bear the thought of leaving the boar behind.

"Fine," she called over her shoulder as Rowan motioned for the animal. A faint set of stairs was carved in the rock, he saw, and they edged forward, keeping to the shadows. The adults were discussing something intently, and a pile of woolens and shaggy furs was being amassed in their midst.

"It was written long ago—" the head miner protested. "You must know we have been warned. There are regular inquiries by the Guild."

"It is mine, this task, and while I appreciate your position, Boxelder, I do not see it your way," Clothilde said.

The miner nodded finally and appeared to wish to counsel her further but, under her direct gaze, seemed to reconsider. Instead, he turned to one of his miners for a report on the mountaintop.

Now nearly to the carved stairs, Ivy started sprinting. She

heard Rowan right behind her as she began climbing the teetering steps.

"*Ivy.*" A clear voice rang out in the chamber. The room became deathly quiet as the voice fell away.

"Go on!" Rowan urged.

The path did not lend itself to speed, and she slipped in her haste, nearly ending their escape in a frightening fall. Dust rained down on Rowan.

"Foolish girl." Clothilde's voice was shrill. "How will you get to Templar without me?"

"Don't listen!" Rowan called helplessly. "You said she'd never take us—remember?"

"There's a treacherous mountain pass ahead, and you'll never make it past the gate." Clothilde sounded pleased.

Ivy slowed. A hint of trepidation crossed her pale face as she turned to Clothilde. Poppy stiffened and snarled at the gathering below.

"What gate?" Rowan challenged.

Clothilde stood, as she so often did, with one hand on her hip and ignored his question. "I'm certain Boxelder would forgive your rudeness if you'd just be kind enough to wait a moment." She looked at them from under a raised eyebrow. "After which I will be happy to escort you quickly—despite your doubts—to Templar."

Ivy scowled, looking about the room. Several of the miners had been inching forward and were within pouncing distance. The large clan of boars, sensing the undercurrent of menace, curled their lips and raised their hackles.

Ivy stared down at Clothilde and wondered suddenly just what sort of mother might let her baby float downriver in a windstorm.

"That's a good girl," Clothilde cooed. "Now get down here, both of you, and after you apologize to your kind hosts, we'll be going. You too, Poppy."

The miners broke free of the huddle, and Ivy found herself meekly in their midst—their heavy scent greeting her nose. With Clothilde by her side, she felt a fleecy wrap thrown around her, and she mumbled something of an apology to no one in particular.

True to her word, Clothilde saw that they departed quickly and by the very same set of steps Ivy had started. She felt her way along the jagged walls and walked carefully, although Clothilde bounded forward indifferently. Poppy's hooves clattered against the rocks behind them. When there was nothing but darkness—a deep mountainous darkness like none other—Clothilde lit the staff Boxelder had given her and instructed Ivy to hold up her bettle. She did so, begrudgingly. A pleasing red light warmed the way but did nothing to lighten the children's mood. Ivy was aching to tell Rowan about her vision on the trestle. She crept forward uneasily, waiting for a moment alone with him.

The path led the group ever upward. Although Clothilde

showed no signs of tiring, Rowan felt it was a fine time for a rest, yet he dared not suggest it. At some point there was a crack in the darkness. The white light was more blinding than Clothilde's robes, and it grew as they approached it. Against the brilliance, she was all but invisible.

"Rowan, hurry yourself," Clothilde demanded.

He rolled his eyes. No one besides himself seemed to acknowledge the lack of nourishing air. Ahead, Ivy kindly stopped to wait for him.

"There's a rope tacked to the wall here, and I want each of you to take hold of it. And don't let go."

With that, they emerged from the semi-darkness into the snow-blinding light. They were near the highest peak of the Craggy Burls, in a world of white snow and ice. And it was cold—so cold that their hands against the rope quickly froze up, despite the miners' best provisions.

The way was marked with flags tattered by the mountain winds—most of which were pointed at odd angles, their poles having shifted in the snow of the ages. Clothilde and Poppy disappeared in the snowscape: the only splashes of color as far as Ivy's eyes could see were these flags and their own hooded jackets, made crudely of some kind of fur.

They hiked the steep zigzagging path, at one point passing through a crevice so small that Poppy needed to be pushed through, grunting with protest. At the top, they were greeted by the austere hulk of the ancient Skytop Abbey.

Before it, a formal gate.

Peering through the massive bars, the children saw the Abbey as it gleamed in the daylight, reflecting off thousands of impressively large icicles hanging precariously from the steep roof. The entire place was set on the clifftop, suspended over the vast cloudscape below.

"The gate you were wondering about." Clothilde stared at Rowan coldly. Rowan glared back, despite the heat rising in his face.

"How do we get in?" Ivy asked, the freezing wind stealing her breath.

"Just one way," Clothilde responded, feeling about in her neat hair. She produced a silver hairpin from somewhere, and it glinted in the stark sunlight.

Ivy relaxed, expecting to see some fine lock picking. Such illegal business made her feel right at home. But rather than turn her attentions to the ancient and unwieldy lock, Clothilde instead grabbed Ivy's wrist and quickly secured her small hand in her icy grasp. She brought the hairpin down and pricked Ivy's little finger.

"Ow!"

"Two drops," Clothilde stated after assessing Ivy. "Just two."

"What are you doing?" Rowan demanded. "Don't you have a key?"

Clothilde led Ivy and her wounded pinky over to the lock

and allowed a large single bead of the brightest red blood to form and then drop upon the casing. There it puddled against the freezing metal and, all at once, vanished inside. Clothilde repeated this and, satisfied, released Ivy's hand and replaced the hairpin, allowing herself a moment to smooth her immaculate hair. But in doing so, a third drop of blood fell from the girl's hand, and instead of finding its mark upon the locked gate, it splashed upon the white lady's skirt hem—a solid blotch of intense color against the brilliance of her gossamer robes.

Clothilde reacted with a sharp intake of breath. For a moment, she looked at the two children with shock, then bent her head to examine the stain.

"What have you done?" she hissed.

Ivy and Rowan were captivated. Their cheeks frozen and their backs buffeted by the wind, they watched as Clothilde's dress made what can only be described as a remarkable transformation.

It began at the hem, the crimson color rolling in like fog—thick and weighty. The small droplet intensified, as if the dramatic whites of Clothilde's dress were calling out for color, thirsty and insatiable. Little waves and curlicues of red surged and rolled, commandeering the fine and delicate weave. Eventually, the entire gown was the color of Ivy's blood, more vivid and commanding even than the white had been. Shocking against the white snow, Clothilde sighed crossly and set her smooth face with a look of determination.

The children stared wide-eyed at the plush crimson gown and then at each other, incredulous. It was only when the transformation was complete that Ivy noticed the gate had swung open.

The group approached the only entrance to the Abbey available to them, a door crusted over with an impossible layer of ice. Spiked icicles creaked above them as they stood on the threshold, waiting. Clothilde managed to free a large brass knocker and rapped loudly, causing a cascade of crystal spears to drop down in an icy symphony.

"If this doorway's any indication, no one's been up this way in some time," Rowan whispered in the silence that followed.

"I somehow think we're not that fortunate," Clothilde responded grimly.

Ivy didn't like the sound of that and reached over to grab Rowan's gloved hand.

At last, cracking, snapping, and finally splintering, the door opened inward. The travelers were greeted with a humid blast of warm air and what appeared to be an empty hallway.

Chapter Thirty-nine

The Hanging Gardens

kytop Abbey was once the lone outpost on the mountaintop, back in Good King Verdigris's time. It bordered on nothing but the ether, and the monks who lived there found it to be as close to their creator as they could get. Their brandywine—some of the best ever to be sampled—was made from a secret recipe and was thick and syrupy, tasting of mountain herbs and nuts. The monks existed in a severe silence, and busied themselves both distilling the brandy and tending to their exquisite hanging gardens.

These gardens were nourished by the hot sulfur springs that bubbled up from deep within the mountain. Consequently, there was an abundance of both heat and water, and with this resource the ancient monks constructed a series of terraces and arbored gardens to rival no other.

But none of this was to be seen—at least immediately.

For the group received an odd welcoming.

Straight ahead in the entranceway appeared a monk of sorts, dressed in deep brown. But—at seeing Clothilde—he gasped with some alarm and attempted to rush the group as quietly as he might up the arching set of stone steps at the hallway's end.

"Poppy, you stay here." Clothilde ordered the boar to remain outside.

"But she'll freeze!" Ivy was aghast.

"Nonsense," Clothilde snapped. "She's a bettle boar, and she will do as I say." Clothilde turned to the animal. "This is for your insolence earlier. Did you think you would not be punished for attempting to leave without me?"

A horrified look passed between the children, but there wasn't time to argue.

Mounting the stairs, Clothilde radiated displeasure. The monk, having ushered the group into a large apartment, shut the door and leaned against it.

"What is this?" Clothilde demanded of their host. Her eyes flashed, and bolstered by her red dress, she looked positively fierce.

The monk looked pointedly at Ivy.

"I think I'd better explain in private," he whispered.

Clothilde's annoyance evaporated, and she agreed to depart with him.

"Don't do anything foolish," she admonished the pair.

"And do not leave under any circumstances, do you understand?"

They nodded, chastened.

As the thick wooden door clicked closed, Rowan turned to Ivy.

"Does she think we're little children?" He scowled. "Who does she think she is to talk to us that way?"

Ivy looked at the closed door.

"My mother," she confessed.

Rowan blinked.

"What?" His mouth was hanging open, and when he finally was made aware of this fact, he snapped it shut, nearly biting his tongue.

Ivy began, breathlessly. Rowan had been right! On a hunch, she had tasted Axle's inscription on the abandoned trestle. She told him about her vision and then fished out his beloved *Field Guide* and returned it to him carefully.

"I knew it!" Rowan was pacing now. "I just knew it! I could have told you. The crests, you see . . ." He stopped in his tracks. "You know what this means, don't you? You're descended from the Good King Verdigris! You're highblood. *Noble* . . ."

Ivy nodded, not wanting him to finish. The Prophecy was troubling in many ways but mostly because it was secretive and vague, and seemed to occupy the arcane realm of adults. It was also the reason behind their current situation and their search for Cecil in Templar. Ivy peeked out the window to the inner cloister. Below, she saw the gardens. She knew they were not supposed to leave.

"Let's go take a look around. What do you say, Rowan?"

Rowan could think of nothing nicer, and the pair left together quietly down the same stairs they came up.

The monks over the years had taken care to extract from their natural settings—whether under moldy floorboards or atop the highest tree—every last variety of flora to be found growing in all of Caux. It was an extraordinary opportunity for anyone with the love of plants (Ivy considering herself in this group) to explore and study.

Much of the vegetation was instantaneously recognized by Ivy, but astoundingly enough, there was much more that was not. She was particularly fascinated by a grouping of bog plants—some small flycatchers and some rather hungry-looking pitcher plants. These plants enjoyed the taste of meat; the smallest was ready to reach out and pluck a finger from her hand. The largest, with its odd-shaped funnel and crooked gullet, was big enough to swallow a man whole and slowly digest him alive. She skirted them carefully and warned Rowan to do the same.

Birds, many free-flying but some in gilded cages, chirped and called out to each other in the humid air. From somewhere in the center of the gardens came the sound of a bubbling fountain.

After passing through a carefully manicured hedgeway, the pair found themselves along a lengthy row of tall and impenetrable yew—little glistening red berries peeking out from the green like pins in a cushion. The floor here was soft with moss and made for a delightful walk. Ahead, the hedge turned off at a right angle, and another grew up beside it—and Ivy realized with some excitement that they were about to enter a maze.

"A labyrinth, Rowan! Let's try it!"

Rowan was less enthusiastic. He could see no reason to purposefully get lost—it was annoying enough to find himself lost by accident, and to pursue it intentionally seemed foolhardy. But Ivy was streaking down the long corridor already, and he knew that he needed to keep her in sight.

He caught up to her just in time; the two met at the corridor's end, beside a peephole. They could choose to walk in either direction, and as Rowan was assessing the merits of their choices, something altogether startling happened.

To their great surprise, the two heard, through the little opening, the ringing peal of a woman's laugh. At first the sound was quite foreign to their ears. It was the laugh of a young woman, a laugh from a time in which laughing happened often, and spontaneously, and was shared with a partner.

Such was its power that it stopped them both in their tracks.

And then, as they turned to each other to perhaps find some answers, there followed a voice, dark and turbulent, one that Ivy had never before heard. But it was a voice that Rowan, having endured the secret Epistle ceremony, would never forget.

Clothilde and Vidal Verjouce—the betrayer of King Verdigris and the merciless leader of the Tasters' Guild—were sharing a private joke a mere arm's reach away from them.

Chapter Forty

The Maze

"I s this what I think it is?" Vidal Verjouce's voice was at once rich and revolting.

"Yes, that's the one," Clothilde responded. "It was in the cellar, overlooked by the sentries."

"Such a gift! And how clever of you to have that pig of yours deliver it to me."

"She remembers her way to Rocamadour," Clothilde said knowingly.

Rowan swallowed, turning to Ivy. There was silence as they heard Verjouce skillfully sipping from a goblet.

"A spectacular vintage. Well aged—eleven years?"

"Very good. What else?"

"Hints of oleander—the bees that pollinate the fruit enjoy fields of other flowers. There is, yes—mistletoe."

"Mmm."

"Fine apples for the wine. Apples, wouldn't you say,

Clothilde, my darling, are a most interesting fruit? I do prefer grapes—more regal. But here we have something. Yes, a medley of apples. But from an old orchard—tended by an undisciplined orchardist. He has other things to tend to besides his fruit trees?"

Clothilde was silent.

"And rainfall? Oh. A good, wet year. But something else—"

"Yes?"

"I taste a stream—no, it's a larger body of water. A river, yes! It flows by the orchard."

"A river, Vidal? You astound me."

"It runs over granite—no, limestone. A chalky taste. The willow rails occasionally dip in for a drink; those I taste distinctly. The cool night air brings a sweetness to the underside of the leaves. I know this river. I do. And I detect a slight char—the applewood smoke this man burned alongside the mill."

"The mill?"

"Your gift is a map, really. I *taste* the mill house by a river, by a small walled orchard. All the information's there; you just need to know how to discern it. It could be tended better, the trees, but the mistletoe that hangs alongside the apples and the ryegrass that is allowed to grow high on the copse floor give this little brandywine its distinct and very valuable flavor. Like music—a young girl's song."

There was a shuffling at the children's feet—and Rowan

looked down to see a small plump hedgehog. Ordinarily, he might have welcomed this unusual distraction, stopping to admire his prickly sheen, but since Verjouce had ceased rhapsodizing and Clothilde was silent, the little fellow's burrowing threatened to attract attention. Ivy cast Rowan a look that could only mean she expected him to somehow shoo the creature away—but as anyone knows, hedgehogs rarely, if ever, listen to what others want from them. It was, after all, his hedge.

But the two were relieved—if only momentarily—to hear Clothilde resume the conversation.

"Your powers of taste never cease to amaze me."

"So I have described it accurately?"

"With perfection."

"Can I assume, then, you have found the apotheopath's tavern?"

Clothilde paused, while Ivy held her breath.

"I have, yes."

"And the girl?"

"Yes."

Ivy looked at Rowan, crestfallen.

"Wonderful—wonderful news!" Verjouce rasped. "You'll tell me everything, of course. But first, let's toast to the occasion! Where is she? With the child under my control, there is nothing to worry the Guild further. To the end of the Prophecy!"

"To the end of the Prophecy," Clothilde toasted.

"And the beginning of the Golden Reign of Taste."

Rowan, for his part, couldn't help but be impressed by Verjouce's tasting abilities—he had heard of his powers to discern the smallest notes in a morsel of food—but to *taste* the trees that dip into the stream? The very air filled with summer pollen? It was a wonderful talent given to an appalling man, and he found himself wishing for even the smallest fraction of that ability.

But it was not lost on Ivy, who had grown rather pale as the conversation continued, that they were discussing her uncle's brandywine—the vintage of her birth, the orchards of her home. Cecil's mill house, his cellars of dusty bottles: Clothilde had been there soon after the sentries and had used Poppy as a messenger. Ivy realized Poppy was probably returning from the dark and evil errand when they met her in Southern Wood.

Here was her home being described so accurately by such a wicked man. An inky darkness crept into her memory of the sun-drenched house and happy meadows, a sinister gloom that left the trees shriveled and air stale.

With the mention of the Prophecy, her heart sank, while everything else inside her told her to flee. Before she realized it, she had leapt to her feet and set off running, but the conversation had a disorienting effect on the young girl. To Rowan's great horror, he turned just in time to see her slip further away into the king's maze.

Chapter Forty-one

The Hedgehog

As she ran along the high walls of the hedgerow, Ivy cursed Aqua Artilla. Its garish scent, its beguiling decanter. She thought of the day she decided to copy it and cursed that, too. She wouldn't be here had she just kept to her poisoning pastimes. Cecil wouldn't have left her, that horrible Mr. Flux would not have been retained, and now—here was the ultimate betrayal. Her very mother delivering her into the hands of the enemy.

Ivy knew from Axle's *Guide* that Templar was close, just down the other side of the mountain. She would finish what she set out to do. She would find her uncle. At once. And alone. Verjouce himself was searching for her, and that meant great danger to all she encountered. Rowan would lose his tongue if the Guild captured him.

The bettle, her bettle, beat a warm rhythm against her palm. She stopped, suddenly.

She had been running the wrong way, she realized, and had no idea which way was out. Every way she turned looked like where she had come, and finally, she collapsed where she stood—crying quietly at a great burden that suddenly felt quite heavy on her small shoulders.

At that moment, the little hedgehog made his way in front of her—hardly noticing her there, carrying on as hedgehogs do in their very slow and methodical way. He snorfled and snuffled as he busied himself with a carpet of moss. Ivy thought she had nothing better to do than to follow him, and that she did.

Being at home in the maze and being at home among hedges, the little creature was impervious to confusion. He ran the maze every day looking for edible tidbits or good scraps of

nesting material to take home. Today was no different, except he had company.

So with his help, Ivy was soon shown the way from which she came, and although she tried, he would hear nothing of her gratitude (nor would he have understood it). How thankful she was to be at the maze's entrance and back in the hanging gardens!

But instead of looking for Rowan, she began looking for a door out of and away from the Abbey. A door! She thought suddenly of the Doorway to Pimcaux from Axle's thick book. Just off to the right, past a lovely collection of twisting vine and an ancient apple tree, she spied a small exit. What would this one lead her to?

Rowan was not easily going to break a promise to a trestleman. He had seen Ivy emerge from the maze and followed her quite hurriedly onto the outer stone terrace and into the bright white. There, to his great delight, he found Poppy at home in the deep snowdrifts. But as he looked around, his heart sank—everything was the same stark, scorching white, and Ivy was nowhere to be seen against it. He thought better of shouting out—he feared more than anything inviting Verjouce and Clothilde along on his search.

"Where is she, Poppy?" Rowan demanded, whispering into the boar's velvety ear.

The beast, well trained with her nose, took no time in

bounding off after Ivy, leaving Rowan to follow her tracks. The drifting snow and rush of winds were nothing to the bettle boar. She soon caught up with her, and it was here that her instinct and enthusiasm for bettles got the better of her.

If asked—if such a thing were possible—the bettle boar might say that she had only meant to nuzzle Ivy's hand gripping the crimson bettle. But this is sadly not at all what happened. What happened was much more of a disaster, one that Rowan, as he was still running to catch up, was powerless to prevent.

Poppy's sudden appearance startled Ivy, and caused her to release her grasp upon the bettle. Were that the end of it, that would be a sufficient tragedy. But no. Poppy was, after all, a trained bettle boar. A beloved and beautiful one, too. And as the red bettle bounced once, then twice, then careened into an icy chasm, Poppy bounded after it and was lost to the snowy-deep cavernous belly of the mountain's core.

Part IV

Templar

The purple of Nightshade—no one can resist it. Even those who bear its name. It calls, dark and inky, its rich fruited soul, so beguiling, so deadly.

—The Field Guide to the Poisons of Caux

Chapter Forty-two

Sorrel Flux

It was nothing short of a state of pure annoyance in which Sorrel Flux found himself currently. The damp of the castle was such that it crept into every corner and aggravated not only his sinuses, but his temper. He had almost given up hope of breathing through his nose while he slept—something about his bedding provoked him into fitful sleep, so that he found himself rising every hour or so through the entire night. He had been ever so successful in ingratiating himself to the queen—it was, after all, his best talent, to make himself needed—and even her gift of a hand-combed flannel nightdress and matching cap did nothing to resolve his insomnia. He found himself with a lot more time on his hands, time in which he was truly in a foul temper.

Admittedly, his disposition was never one of sunshine and rainbows, so for the entire castle's staff, the days that Sorrel Flux was most unhappy were their misfortunes, too. But on a good day, when one was to be found, Sorrel Flux would readily concede that his time had been well spent in the castle. Flux found it quite ironic that his former master, Vidal Verjouce, had meant this position as a punishment—when almost immediately the potential for real, true accomplishment made itself known (not the kind that Verjouce promised, the kind that never seemed to materialize). For Flux was a man privy to all of Verjouce's secrets and therefore all of the Guild's as well. And he knew many things, many more things than his master might like him to know.

Simply by being gifted with sight, unlike his master, he had been able to keep to himself little tidbits of information that had come across Vidal Verjouce's vast leather-topped desk at the Tasters' Guild. He had perfected his signature—this, with Verjouce's blessing—and often signed Guild-related documents when his master was indisposed. He had free access to Verjouce's drawer of wax and special seal, so with his signature and crest Flux might send off even the most secret of messages representing himself as his employer.

And it was in this drawer—or rather, behind it, in a hollow void that served as a secret cabinet—that Sorrel Flux had made himself familiar with some very old and cryptic documents he had found while exploring. The sheets of paper were hastily folded and quite enormous, as it turned out. They had been ripped from their binding; he could see on one side a ragged border.

Flux needed to put them on the floor to make them out—and then, to his great chagrin, he was greeted with some sort of ancient impenetrable script. But spending a little time with the pages, he suddenly (accompanied with a severe feeling of light-headedness) felt that he could perhaps read a phrase or two. It was as if his eyes were twisting the old handwriting into the proper shape; the sepia ink wriggled and collapsed upon itself in knots, and was born again—briefly—as legible writing.

It took tremendous concentration on Sorrel Flux's part to discern that he was reading the location of some sort of doorway, and after the event he was left with a blinding headache—so much so that he found the whole experience nauseating, and never again attempted to translate the remaining papers. But he took with him the knowledge that this must be something of some import, since his master had never once mentioned the existence of these documents, nor had him chronicle them for him, as was his duty.

So it was that this experience of his came back to him one late night as he tossed and turned in his servants' quarters at the castle. And he realized something. Something that disallowed sleep for him for the remainder of the night—and for once he cared not at all. He realized that he had been privy to an important piece of information.

He knew where the Pimcaux Doorway was to be found, and he knew he was very, very near it.

Chapter Forty-three

The Knox

The dreadful King Nightshade stared out the window from his private chambers. He was looking at the mountains in the distance, particularly at the snow that draped itself over the peaks in a way he found intruding, encroaching—perhaps even invading. It was no accident that most of his time was spent in the south, on the sandy shores of the tropics there. He pictured his good foot, hale and hearty, alongside his horribly disfigured one, pale and ineffectual, walking in the white powdered sand of his favorite beach.

He thought of his beloved Kruxt now, during this Windy Season, being battered and bruised. The fruity palm trees flailing about in the gusts. The thought saddened him, so he turned his homesickness into anger once again at the looming mountains. His thoughts often went round in circles this way and might continue on for some time, after which extruding themselves in the form of a poem.

But today he was bothered by another thought.

His wife, the queen, had been single-mindedly focused on the Festival of the Winds, particularly her favorite part—the execution—and he hadn't seen much of her at all. He felt neglected. And everywhere she went, that awful yellow man was by her side, anticipating her every need and sharing, often, a private joke or two with her. A joke, he couldn't but somehow feel, at his expense—he was sure he'd caught the man imitating his limp. This smarmy taster was everywhere the queen was—particularly since the Royal Perfumer, once glued to Artilla's side, had seemingly disappeared overnight. If Artilla missed her advisor and perfumer, she didn't show it. She seemed utterly satisfied with her new taster's attention.

And then there was the rash of poisonings he had to contend with. More than usual, by far. The servants were upset and nervous. These things rarely distressed him—if ever. But they had been affecting his quality of life, and that would never do. The king sighed.

The butcher—gone.

The last of five generations of bakers—gone, too.

The iceman—sick and unable to make his deliveries, causing vast amounts of good food to spoil, which in turn was causing a great deal more illness.

The fishmonger, the milkmaid, the stable boy—all unaccounted for.

Had the queen succumbed to her own overenthusiasm?

Was she poisoning willy-nilly? And—this thought was a particularly difficult one for him—*was he perhaps next?*

For once, he grew suspicious of her and regretted his choice of his twin as sole taster. The logic of using only his sleepy brother was wearing thin in this time of extreme need. He made a note to inquire to Verjouce for an understudy from the seminary.

And with that, he turned his back upon the hulking mountains, and the town of Templar below, and made his way over to his writing table, with some foul poetry on his mind.

It was these offending mountains off of which both Ivy and Rowan had successfully found their way.

They had sat, freezing, by the chasm's edge, calling for Poppy to no avail. The crevasse was deep and icy blue and seemed to open up into nowhere and extend down forever. Finally, it was Rowan who insisted it was time to get warm. Ivy left behind her last token of her home, and source of great comfort, and Rowan, his new and faithful friend. A traveler passing by them (although, of course, there was none) might have seen two of the saddest faces ever to be seen before in Caux—a land, admittedly, full of forlorn faces.

The thought of Verjouce and Clothilde united against them was a chilling one, and eventually drove them into the Abbey's carriage house. There they found a dark sled, and frantic with fear and worry, Ivy unlashed its tethers while

Rowan flung open the wide doors. Paying no mind to their vehicle's sinister ownership, they pushed off.

Axle had once said it would be an odd sort of carriage that could convey its passengers in both swiftness and stealth without the aid of steam or rail. But as a trestleman, he can be forgiven for this oversight, since not once had he found himself aboard a grand sled. And what a sled it was upon which Ivy and Rowan now embarked! Rich in detail, and no expense spared: it pierced the snow with a mighty stallion's head carved of ebony, as if ready for battle. The beast's wild eyes and frantic grimace were flecked with white as the children pushed off down the mountain pass. The cabin was warm and neatly kept, equipped with upright seats and thick woolen lap blankets, but this finery was lost upon the children, for they were each mourning their great loss. They sped down the Craggy Burls in Vidal Verjouce's personal snow carriage, the edges of the runners honed and sharp as knives.

Finally, they came to a place where the sled could go no further: the snow was scarce, and rocks and rubble littered the pathway. An awful grating noise emerged from beneath the carriage. They left behind the black horse head to a gallery of sharp rock and to the company of no one, a wisp of fine snow swirling about its dark nostrils and lolling tongue.

The remainder of the trip was left to their own feet, and since it was not far, they were quite agreeable. By then the view of Templar was clear, and the thought of arriving at the Knox bridge—Axle's favorite place, after all—gave them the energy they needed to complete the journey.

The Knox! The bridge was impossible to miss. It spanned the Marcel, which here was quite wide, and harkened the beginning of the city of Templar. The Knox was like a village to itself, its tenants draped over the river with ingenuity and daring. The bridge was almost as wide as it was long, and either side of it was populated with stores and watering holes where a railing or barrier would normally be found. Some of the more outrageous buildings even reached up several stories high over the water, claiming every last inch of real estate in extreme feats of engineering.

And the din. It was a place of commerce, true, but also discord. Both Ivy and Rowan had been so used to long stretches of silence in their travels that the pandemonium they encountered at the city's edge took them aback. As their ears adjusted to city living, their eyes were treated to a dubious breed of Cauvians—true, there were merchants and tavern keepers, as well as other similar citizenry. But they mostly kept to their storefronts and apartments. No, the Knox bridge seemed to attract little of the fine and respectable folk to its wide cobbled street, but rather, shifty-looking individuals, city dwellers up to no good.

Everywhere vendors called from movable carts. Wheelbarrows of poisonous mushrooms and droopy, suspicious-looking herbs blocked walkways. Small vials of vicious syrups clinked seductively on top shelves. Ragmen sipped pitchers of flat ale while trading in tabletops of patched clothing and old and moldy shoes from the recently deceased. Rowan was appalled to see ersatz tasters—impostors not properly trained by the Guild—floating about looking for dangerous work.

A murmur rose from the crowd ahead, and Ivy looked up in time to see a ragged man fall to the ground and a circle form around him. This man, in his short life, had been called Klaxon, and Klaxon had made a surprising number of enemies. He was common to the bridge, and once the crowd saw there was little else to see, they dispersed.

But no sooner had the dead man hit the street than a gaggle of undertakers—Rowan knew them instantly from their beaverskin top hats and dark suits—appeared, elbowing their way in to inspect the unfortunate. They came to an agreement among themselves, and after much nodding and negotiating, an apprentice was ordered to load the deceased into a plain wooden cart.

"Watch your pockets," Rowan advised Ivy in her ear. He knew in tight places with people like these, a pocket might be emptied of its valuables quite expertly. He clutched his tasters' robes tighter to his chest; with the other hand, he reached for Ivy's.

"There's nothing to watch," she replied dejectedly, and Rowan felt his heart sink again at their loss.

"Here." Rowan tried to press his small green bottle into her hand, hoping to make her feel better, but Ivy refused it.

She turned her attention back to the bridge. There were so many doors, some in the most surprising of places—every last inch of space was being used in a marvelous tribute to commerce. The little storefronts and their upstairs apartments existed in borrowed space and jutted out precariously. Laundry waved like flags, drying in the open windows.

They were standing nearest to a tavern, the Mortar and Pestle, and from inside came the notes of a lively drinking song.

Rowan was enthralled—although he knew the bridge, he had spent his previous time in Templar avoiding it (at the urging of his charge, Turner Taxus, who believed himself respectable and wanted his taster to be so, too). He had to admit he felt happy to be back in society. Not quite polite society, but it would do.

"Didn't Axle say that the Knox was 'an ancient place for honest trade and exchange of conventional ideas'?" Ivy asked, looking around her.

"I guess he doesn't get out much."

"Where do you suppose his brother lives?" Ivy wondered. There were so many places to look, and she had no idea where to begin.

"He didn't say," Rowan recalled. He paged through Axle's *Field Guide* in hopes of finding a clue to the topography of the Knox. "Something strange is going on—" He frowned, perplexed. "I can't seem to find anything. It's all muddled. The pages are out of order in places, and look—this one's upside down!"

"Er." Ivy cleared her throat. "That must have happened on the trestle, when the book broke."

After several frustrating attempts, he indeed found a small map of the establishments on the bridge, tucked into the chapter on Cauvian constellations and evening songs. Turning to a storefront beside him, across from the Mortar and Pestle, he looked around for a signpost. He found none, but from an archway above the entrance dangled a particularly lifelike spider. Yet Axle's map contained no mention of such a store, and peering up again from the page, Rowan stepped back from the window display—unfortunate insects of all shapes and sizes, each speared uncomfortably with a large silver needle.

"I think Axle's map is slightly outdated," Rowan admitted.

But with the departure of the undertakers came a new

menace. Rowan straightened up, the *Field Guide* forgotten, and nudged Ivy's elbow in alarm. Patrolling in front of them, causing the riffraff to give them wide berth, was a pair of Nightshade sentries. They were dressed in the pomp and purple of the regime, and with a jolt, both Ivy and Rowan were reminded of the last time they saw this uniform at the Hollow Bettle, on twenty doomed men.

It was midafternoon, and the two Nightshade sentries were both slightly dull from hunger. The pair had no intention of pursuing the individual behind poor Klaxon's early demise. Theirs was not the duty of crime-solving; their orders were to intimidate and if at all possible practice a little extortion on the side. They paraded menacingly and reminded the sad citizenry of their miserable lot in life. If Klaxon looked like he might have owned even one minim in his sorry days, they would have claimed it for the king (if he had had two, they would have quietly kept one for themselves).

Rowan hid himself as best he could beneath his hood.

"Split up," he whispered. Tasters were common enough in Templar, but Ivy and Rowan together might raise suspicion. Their capture would make for a hearty promotion for these guards and a pleasant change of lifestyle. Maybe a taster of their own.

This particular patrol, as with all Nightshade sentries, had been briefed that day on the missing taster. They strolled slowly, eyeing the crowd with obvious distaste—making their way right toward the pair. The children's hearts sank as they watched the men begin to advance on them.

But the bridge was suddenly alive with footsteps, and the sentries were quickly joined—and nearly broadsided—by a large detail of their own kind, trotting across the Knox.

"You two!" the officer ordered. "Fall in! By order of the queen—we need every available hand! We must capture the beast! An escaped beast of enormous proportions!"

And with pointed staffs lowered, the army departed.

"That was close," Rowan whispered.

"Yes. A little too close."

"Better get inside somewhere before they return. They don't seem to be entering any of these stores."

"No—just menacing the crowds."

The pair turned in time to see a small man wearing a sandwich board walking up and down in front of an inn. The man turned, and the two could make out what it read: The End Is Here.

As good a place as any, they thought, and together they approached the inn, called the Bitter End, and ducked inside the small wooden door.

Chapter Forty-four

The Estate

The Bitter End was never a place of high society. Its clientele could not claim to be in possession of anything remotely resembling good manners. It was, in essence, a flophouse—a place where you slept if you had no other place at all to stay. The rooms for rent were up a ladder that leaned against a far wall and disappeared into a dark hole in the ceiling. Between the door and this ladder was a small dance floor (empty) and a long bar (also for the most part empty). Inhabiting the emptiness were but two visitors that evening, and they huddled together in deep conversation.

As Rowan and Ivy stood uncomfortably in the center of the lonely dance floor, they drew the attention of the regulars.

One of the more outstanding features of the Taxus clan, which Rowan's former charge, Turner Taxus, had shared, was an extraordinarily long and sausage-like nose. It was unmistakable and marked the family members as Taxus descendants from afar. On Turner Taxus it hadn't been so bad, but on the women of the family it was a severe source of shame. The Taxus nose jutted from the forehead out into the room and had a weight and mass to itself that made it wiggle with the slightest step.

Once Rowan's eyes adjusted to the dimness of the Bitter End's lighting—just a few stubby candles and an old gaslamp—he peered at the strangers at the bar. Rowan froze. The men, and their Taxus noses, had been drinking here rather than at the more popular Mortar and Pestle because they were hoping to find a place where they might talk. The Mortar and Pestle had been overly lively that evening, perhaps with the expectation of the coming Festival, and these two needed a little space for a private discussion. It was Rowan Truax's extraordinary misfortune that the topic of their conversation was the search for the errant taster who was responsible for their relation's early demise.

And it was the Estate's good luck—certainly they were not guilty of any hard work this evening, or any other, for that matter—to have their man walk right into their tavern.

The Estate and the former Taxus taster recognized each other instantaneously. To Rowan's horror, he watched as one and then the other man pushed himself sloppily to a standing position from the bar. But the drink the Bitter End commonly served, a green syrupy thing, was more potent than the Estate had figured. And they had been working on their third by the time Ivy and Rowan ducked in.

The taster made a split-second decision. He did not want to be caught between the Estate and the Nightshade sentries outside on the bridge.

He ran with Ivy for the ladder on the far wall and, grasping both sides, helped her up it as fast as he could.

They reached the top in short time, and the two stood on the creaky floorboards in the dark—affording them a perfect view of their pursuers.

Chapter Forty-five
Mithrodites

Quickly, Ivy's eyes adjusted to the dark, and she felt around near her where she thought she perceived a ledge. Indeed, the wall stopped where her hand rested and receded into a small dusty cupboard. Normally, she would have possessed little enthusiasm for sprawling around in the dark—especially since it seemed this section of the flophouse was never cleaned and cared for—but times like these called for desperate measures.

From her days at the Hollow Bettle, she knew occasionally a cupboard was a good way to get somewhere. She found a knotted end of a rope and pulled the cupboard door toward her and then, when it wouldn't move, pushed it in with all her might. It opened and clattered to the floor of the dark space beyond.

"In we go!" she called to Rowan, who was in complete agreement.

The Estate was settling their disagreement below as to just who should climb the ladder. They were in little hurry since by all outward impressions, there was no place for the children to go. The barkeep, a man of little curiosity, was unacquainted with any places of egress, and affirmed that there were no windows to brighten the misery up there. So there was left between the two Taxus men only the decision as to who should make the capture.

The larger one, Quarles Taxus, felt he was deserving enough (he was directly descended from Turner Taxus, making him a closer relative) that he resolved the argument with one large shove. He climbed the ladder remarkably well for a man dragging a distant cousin on his right leg. But to the complete chagrin of both representatives of the Estate, when they arrived and at last turned on the dim and flickery filament bulb, there was no one to be seen.

The storefront that happened to neighbor the sad Bitter End was the supply shop Mithrodites, wherein anything poison-related could be found for a price. At one time, during the boom of the early Nightshade regime, this store boasted two entire stories of poisoning material—empty capsules, dried herbs, peculiar powders, and early collector's editions of *The Field Guide to the Poisons of Caux.*

But as the novelty of the world they lived in faded and the sad reality of its dangers emerged, the proprietor of

Mithrodites was forced to shutter up the second floor and carry his wares—still with a healthy clientele, it should be noted—in a more modest way. He was satisfied to leave the second floor as an occasional office and storage space for extra inventory.

So it was that through the dusty cupboard at the Bitter End, Poison Ivy and Rowan Truax found themselves emerging into a storehouse of sorts. Everywhere they looked, there were shelves carrying anything and everything that was harmful or fatal if swallowed.

Ivy couldn't resist a look around.

There were dusty glass canisters of dried herbs, shriveled roots, and knotty flower heads, the labels in a faded chicken scratch.

"Axle always said, 'Plants—all plants—have secrets,' " Ivy said respectfully. " 'To unlock them is power, as the apotheopaths knew.' "

Rowan thought of the Mildew Sisters and scowled.

"The day will come when all the plants will awaken to their true natures," she said thoughtfully.

"Is that a good thing?" Rowan was reminded again of his encounter with bindweed in Southern Wood.

"Yes." Ivy laughed. "Because it's how it should be. How it once was. But it's up to the apotheopaths to harness that power—for the good."

"What's this?" Rowan eyed a jar of deep-green dried foliage suspiciously.

"Snakeweed. You—well—don't want to touch that one."

Rowan pulled his hand back from the jar's opening, but not before he thought he heard what sounded like a hiss.

"Look—bittersweet," Ivy noticed. "It makes everything taste the opposite of how it should. And boneset—I bet you can figure out what it's good for. Eyebright and feverfew, for illness. Lungwort, snoring. And, oh! The blights—if you boil their leaves in lye, they release an awful choking smoke."

Ivy was now occupied with the displays of glassine capsules and a collection of eyedroppers. Charcoal, tins of exotic incense, poisonous puffballs. Corks of all sizes and silver pins. There was a cask of hollow rings in flashy colors, and Ivy stopped to try one on. A gaudy red one caught her eye—it reminded her of her lost bettle. After a moment's thought, she slipped it into her pocket.

A bottle distracted Rowan, and he examined a fine brown powder labeled *Poison Ivy, Minced.*

"Look here! It's your namesake." Reaching for it, he quickly thought better, and his eyes arrived upon another tin. "Hey," Rowan said excitedly, "this one here's called King's Cure-all!"

"If only it were that easy."

She turned, half examining the dark leaf. Her thoughts returned to the lost elixir, and any excitement at their current surroundings was extinguished.

Rowan was suddenly thoughtful.

"I think I see why you like apotheopathy so much," he said. "I never knew how helpful plants could be—at the Guild, we really only learn about the harmful ones." It was occurring to Rowan that Ivy might be able to help him with a lifelong problem. "Um, Ivy?" His face, as if on cue, began to warm and redden, and he was thankful that Ivy was otherwise distracted. "Got anything for blushing?"

She looked up, quickly surveying the room.

"There—" She pointed at what appeared to be a lifeless potted plant. "Bloodroot. In small doses, it will help your blushing."

"What about large doses?" Rowan asked hesitantly, taking a step away from it. If his experience in Southern Wood was any guide, he expected red ooze to pour out of the withered thing.

"Too much of anything—even water—is poisonous." Ivy shrugged.

Bloodroot, he thought. While tempted, he was determined to avoid any more disastrous encounters with the plant world.

Ivy was now in front of a display of small bottles labeled *Nightman's Skullcap.* Before Rowan could ask her about it—indeed, before he saw anything at all—she had pocketed one. She continued down the row.

"I'd love to stay here longer," she said wistfully.

But the two remembered the reason behind their haste.

"We'd better find a way out."

The exit turned out to be a respectable one, considering.

Around the last row of tall shelves was a set of stairs, at the bottom of which stood the door to the reduced Mithrodites storefront. And Mithrodites was throwing a sale. No one, during the rush to purchase supplies for the Festival, seemed to notice the double doors at the rear swing open and produce a pair of children—who quickly blended into the crowd.

Chapter Forty-six

Peps D. Roux

The shoemaker Gudgeon's family had owned and operated a business from the same building for many generations. It hadn't always been such a respectable one—you can't get much more respected than to be the king's Royal Prosthetic Cobbler, with an imperial seal to prove it—but the family business had operated for centuries in one form or another in the slim but desirable location on the Knox.

Gudgeon had built it up from a run-down, second-rate crispin shop to what it was today, and of this he was quite proud. But his work with King Nightshade—specifically, his intricate shoe creations—was not his first love. Although he had created a display of King Nightshade's formal footwear for all to see, he preferred to dabble in the oddities that he showcased in his other windows, which were lit with spotlights and spun on mirrored carousels. Gudgeon created prosthetics: not just shoes for clubfooted kings, but anything from intricate hernia belts to artificial limbs. A passerby might stop—and many did—to wonder at Gudgeon's peculiar skill. And most would find it a little off-putting. Most, of course, except the king.

But behind his brightly displayed spinal corsets, neck braces, wooden teeth, miniature wheelchairs, and tastefully arranged skeletal feet was another more ancient secret: Gudgeon's storefront also doubled as the entrance to the Knox's nether regions—that is to say, to the living compartments of many a trestleman. Over the years, though, their numbers had dwindled. And today, the bridge's lone occupant—one Peps D. Roux—still could be found beneath the Knox carrying on in the trestlemen's tradition.

Not that Peps was at all upset about inheriting the entire bridge as his own. It was, in some respects, his own orchestration. Over time, he had widened and expanded his once-small apartment into what was now an enormous and quite grand loft, with river views on either side and all the latest of luxuries one might find in a bustling city like Templar. He was inarguably very much at home with the finer things of life, and his friend Gudgeon, as it happened, was happy to provide him with the flashiest tailored clothes that he could create.

But today was not the best of days for Axlerod's brother.

He had undoubtedly been favored by great success over

the years—if measured in material wealth—but today it had caught up with him.

For years, Peps had taken advantage of his famous brother's reclusiveness. He had benefited immensely, and without Axle's knowledge, by pretending to be the famed Axlerod D. Roux when it suited him and his pocketbook. It was an innocent enough crime—Axle never left his quaint little trestle in the middle of nowhere and seemed to desire nothing in return for his writing efforts. In Peps's view, his brother was an odd homebody, forever tinkering with his retractable pincers and ancient volumes of unreadable gobbledygook. Now and then, in an act of contrition, Peps would come across some obscure and impenetrable encyclopedia and send it off to his brother, a gift purchased with Axle's own money.

Over the course of Axle's long career, Peps had arranged for the royalty checks for the *Field Guide*—a great sum—to be directed to his own address on the Knox. And it wasn't beyond him to impersonate his brother should he dine at an upscale and expensive restaurant. When asked directly by an adoring fan—or a banker—if he was indeed the reclusive author, Peps would merely shrug and bow his head in a much rehearsed fashion. People, Peps knew and often took advantage of, believed what they wanted to believe. He just helped them along.

And now, as he sat in his sitting room with his friend and

advisor, Gudgeon, he lamented the years of borrowed identity. He held in his hand an invitation from the queen.

"What am I to do? There's hardly a way to refuse such a summons."

"And if you go, you're likely to be exposed. . . ." Gudgeon was nervously twisting his hands, in which was a moist handkerchief.

"Not necessarily." Peps shot his friend a look. "Give me a little credit, please."

"I only meant—"

"Never mind. I obviously can't go—what will I wear? I'll need a taster; have you considered that? Where will I get one of those? And not one of the raggedy ones for hire outside, either. Someone believable."

"What does it say again?"

Peps read from the gilded card.

WE'VE LONG BEEN A FAN OF YOUR WORK
AND WOULD GREATLY ENJOY A
STIMULATING CONVERSATION. PLEASE BE
OUR GUEST AT OUR COMMEMORATION DINNER
AT THE PALACE ON FESTIVAL'S EVE.
NO EXCEPTIONS.

"No exceptions."

"No. No exceptions," Peps said miserably. "I particularly dislike that part."

"Festival's Eve! But that's the day after tomorrow!" Gudgeon's reminder was met with a cold stare.

Upstairs, a distant bell rang, signaling a customer's arrival. The shoemaker was more than happy to excuse himself at the current juncture—he had experienced Peps in this mood only once before in their many years of friendship, and he wished never to again.

He trundled up the grand wrought-iron spiral stairs that Peps had installed years ago and was greeted by the youngest pair of customers he had had in some time.

"Excuse us," Rowan said to the impeccably dressed man who greeted them. He had been hoping to find a store a little busier than this in which to pass some time.

"Yes, young man. What might I do for you today?" Gudgeon looked him up and down for any sign of a limp.

"Well—" Rowan didn't really know where to begin.

"I practice the utmost in discretion," Gudgeon assured the boy. Perhaps he was here for his sister? She seemed, although a touch pale, quite well herself. They both were too young for a hernia. Neither had a hunchback that he could see.

"You really need to confide in me if I am to outfit you," Gudgeon prodded. This was the tedious part of the job.

Ivy cleared her throat.

"Could you tell us where we might find a trestleman named Peps? Peps D. Roux?"

Gudgeon was so unused to questions regarding Peps that he blinked once, then twice, very slowly. Hardly anyone knew Peps as Peps, and the few who did were not small strange children. But Rowan quickly clarified.

"This is Ivy Manx. His brother sent us. He said Peps would help us."

Chapter Forty-seven

The Invitation

"I vy Manx? Ivy Manx . . ." Peps was mulling over her name, trying to revive a distant memory.

Ivy, meanwhile, was recovering from the startling family resemblance between the two trestlemen. Indeed, for a moment, as she laid eyes upon Axle's brother, she thought she was seeing her old friend once more—a welcome sight. But Peps was in every way a sophisticate to Axle's studious personality, and their similarities ended at their faces.

"Yes, I think I know now. There was that little girl my brother was so fond of. Rescued her from the river, I seem to remember. A lot of fuss—never could understand what he was on about. Yes, it's coming back to me now." Peps peered closer at Ivy. "Is that you, then? I seem to remember he had quite a soft spot for you."

Ivy and Rowan had been shown down to Peps's spectacular living quarters only after Gudgeon had checked with the trestleman first.

"Have you ever seen anything like this?" Rowan whispered in Ivy's ear. This sort of luxury was usually reserved for the Guild's most favored subrectors.

Peps looked from one to the other of his little visitors expectantly.

"Well, what is it that I can do for you?"

Ivy's heart sank.

"Axle didn't send word? A letter, perhaps? Anything, maybe, about my uncle?"

"Send word? Whatever for?"

Peps's mind suddenly entertained the thought that his brother might have sent these two as collectors for his years of trespasses, but he soon realized the absurdity of sending children for such an end. He scanned his mind for any word from Axle. In truth, he was in the habit of ignoring anything that came from his brother—so tedious and wordy were his missives.

"Sir—I think perhaps Axle thought you might—"

"And who are you?" Peps turned to Ivy's companion, interrupting him impatiently.

"This is Rowan. Rowan Truax."

"At your service." Rowan bowed politely.

"Hmm," Peps sniffed. Rowan was still quite a spectacle in

his tasters' robes, and Peps looked him up and down. "Young man. You are a taster?"

"*Was* a taster," Ivy clarified, assuming Axle's brother would possess the same dislike for the Guild position.

But the news of Rowan's training had an unusual effect on their host. Peps suddenly spun around from where he was standing—beside a small coffee table tastefully piled with rich, lush-looking illustrated books—and produced for the pair an incredibly winning (and quite surprising) smile. It positively sparkled, and Ivy was made acquainted with Peps's prized golden tooth. And whereas his initial welcome was one of distraction, now he deigned to focus his entire attention upon the two—in a way that brought Ivy, for one, incredible relief.

"A taster! A taster, you say? So young. Are you a recent graduate of the Guild? Please, sit down. The two of you. Gudgeon—what are you waiting for? Get the tea tray!"

As the pair set about trying to get comfortable in the miniature chairs, Ivy couldn't help but ask again of any news.

"Excuse me, sir. But are you sure you've heard nothing about Cecil? Nothing's come from Axle—nothing at all?"

"Hmm? No. Nothing, I assure you, my dear. Not a tidbit. Do tell me, though, how is my brother faring? Well, I hope."

Ivy nodded, crestfallen.

"Good, good. You're not a taster, now, are you, dear? No,

of course not," Peps muttered, annoyed at Gudgeon's slow progress. The cobbler was carefully balancing the heavy tray.

Ivy sagged and looked miserably at Rowan.

"Your uncle, you say. Is this that outlaw—that apotheopath my brother was friendly with?"

"Yes."

Gudgeon was seeing to the tray's contents. He carefully placed the colorful sugar cubes favored by Peps into a bowl beside the fresh cream. But something occurred to him now. He hadn't bothered to mention it to Peps before—there were so many prisoners he'd encountered working for the Nightshades. At times he had even been forced to step over them, if the queen's dungeon overflowed as it sometimes did. But Peps had said something about an apotheopath, and that reminded him. It wasn't a word one often heard these days, and perhaps it was no coincidence.

"Peps," Gudgeon began casually. "I meant to tell you. At the last shoe fitting there was talk of a prisoner the queen discovered in the dungeon. He'd been there all year, completely forgotten! Funny—they said he was an apotheopath."

"A prisoner!" Ivy gasped. "Where? What did he look like?" She looked from Peps to Rowan hopefully.

"Well . . ." Gudgeon struggled. "I thankfully left before they summoned him. But if he spent the whole time in the dark, dirty basement, I'll bet he was in need of a bath."

"Really, this sort of information is something you don't

just forget. How very irresponsible. An apotheopath! Hardly an ordinary prisoner. What *else* have you neglected to tell me?" Peps admonished. "What do you have to say for yourself, Gudgeon?"

Gudgeon felt his temples constrict in a familiar way that he knew meant a migraine.

"Oh, it must be him! It must be!" Ivy cried. "A whole year—that's just when Cecil left!"

"Let me think, let me think! Stop chastising me so, Peps." Gudgeon looked quite upset. But he thought for a moment.

"They were going to have him brought up as soon as I finished my measurements for the king's newest pair of shoes. The green ones. The queen said he had come to cure the king's foot but was thrown in the dungeon before he could get the chance. The whole thing made me quite uncomfortable—and I was ever so relieved when I left the entire scene behind. But I remember now, the queen said something about a speedy execution and how sorry they should feel for keeping him waiting like that."

"Execution?" Ivy panicked. "When?!"

"I think . . . I think it's set for the Festival. For the big celebration."

"Oh, Peps—you must help me save him! Axle said you would! How do we get into the castle? It's a fortress! That's why the Nightshades come here during the Winds—it's the only safe place!"

"And all those sentries," Rowan added.

Peps gathered himself up and leaned back with his short arms behind his head—a great look of satisfaction upon his face.

"Well, it just so happens I have an invitation right here."

Chapter Forty-eight

Not One, but Two

I t was quickly decided that the three-some would attend the dinner to-gether and that Axle's reputation for eccentricity was such that arriv-ing with not one, but *two* tasters to the grand affair would not be out of character for someone of his high regard. Peps liked the idea of showing up at the palace with an entourage and quickly set about making preparations for outfitting Ivy as a junior taster.

Gudgeon scurried about here and there along the Knox, making purchases for the three. But he was, if he stopped his hectic pace to admit it to himself, of two minds about the whole business. He was not a man who enjoyed taking risks and didn't like to see his friend do so, either (although how he overlooked Peps's questionable dealings for so long is another matter entirely).

He found the appropriate robes for the young girl, as well

as the requisite tools: tongue scrapers, atomizers of distilled water, and golden flatware. And then he set about on more pleasant tasks. Peps had requested a glamorous suit for his debut at the palace. And everyone agreed there were a few alterations the children would need to their appearance—something that Gudgeon, who was, after all, the Royal Prosthetic Cobbler, might see to nicely.

At the Knox, the guests strategized.

"So you take the smallest bite—always with your right hand—and play it about on your tongue."

Rowan was giving Ivy a crash course—an irony that was not lost on the two, considering Rowan's past tasting failures.

"Why your right hand?"

"It just *is*. Ivy—" Rowan was getting flustered with explaining each minute detail. "It's always been that way. Stop asking questions! I've got to impart eight years of training into one lecture!"

Ivy apologized, and shifted in her seat. She was left-handed, and it would be a task to remember to use her right. She couldn't wait until the day after tomorrow—with her uncle so close, her stomach was in a constant state of butterflies.

"You're looking for anything, any hint of taste. But let's focus on behavior, since we'll agree that taste is not my strong suit. It's sufficient to nod, like this"—Rowan nodded to Peps wisely—"to indicate the food is fit to eat. At large dinners—especially ones that follow all the courtly protocols—it would be too distracting if each taster were to speak to his charge, so in the politest of society, like here, tasters are expected to observe the Rules of Silence."

"How do you tell your charge the food is poisoned, then?" Ivy wondered.

"If you detect something, there is a sign. Usually, the taster will drop his fork on the table."

"Why not just say something—after all, the food is poisoned!"

"Well, often enough the food has been poisoned by someone at the table—and intended for one of the guests. The poisoner could even be your charge, and it is not our job to judge—merely to taste and inform. That's the Tasters' Credo: 'Taste and Inform.'" Rowan smiled.

"I'm familiar with it." Ivy grinned.

She popped a small bite of potpie in her mouth, trying her best to taste the morsel—to really *taste* it in a new way. And indeed, something interesting happened. For a moment, the world dropped away, and Ivy was aware of only the medley of flavors on her tongue. The butter, the salt, the thick gravy—each one was distinct, yet together a symphony of taste. The components disassembled further on her tongue (the cream of the butter, the flour of the pie, the plump, juicy fowl), and instead of immediately following it with another bite, she felt no need to eat more. And as the complexity of flavors drifted away, she could sum up quite successfully the ingredients of each, because she had truly and successfully tasted her food.

"Your years as Poison Ivy have well prepared your palate." Rowan was appreciative. "You're a better taster than I am— without a day of training!"

"Let's eat," Peps interrupted impatiently. "The problem with tasters is that by the time you can get a bite in, everything is cold!"

The meal was indeed one of great delight and temptation, delivered in person by the chef of Templar's most luxurious eatery, Trindlesniffter's. The chef, a round man named Trindle with flame-colored hair, was delighted to see the trestleman. Apparently, this was Peps's regular fare, since by his own admission, he was the only trestleman he knew who couldn't, or wouldn't, cook a bean. Peps nodded appreciatively at his plate, and soon the two old friends were boisterously cheering their fortunes.

Rowan, sensing a private moment, leaned across to Ivy and whispered, "You still haven't told me how you plan to cure the king."

This was the question that had been plaguing her since the elixir bottle broke. She didn't have a plan, but more of a hope . . . an idea. But not one she was about to share—yet.

First she needed to get herself into the fortress-like palace, and just as Axle promised, Peps was helping her.

"I need to use your kitchen, Peps, if you don't mind," Ivy said, fingering her stolen vial of nightman's skullcap through her pocket.

She was excited to get back to her old tricks.

Chapter Forty-nine
Arrivals

Outside Gudgeon's store it was a pleasant temperature, and although the Winds had yet to ebb, there was an unusual amount of citizenry walking the bridge this early evening. Peps—as Axle—and his two tasters slipped out the front door and onto the cobblestones. The trestleman, with his richly dyed purple cloak wrapped tightly around his stout body, was dwarfed by his two friends, who flanked him. They set off through the crowd.

The tasters were outfitted in generous fashion by Gudgeon's talented hand, and Ivy considered herself lucky to not be wearing the restrictive corset he had hoped she would. Rowan, too, had dodged some of the more eccentric looks—Gudgeon was hoping for the chance to outfit him with a lump somewhere, a hunchback or perhaps a throaty goiter. Instead, the children managed to look presentably healthy. Ivy, head covered by her dark tasters' robes, wore a change in eyelashes and a becoming beauty mark that Gudgeon had added in a flourish of theatrical makeup to her cheek. Rowan stumbled along in a pair of ingenious shoes that made him several inches taller and a small fashionable beard. Together they made a respectable team, and if they kept their heads down, no one would recognize them.

If possible, the Knox crowd had grown rowdier since the last time Ivy and Rowan were on the bridge. And it was clear that it was the anticipation for the Nightshades' annual Festival that drove most of the bridge's visitors. The wind—never one to be ignored—was clacking street signs on their high poles and whipping everything not tied down into a frenzy. Garbage and debris blew against the threesome's ankles and swirled off into the night. Ivy managed to catch an eyeful of a yellowed parchment pamphlet as it struggled to free itself from a lamppost. It featured an engraving of a madman—hair flying and twisting in every direction, his eyes inscribed with a look of complete cartoonish lunacy.

With a jolt, Ivy was reminded of their desperate errand.

FESTIVAL OF THE WINDS

FEATURING THE SCHEDULED EXECUTION

OF DIABOLICAL OUTLAW, FIENDISH QUACK,

AND AWFUL HERMIT APOTHEOPATH

FESTIVITIES START AT SUNRISE

It was just over an hour later, as the last of the dusty gray light was being swept away by the wind, that Gudgeon found himself still standing in Peps's darkened loft, staring at the magnificent view of the Marcel. The scenery comforted him. That is, until he saw a small boat drift into view—from the north—and dock haphazardly on the city side. That was unusual. With the dockmaster celebrating, there was no one to collect the tariff, and Gudgeon peered more closely at the curious arrival. From inside the cabin emerged an odd threesome. A tall, aristocratic lady in a thrilling red ball gown, quite a sight even on her own. Next the small unmistakable form of another trestleman—the two of them were enough for Gudgeon to gossip about for weeks. But the third—the third figure to disembark made Gudgeon's blood run cold. Someone—something—rarely seen, even in the city. And then only at night. A hulking figure in a ragged robe, wild hair escaping the hood on all sides.

An Outrider, Gudgeon realized, an Outrider was here in Templar!

Turning quickly from the window, however, he missed the last arrival. A clever eye indeed was needed to catch the figure of the sleek black stowaway keeping mostly to the shadows, flapping his tired wings into the city's night air.

Chapter Fifty

Preparations

The thing about taste, as any first-year attendant of the Guild might tell you, is its close reliance upon the sense of smell. And, of course, miserable Sorrel Flux and his swollen sinuses could smell not a thing—not his own foul breath, not the musty curtains on his bedroom wall.

Any taster in this predicament, other than he, would be in a state of high anxiety at performing his duties for the queen. He knew she would take pleasure in testing him publicly; it was her very nature to poison—she could hardly be expected to resist her treacherous urges.

But Sorrel Flux was long past worry. He was of equal scheming temperament to Her Majesty. He had consulted his friend Lowly Boskoop, who in turn kept a close inventory on anything unusual that went into the king's kitchen. (Flux was expert at humoring Lowly's servant's pride and gleaned various tidbits concerning the menu for the evening.) The meal tonight promised to be a momentous event—dining with the royal family, after all, appealed to Flux's vanity, and for it he was well prepared.

Now, with the final event nearly upon him, he sat with a towel over his head and a bowl of hot water beneath his yellowed face. He was attempting to clear his sinuses, but as soon as he rejoined the stale air of the castle, it would be all for naught. Condensation dripped from the tip of his long crooked nose.

If the evening was going to be any success, he needed the coast to be clear. It was imperative to his grand plan. Now quite accomplished at poisoning sentries, Flux administered a basket of particularly potent mushrooms to the large population of the castle's guards—sprinkling it in their fragrant stew—and the resulting quiet was well worth the effort. Next Flux poisoned the staff supper. The palace was nearly vacant.

As he readied himself for the dinner party, Flux could barely contain his growing excitement over his own cleverness. Tonight, he would be putting his sorrowful years of servitude behind him. Soon he would walk free in paradise—the Doorway's secrets now were his.

He had but one more person to call upon before the guests were set to arrive. Sorrel Flux, after smoothing down his thin wisps of hair with a remarkably calm hand, went out into the corridor in search of his associate Lowly Boskoop.

King Nightshade detested his wife's get-togethers.

The anticipation gave him indigestion, and the polite chitchat was always so forced. He craved a more entertaining setting, where he might find himself accidentally amused.

Remembering the guest of honor, he yawned. It was to be some small and dislikable trestleman, someone, no doubt, who had little if anything amusing to say. Hadn't he tried to outlaw the entire lot of them? He would have succeeded, too, if he pressed the issue, but Artilla had a soft spot for the author of that poison book she so admired.

The trestleman was a writer, thought the king, and undoubtedly the conversation would be very high-minded and bookish—unlike his own brand of prose. It was just these sorts whom the king shunned. What he really needed was a court jester, but his last attempt to fill that position had been such a shocking disaster.

He allowed himself a moment to recall the likable fellow. The man had an ear for rhyme—a true and enviable gift. He was also quite hairy, an amusing trait in anyone, especially a jester. So completely covered in hair was he, he resembled more wolf than man. After the jester's eventual demise, the queen, inspired by the man's animal appearance, had the Royal Taxidermist set to work upon him. So convincing was the Taxidermist's work—the glint in his eye, the pep in his frozen step, the reach of his arm as he forever grasped his flute—it took the king a fair few hours to realize the man was no longer of the living (all the while the king was waiting politely for the stuffed man to amuse him). Sadly, that led to the king's next horrible realization: his hairy jester had been preserved very much like an *antique*! This conclusion so frightened the king, so completely revolted him, he resolved never, ever to find humor in someone funny again. (All was not lost on the experience, however, as it provided the inspiration for one of King Nightshade's particularly morbid poems.)

The king pondered his ability to turn shock and misfortune into poetry as his brother snored from across the room.

Which reminded him.

Earlier, he was relieved to have received a message from Vidal Verjouce, answering his query concerning a new taster. Verjouce had written to assure King Nightshade he was sending only his best for tonight's occasion—a note that both pleased the king and made him nervous. Vidal Verjouce wrote in vagaries that confused him, often making him irritable.

In the meantime, the king thought he might compose a toast for tonight's meal and sat himself down at his elegant writing desk with a blank mind.

But how elusive was his muse! As he waited, and indeed nothing came to him, and indeed nothing again still, he wondered offhandedly if he might, with some help, be able to find a mite-infested mattress in the castle. He pictured himself reclining upon it, pen in hand, and experiencing the plight of the poor and downtrodden in a fit of inspiration.

But seeing as the king was not one for sympathy or sacrifice—even for his poetry—he did not ring for a sentry.

Of course, none would have answered.

Chapter Fifty-one

The Guest of Honor

Peps D. Roux and his two tasters arrived at the Palace of Templar, at the invitation of the queen, to find the guard booths at the castle door quite empty and unwelcoming. In fact, the entranceway was so lonely, with no one there to receive them at all, that Peps grabbed the invitation from his breast pocket and rechecked the date and time. It was in order.

"Hello?" he ventured, and was answered only by the murky bubbling of the moat.

Sorrel Flux's slow and methodical elimination of the castle's staff had been comprehensive. Finally, it was a scullery maid, flagged down by Peps, who led the threesome, unceremoniously, to the large ornate doors that marked the court's receiving room. There she quickly departed, leaving the visitors in an awkward silence. Then, following the flamboyant trestleman's example, Ivy and Rowan made their own way before the fearsome and despicable rulers of Caux.

"Well, then . . ." The king cleared his throat. He wasn't very good at small talk. "Which one of you is that trestleman writer?"

"Darling." The queen rolled her eyes. "It's obviously the one in purple. The little man."

"Ah, yes. Now I see. He is a little fellow, isn't he? Does he do anything? Dance?"

"I don't think so, dear."

"Still, I'd like to see him dance."

"We have your book right here, Mr. D. Roux." The queen patted a copy of the *Field Guide*. "Lovely little thing. We are so very happy to meet you."

The room was filled with various guests—a few of Caux's more terrible ladies and gentlemen who were in the queen's favor—and Peps thrilled them all with a flouncy bow. Ivy's eyes couldn't help but be drawn to the queen's enormous ring, and she nervously twisted her own sorry reproduction from Mithrodites she wore on her finger.

"You bring to the table two tasters tonight, Mr. D. Roux?" asked the queen.

"Indeed, Your Majesty. It is my habit to never dine without them. I am, after all, a . . . celebrity." Peps nodded and smiled at the starched and disapproving faces that lined the ornate wall.

"A *celebrity*, you say?" inquired King Nightshade.

"Yes, Your Highness. A celebrity."

There was a pause, and Ivy held her breath.

"Highly irregular. Wouldn't you say, dear?" The queen turned to her husband ever so slightly.

"Hmm?"

"I asked if it wasn't highly irregular that there are two tasters for one such smallish man."

"Correction, my dear. A *smallish celebrity*. But really, Artilla. I would hardly hold it against your miniature guest. You do have a reputation that precedes *you* as well."

The queen, complimented by her husband's words, returned her gaze to the threesome, and just then a voice—a shrill, yet gratingly *nasal*, voice—bubbled up (as if from under a rock) behind them. A voice that Ivy knew at once and could never in her life forget.

It was, of course, the voice of her former taster and unwelcome lodger, Sorrel Flux.

"Dinner, they tell me, is served," he oozed.

Chapter Fifty-two
The Tapestries

There remained, in the castle, only one thing—or rather, one set of things—that could be attributed to the Good King Verdigris that had not been thrown into the moldy basement at least once. They defied the king's decree against antiquities and heirlooms and were displayed on every available space of wall in the formal dining room. They were enormous, and spectacular.

And since they were favored by the queen (indeed, by anyone who was fortunate enough to see them), on the walls they remained: a magnificent set of seven tapestries, made long ago by an unknown hand. Artilla, in a fit of inspiration, had decided that they would serve not only as a wonderful backdrop to the night's festivities, but as the theme to the entire meal.

Needless to say, the king despised the tapestries. He was made positively ill at the thought of them lurking over his shoulder and materializing within a sidelong glance. He insisted, as with all antiques, that they smelled funny, and could see no artistry in their woven threads—rather, infinite places for dust mites to hide and multiply. He hated that his wife demanded eating beside them, but try as he might, she was not going to let him off the hook tonight.

He took pleasure in the fact that he would have some revenge to exact upon the party when he gave the toast—he finally had put pen to paper and composed a little something for the evening.

The guests were shown into the formal dining room ahead of the royal family.

Ivy's heart was beating hard, and its echo pounded in her ears. The surprise of seeing Sorrel Flux caused her legs to weaken momentarily, and she found herself wishing—not for the first time since the Abbey—for the comfort of her red bettle. Gudgeon's genius at cloaking clubfoots and hunchbacks translated into an equal ability at disguise, but even though the children were well augmented and prepared, Ivy—draped in her taster's cloak—wondered in one horrible moment if Flux might see right through her.

Tonight, what little remained of the castle staff were dressed for the hunt. Indeed, the party could have been occurring in a picture-perfect woodsy clearing, except for the fact that there were four walls and a ceiling (although the camouflage was nearly complete). A chatter of caged birds—mostly woodland songbirds and some odd waterfowl—rose up in a thunderhead of sound to greet them. Once the noise had subsided somewhat and the smattering of floating feathers had settled, a lonesome lute took over. Everywhere were the markings of an outdoor meal; even the floor was strewn with reeds and twigs and crunched convincingly underfoot.

As the threesome made their way to the enormous oval table, they were joined by a few of the other guests: a handful of visiting dignitaries and a low-level ambassador from Kruxt waiting out the Winds, each with his taster. Peps stopped to nod and greet them while Ivy and Rowan stared impassively at their counterparts. Ivy stole a glance at the room. The cloth that draped the dining table was exquisite, hand-stitched of delicate leaves in a living patchwork. The table was set with wooden platters and polished bowls, while dark moths fanned their wings on the centerpiece—a heap of skulls upon gnawed crossbones. A jagged vine snaked in and out of the empty eye sockets.

With a nudge from Rowan, Ivy tore herself away from the scenery, trying to remember her hasty lesson in protocol. There, on the table, in golden ink, was a succession of dried fig leaves scrawled with the names of the invitees. Ivy scanned for Axle's, and Peps took his place—the place of honor—beside that of the queen.

The side door opened, and through its archway came the Deadly Nightshades. Queen Artilla had changed into a spectacular deep-green gown—a hunter's green, she called

it—which was little competition for the greenery of the room. Her crown shone evilly, amassed with dozens of crystal-clear gleaming bettles.

The queen had had less luck outfitting the king.

For him she laid out a matching hunter's costume, but he had been unwilling to wear it. She had, however, been successful in convincing him to don a crown of antlers—this he wore *only* because they were dipped in gold—and she had done her best not to produce a mirror in which he might glimpse himself. The effect of the crown was a startlingly ridiculous one: it was ill fitting and caused the ruler of Caux to resemble a drunken stag. Plus, it tended to catch upon everything it could, and the scenery in the room was quick to fetch a ride atop his head.

So it was that the king's entrance was less spectacular than his wife's. Having to do battle with the mean and gnarled branches of a tree, he came away with a wisp of hanging moss dangling from an upper antler. He wore on his feet Gudgeon's new green shoes and might have generally admitted to the room that he found them to be the most comfortable thing about the entire event.

"May I present for your admiration the king and queen of Caux!" announced Sorrel Flux, performing a job normally reserved for Lowly Boskoop.

Peps was the first to rise and bow, and with his tasters by his side, finally drew Sorrel Flux's consideration. But Flux's mind was on other matters, and his fancy was caught not by Ivy, but by the other taster. The young man beside the teensy author seemed vaguely familiar. His hair seemed different, true, and the unusual beard he possessed for such a young man was confusing. The youth's face blandly resisted recognition—it niggled at him, but soon the furrow over his waxen brow was eased by the commencement of the meal.

A lone hunter's horn sounded from somewhere far off—cheerless and forlorn. Again it blew, and Ivy realized it was a mournful indication that dinner, and with it her taster duties, was about to begin.

Chapter Fifty-three

The Hunt

"It pleases the queen to dine tonight with the theme of the hunt," Flux announced with a smile that showed off his large and crooked teeth.

Even with his arms open wide, Sorrel Flux could not fill out his robes. If the king had earlier been wishing for a jester, he might have been satisfied with Flux in his dress attire—a sight rife with hilarity. (The king, however, would have been quick to discover that of the many virtues lacking in Sorrel Flux, a sense of humor and the ability to turn a phrase were two.)

The queen drew their attention to the famed tapestries, and Ivy realized what she had mistaken for a mossy and inviting glen was actually a wall and, in turn, mere woven thread upon that. There was no doubt that these tapestries were crafted with an ancient and lost art. With a low voice, Queen Nightshade lectured on the various plants she found amusing, taking particular care to point out the depiction of her namesake, the deadly nightshade.

"The tapestries, so very realistic, no?" she purred.

The king muttered something under his breath.

"The king has a completely different word in mind!" the Royal Diarist announced brightly.

In total, there were seven panels depicting a series of gardens. But what gardens were these? Some were lush and welcoming, while others were eerie and uninviting, and in the last of them stood a beautiful maiden in white. Yet, in all, the colors of the woven threads, after so many years, were still vibrant and remarkably preserved, and the very air around the tapestries seemed to pulse.

"If you would be so kind as to take your seats, the dinner will begin at once!" Flux announced, seemingly from behind a shrub.

The lush table was populated, and Prince Francis, snoozing comfortably, was wheeled in beside the king. Sorrel Flux moved to take his position as the queen's taster while the servants tended to the preparation. There was indeed a shortage of staff, and the few that now appeared looked harried and overworked.

"The king will now grace us with his genius!" the Royal Diarist called from the corner.

"Yes, indeed, I have written a toast in your honor for this occasion, my dear." He cleared his throat. "Do you wish me to begin?"

"No," the queen replied hastily, thinking of her guests' appetites. The ruler of Caux looked cross.

"The king will now remind the queen just who's boss around here," the Royal Diarist predicted.

"Darling"—Artilla recovered smoothly—"shouldn't we wait for the drink to be poured?"

A cask containing his favorite brandy sat invitingly beside the king. It did seem wise to wait for it before making the toast. After a moment's pause, he agreed.

At this juncture, while the hopes for the evening were still high, the appetites of the table's occupants were pleasantly alive, and their senses were not yet spoiled by overbearing perfumes or the like—at this juncture, it was possible to forget one's bearings and lower one's guard. Rowan knew this. He was taught this at the Guild, that distraction from the simple act of tasting was the taster's biggest challenge. He tried very hard to steel himself against anything that might divert his attentions, and he felt suddenly light-headed at the task. But he had little time to contemplate much else as the room suddenly erupted into chaos—in the form of a large pack of hounds that had been loosed on the chase of some seemingly invisible prey.

The chamber was filled with their barks and howls, and they streaked after one another so quickly and furiously that they appeared to be one blurry mass unto themselves, snarling and growling in their mad rush. Foam slathered their jaws and was thrown about the air.

It felt as if they might carry on this way until they'd exhausted themselves, but just then the dogs suddenly halted, to the apparent surprise and displeasure of the queen. Something had spooked them greatly, and now, with their tails between their legs, they huddled together, whining.

From the entrance where they had made their way not long before came a voice that so terrorized the hounds.

"King Nightshade," Vidal Verjouce said, "I do hope dinner has not begun without me."

The terrible effect of Verjouce's presence was not felt solely by the hounds. Sorrel Flux was clearly unhappy at the sight of his former employer, and this time it was difficult disguising his shock. He had a horrible moment when his suspicion got the better of him, and he allowed himself to wonder if somehow Verjouce knew what he intended, if his former master had somehow intuited his plan—and a private terror rose up inside him.

"What is the meaning of his presence?" the queen hissed at Flux—although Flux was not the source of the trouble.

"Your Highness, I assure you—" Flux stammered.

Verjouce made his way over to the table, the tip of his ruthless cane barely grazing the ground. (If the theme of the dinner and the occasional tree in his way surprised the blind man, he showed it not in the least.)

The dogs were cowering under the table, making a general nuisance of themselves—stepping on toes and pulling down a corner of the tablecloth, causing an arrangement of poisoned apples to clatter to the floor.

"Forgive my tardiness." The Director addressed the king. "I was delayed on the mountain. There was a little incident with my sled."

Ivy allowed herself a quick peek at Rowan, who looked pale and sick.

Queen Nightshade sighed and clapped her hands, and several costumed staff appeared and began coaxing the hounds out from their hiding spot—an ungraceful process that took much longer than she would have liked and involved bribing them with scraps of raw meat.

It was now time for the entertainment.

"Bring in the prisoner," she ordered.

Chapter Fifty-four

The Menu

What a year in a Nightshade dungeon could do! Ivy's elation turned to heartbreak as the lone prisoner was ushered in before the queen. Cecil Manx was a sad sight to see. The apotheopath had received far better treatment over the off months when the royal family was sunning themselves in Kruxt and the guards and local staff were able to care for him. But now, with his presence known, the cruel tortures of dungeon life had quickly overtaken him, and he was distressingly feeble. He trudged into the forest glen.

"Ah, the apotheopath," King Nightshade noticed. "How cleverly wicked of you to invite him to dinner."

"Yes, I thought you'd approve." The queen smiled.

Cecil was in no condition to notice his niece. Rowan managed to nudge Ivy's ankle under the table in sympathy, and she felt some strength from that kindness. Her uncle was led to a small clearing where his presence wouldn't be overly intrusive to the mood of the diners but where he might still be called upon at the whim of the queen. He stood bound at the wrists with his head lolling slightly. He mumbled under his breath.

Vidal Verjouce was silent, the holes of his eye sockets betraying not a thing—but there was a new keenness to his countenance, as if the evening had just become a little more interesting.

Ivy didn't have much time to consider her uncle's plight, for the meal charged on, and she knew she needed her wits about her. She glanced down at the golden dinnerware beside her plate—an appalling collection of strange and foreign utensils like none she'd ever seen. Beside them, a card.

MENU

Raw Eel and Kruxious Sea Snail

Dormouse à la Artilla

Pheasant in Shell

Salad of Boiled Tongue

(and Other Unpleasantries)

**

Burgoo of Beast

**

Toadstool Truffles

When it came to food, Queen Nightshade's tastes could only be described as gruesome. She took distinct pleasure in others' discomfort in all aspects of life, and the dinner table was no exception. She was known for her awful experiments with turtledoves baked in pies. She did terrible things with cute bunnies and vinegar. She raced turtles into the soup pot, allowing the victor the horror of seeing the others to the kettle before he, at last, joined them. In short, it was the stuff of nightmares.

It will remain forever unknown, however, if the queen actually *knew* that the main dish on her menu would produce the greatest horror in her guests—or if she stumbled upon it simply by accident. It was one that, when announced, drained all the life from both Ivy's and Rowan's complexions.

"We have for your enjoyment this evening quite a rare treat," announced Sorrel Flux.

It had been only the day before yesterday when the great beast arrived at the walls of Templar and was caught by the sentries and immediately turned over for the pleasure of the queen. It was a rare find indeed, one that was not ever seen below the cloud line of the Craggy Burls. And one that quickly became the star of the menu.

"Have any of you ever had the pleasure of dining upon bettle boar?" The queen smiled, looking around. There was an approving murmur from the ambassador, while King Nightshade perked up at the mention of the priceless jewel.

"I thought not."

Ivy's breath caught in her throat. Then, with a wet *plop*, her attention was drawn to her plate and away from the spectacle. A large and warty toad had just landed in the middle of it, and she was pretty sure he had come from behind her, from the tapestry. She thought of nudging him gently away—he seemed quite at home—and she tried to decide which of the many surgical-looking utensils might do the trick. She settled on one that seemed to be made for toad-pushing, but by the time she returned her attention to her plate, he was gone. In his wake, the merest spot of mud. Ivy peered about the table, but he was lost to the arrival of the appetizers.

It took the strength of several servants to place a large curled horn in the table's center. As they stepped back, live eels and sea snails cascaded out, slick and gooey. The eels slithered busily around the tabletop, leaving the diners the unpleasant task of spearing them with their forks. With dismay, Ivy watched Flux use the golden nutcrackers beside him to crush a snail alive, while another traced Rowan's dinner plate, leaving behind an unsavory trail of slime.

"Really, now, Artilla. I must insist on reading my prepared toast!"

"In a minute, dear." The queen brushed away a stray leaf on her husband's shoulder, only to have another replace it.

Queen Nightshade smiled as a new platter arrived before the diners. It contained small, delicate pheasant eggs, and Ivy watched as the ambassador's taster selected a tiny pearled spoon and expertly cracked one open. Inside, to Ivy's distinct horror, was a nearly hatched bird.

Beside Peps a plateful of live dormice were protesting. Their tiny squeaks were sad and mournful, for they had been dipped in honey and were, as a result, quite sticky. They were then invited to a further indignity by being rolled in poppy seeds. Stricken, Peps covered his mouth with his silk scarf as they swam dully about their bowl.

Ivy perked up momentarily, seeing that there, hiding behind a gelatinous blood pudding, was the toad. He navigated

the busy tabletop successfully as the last dish arrived. It was set in front of Rowan, in the only free space. The servant removed the golden dome from the platter, revealing what seemed to be a mass of velvety sausages, boiled and tossed with an unappetizing greasy dressing. Not one was alike.

"Salad of tongue." The servant bowed, pointing out various components of the truly awful dish—from the lolling ox to the tiny hummingbird tongue.

Rowan nearly fainted, thinking of how many animals had lost their voices for this dish. He looked helplessly at Ivy. His hands shook and his own tongue felt slightly swollen in his mouth; a bead of sweat appeared on his forehead. He thought of the Outrider—his harrowing grunts—and his mind turned to his great attachment to his own tongue.

Sorrel Flux, always one to pick up on another's discomfort, was amused at the young taster's distress. Rowan held his breath—something entirely against his taster's training—and took a small bite under Flux's gaze. Although he tried to concentrate, he found himself returning to the awful scene at the Hollow Bettle, when he tasted the soup Flux had poisoned. He thought of how many people he'd let down that day, the start of this long adventure. The tongue's texture was springy and dense, and it sat like a lump in his mouth. He tried hopelessly to muster his education. Everything rested on his pronouncement—their very lives, perhaps even Caux's future.

"Fit to eat!" came Ivy's clear voice beside him.

So much for the tasters' Rules of Silence. But Rowan was grateful. He trusted her pronouncement more than his own, and he quietly spat his mouthful into the small spittoon beside him.

Ivy's voice, the buoyant voice of a child, was a breath of fresh air in the stale protocol of a royal dinner party. Indeed, Cecil raised his head from his state of despair and looked in her direction. Ivy's heart leapt. Had he recognized her voice? Sure enough, there was a gentle twinkle in the corner of his eye—she had missed it so much. It was all she needed to bolster herself against what was to come.

Yet across the table the queen's taster frowned.

That voice—infused at once with annoying innocence and wisdom. Cecil was not the only one to find it familiar.

Chapter Fifty-five

Poppy

Deep within the dark blue light of the snowy chasm, after tumbling a great way and skittering down a frozen gorge, Poppy made it back through an icy passage to the mines and then to Skytop Abbey, as only a bettle boar might be expected to do. The chasm pit was a series of snaking tight squeezes, but she just followed her nose. In fact, she had made it there rather easily and found it not at all troublesome to do so with Ivy's bettle in her large mouth.

From there, it was a snap to follow the children's trail down the Burls, and Poppy had been trying to figure out a way into Peps's apartment beneath the bridge when she was captured. Her snout had told her that her friends were near. The boar had put up quite a fight—in the end, it had taken many lengths of rope and the whole battalion from the bridge to subdue her.

Had everything gone as Flux suggested, the hounds would have chased and terrorized the snow-white boar around the room for the amusement of the crowd. But the hounds had been returned to their lair beneath a back set of stairs, and for no amount of coaxing would they emerge. There they stayed for months to follow, in fact, until they were almost forgotten—for the fearsome scent of the Guild's leader hung about the castle as if there to torment them.

Flux's plan had been to exhaust the boar with the dogs, thereby disabling her, and then she was to be tossed into the boiling cauldron—along with various savories—and become dinner. It was to be a particularly vicious dinner, one of his greater triumphs.

But it was absent any hunting dogs nipping at her feet that Poppy made her grand entrance. She was a beast transformed, though: her hackles were raised and her lips pulled back in a grimace—snapping and snarling at the room full of spectators. Ivy kicked Rowan so hard he almost cried out.

"Artilla! What a thoughtful gift! What a treasure she is— look how she sits there with her teeth clenched and that cute snout all wrinkled up! Almost as if—" The King of Caux was on his feet, advancing on Poppy with great enthusiasm.

"Behold, the king does bravely battle the beast!" cheered the Diarist.

"Careful, dear," Artilla warned. "This one appears to have a temper."

"—almost as if she has something in her mouth! Why, look—she does! The boar has a bettle! A red one! Right here, in her teeth! Artilla, you've outdone yourself again!"

But there was no amount of cajoling to get Poppy to release her prize, and for his efforts, the king nearly lost a royal thumb. The queen was forced to suggest they just throw the animal into the pot and collect the bettle after supper.

"We'll serve her with the red bettle stuffed in her mouth," Queen Nightshade suggested. "Like an apple."

At that, Rowan stood up and offered to try.

The room's attention was directed at the trestleman's taster, a taster who seemed uncommonly familiar with boars. The beast turned on him, and to Flux's great delight, it seemed like he would soon be mauled. But, sadly, this taster apparently possessed some inexplicable talent for animal training, and the beast was soon clattering about his robes in excited circles.

As Rowan coaxed Poppy to release the hollow red bettle, Ivy had just the moment she had been waiting for. She approached the king's cask of brandy, but the cork she had noticed earlier was gone, replaced with an odd, furry moss. It covered the entire oak barrel. With the room still enthralled by Poppy, Ivy began frantically pulling off clumps of the advancing greenery. Fistfuls of springy turf fell at her feet, and still she could see no opening. And then—there it was! With

354

a surge of relief, she flicked open her garish red ring and introduced its contents to the barrel.

And as the king examined the unusual bettle, he was reminded again of his own thirst. He poured himself a glass and, inspecting it, swallowed heartily. The guests were served.

"Now, this really does call for a toast!" He wondered whether he might ad-lib in light of the new events.

Along with the encroaching green moss, something ever so odd was happening around the walls of the room. Cecil Manx's mutterings were having their intended effect. It was all but unnoticed by the partygoers—a vague tingling of movement from the corner. Ripples of air seemed to gather and disperse in secretive ways, centering around the tapestries. Other things, too. A spotted red toadstool that Ivy was sure she'd seen in the woven fabric suddenly popped up larger than life beside the king's plate. (The toad made himself happily at home beneath its fluted edges.) A tidy growth of violets bloomed from Rowan's drinking glass, and a lively carpet of yellow cinquefoils burst up at her feet. Yet no one found this remarkable.

While everyone quenched their thirst from crystal goblets, Ivy caught her uncle's eye again—this time for longer, and she was rewarded with a slight, yet distinct, smile. And she was reminded of one of the things she knew about apotheopathy. The Good King Verdigris had also been an apotheopath, like her uncle, and perhaps her uncle was not as distant from the king's magic as the rest of them. Hadn't Clothilde said he was a Master Apotheopath?

King Nightshade, meanwhile, thought it high time to reward the group with his newly penned poem and was rising from his makeshift throne unsteadily to do so. He unfurled his long parchment and cleared his throat—as he did, Ivy saw a cloud of small flies emerge from his mouth.

The woods were invading from the tapestry.

The king's beard was sprouting twigs and small branches, his shoulders a nest of leaves. A hairy spider wove a web on the queen's crown, crawling across her ivory face. Even Peps was not immune—a fiddlehead fern had sprouted from his tailored buttonhole and was unfurling its spiraled head.

King Nightshade cleared his throat to begin his composition, one so terrible he had himself been made ill while writing it. He raised his glass to his wife to begin.

Thankfully, Ivy would never hear this composition of the king's or any other, for it was then that her potion, mixed with the potent brandywine, chose to work. King Nightshade sagged backward into his temporary throne, quite comfortably and slowly, while the rest of the table succumbed to the intense sleeping draught she'd concocted in Gudgeon's kitchen with the stolen nightman's skullcap.

Where before there was lively conversation, now a simple chorus of snores. Peps and Rowan leaned cozily on each other, draped in a blanket of pine needles. The queen's mouth sagged

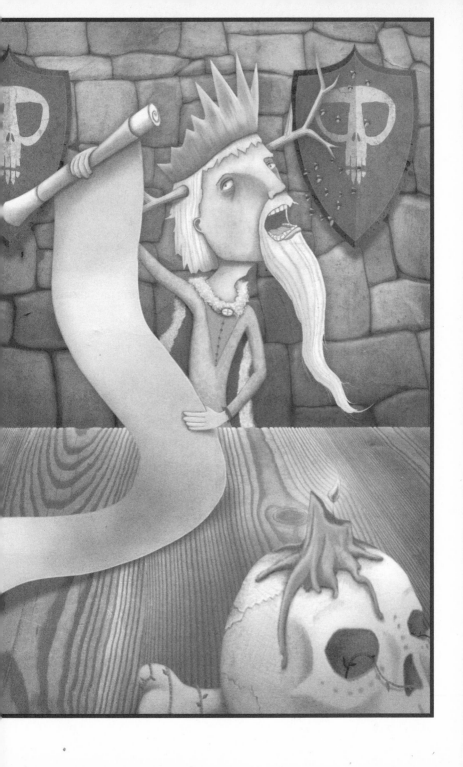

open and soon became a nest for honeybees. Her terrible lady friends withered and cracked as their pale skin was transformed into birch bark.

Cecil's mutterings had ceased, and he sat placidly regarding the slumber party.

Yet two remained at the table who, like Ivy Manx, did not sleep.

Verjouce had not drifted off, having the only palate sharp enough to detect Ivy's concoction. And Sorrel Flux was wide awake; having noticed his former master not partaking of the beverage, he had wisely abstained as well. And Flux was looking evilly at Ivy.

It was old magic—potent Verdigris magic—that was in the air. It was dissolving the very borders between woolen pictorial gardens and the dining room. The room seemed to wiggle and pop with invisible currents.

Moss grew up quickly over the place settings and crystal goblets. And into the queen's coiffed hair. For his part, the king's antlers had lost most of their golden luster and were returning to their natural state, covered in a springy fuzz. Sorrel Flux, a man already jaundiced, grew a mane of yellow marigolds from the folds of his turkey neck.

Then, from an outcropping in the tapestry, came the bindweed, and it snaked itself up the chair legs, fastening the various guests' legs to their chairs, moving on to their arms.

Verjouce, blind to his plight, was the first to feel himself secured to his seat by the snaking vegetation.

The forest had emerged from the tapestry quite completely.

In the end, a few of the guests opened their mouths—perhaps in vague protest—but nothing was heard but a cricket's *chirp-chirp-chirp*. The queen, murmuring contentedly in her sleep, sounded vaguely like a guppy.

"Really, Flux," Verjouce chastised after a moment of silence. "You surely overdid the narcissus on the snails. I thought over the years you might have learned something of the value of delicacy from me."

"You think I learned anything but servitude from you?" he snarled.

"So ungrateful."

Flux, with his position furthest from the wall, had managed to fend off the encroaching bindweed—the longer it was growing, the thicker it became and the more securely it was restraining its victims. He stood haughtily.

"You blind fool—it is I who shall succeed tonight! You can make merry while I make for better lands. I've found the Doorway, you worthless conjurer. The Pimcaux Doorway! And it's mine."

Ivy was on her feet, running over to King Nightshade's sleeping form. A small red-crested woodpecker was at work on his right antler. She uncurled his hand and reclaimed her red bettle and was immediately infused with a warm sense of well-being. Taking advantage of the growing disagreement between teacher and pupil, Ivy snuck over to her uncle.

"Cecil!" Ivy whispered urgently. "Tell me how I cure the king!"

Verjouce was sufficiently bound that turning his head was impossible—but a blind man need not have bothered. His ears performed better than most, and he had not missed the fact that a young girl was calling the prisoner apotheopath by a name he well knew. A name that at one time was very familiar to him. The Guild's Director realized the child he sought, the child Flux had allowed to slip through his fingers, was in the very room.

"Not that king," Cecil said evenly. He, too, was being quickly anchored in place by the weeds.

"What do you mean?" Ivy cried, skirting a vine. "Axle said—"

"Not King Nightshade. The *other* king."

"What other king?" Ivy was at a loss, searching the crowded woody room.

"The real king—*King Verdigris*. You are meant to cure King Verdigris, Ivy." The calmness of his voice was helping Ivy not to panic but was having the opposite effect on Vidal Verjouce, who began struggling mightily against his bonds.

"King Verdigris is alive? Where?" Ivy was both stunned and relieved.

"In Pimcaux," Cecil replied more urgently. "You must go!"

Sorrel Flux was at the door, a wake of orange petals floating in the air behind him.

"Follow Flux!"

It was here that Sorrel Flux's enthusiasm for eliminating sentries (and everyone else who got in his way) caught up with him. Had he kept but just a few to patrol the castle's grounds, they would have stopped the surprised threesome who greeted Flux now as he flung open one side of the immense arched doors.

But as it was, Flux was a man on a mission, and nothing could stop him.

Not the Outrider whom Flux nearly ran into. Not his prisoner, the tall and royal Clothilde. And certainly not the diminutive trestleman by the side of her red skirts.

Chapter Fifty-six

Axle

xle had had a horrible time of it—the trip, the boat (normally the Marcel was a smooth ride, but during the Winds he suffered from motion sickness terribly). And the rigid fear he experienced at being away from his home—indescribable panic at times. Much harder than the fact that he was being taken against his will. He had no wherewithal to enjoy what is ordinarily a beautiful trip down the Marcel, through the pastoral countryside of Caux, to Templar.

He had finally completed the thirteenth edition of the *Field Guide* and was allowing himself a moment of congratulation in the form of a vintage bottle of excellent brandywine when the first uninvited guest arrived at his home.

Clothilde had been frantic, stating that the children were in danger. When she arrived at the trestle, Axle was surprised at her state. Her attire was somehow red—startling in itself—and was filthy with the effort of her escape from Verjouce. Her constitution was haggard, and she was frail in a way that frightened and confused the old trestleman. For a bewildering couple of minutes, Axle had no idea of what she spoke, and then, after taking a prescribed gulp of brandy, she calmed somewhat. She had interrupted him in his study, and they were therefore surrounded by the comfort of his old and massive books. But one look at the Verdigris tomes sent her immediately into relapse. Just when he had her calmed, she began pacing and wringing her hands, crying out at times in utter despair—pulling at her hair and behaving in every way unlike any guest he'd ever entertained. She was obviously ill. Finally, with the help of some salts, she regained herself, and he managed to calm her enough to extract a story from her.

At first Axle was greatly pleased with news of his young friends, but quite soon, with Clothilde's telling, his alarm returned—tenfold.

She explained she'd been leading Ivy and her taster companion by back roads to Templar—and on to Pimcaux. They had gone by way of Underwood and the Eath. But Verjouce had been clever and caught up with them at Skytop Abbey. Clothilde lost Ivy there in an attempt to trick the Guild's leader. She had wanted to keep them apart—knowing that if he was to ever meet her, all was lost. When Verjouce discovered her treachery, he imprisoned Clothilde there in the Abbey. He was in a fury.

"Am I really to fail? We must find the girl! You can convince her to go to Pimcaux—she'll listen to you. Time is of the essence for my grandfather. If Verjouce finds Ivy . . . he'll destroy her—and any chance of the Prophecy. Axle, he will destroy us all."

Although Axle possessed few warm thoughts for Clothilde, he knew he could not refuse her.

It was decided they would set off that night. Axle kept a small boat lashed to the underside of one of the footings, and it could be readied quickly. It was not a desirable time to travel, with the Winds still blowing steadily, but they had no choice.

It was just not part of their plan that the Outrider would commandeer their craft and deliver them in chains.

Verjouce's servant had not left Southern Wood or the grounds near the Hollow Bettle. He lurked there in hopes of finding his prize, thinking that it was quite possible the child would make her way home at some point. He was of a sinister temperament that did not much mind waiting for his prey. In the Wood, he lurked among the flora and fauna, eating small game whole and at times without a fire and drinking from mud-caked streams.

He sometimes slept in the white gossamer tent where he had tracked the travelers. The tent was the only marking remaining of Underwood, a place that held little interest for him. He had tracked the children to its entrance and was preparing a fire with which to smoke them out. Oddly, before he could do much of anything, the hole inside the tent had closed up completely—quickly, as if the earth were weaving itself back together. Nothing was left, no mark at all, of the tunnel into the lost world. But having never known Underwood, he experienced no sense of loss—and in the tent had gained a shelter from the ravaging Winds.

Had he not been back to the small footbridge to spy upon the Bettle, he would have missed her.

His eyes narrowed, watching her slip down below the trestle, her dress streaming behind her in the dark sky like a scarlet flare.

He knocked in the little red door easily and collected the fugitives.

"Axle!" Ivy called—she had only been happier to see her uncle.

The Outrider, Axle's captor, was confused. He thought he had left the Wood behind—but here it was again, and everywhere, all at once. Why, it was growing up and over his master before his very eyes!

Sorrel Flux had easily slipped by the confused Outrider and was sneaking down the polished hallway, marigolds blossoming feverishly upon his shoulders.

Ivy Manx was not detained long, either. Unfamiliar as she was with the castle's sly layout, she needed to keep Flux in sight. It was no time for a reunion. Thankfully, Flux left a trail of petals in his wake.

Chapter Fifty-seven

The Kitchen of the King

Flux had spent most of his sleepless nights eliminating potential sites for the Doorway, but it wasn't until he'd pried the key to the kitchen off of Lowly Boskoop that morning that his quest was successful. It was exactly where those ancient vexing pages had said it would be, hidden in plain sight.

In the kitchen, Lowly Boskoop was securely bound to the chair where Flux had left him.

If King Nightshade hadn't been so panicked about being poisoned—with a single kitchen key allotted to Lowly Boskoop—the Doorway might have been discovered long before now. (Or perhaps not, since those who had scoured the castle for the missing King Verdigris would later swear it was not there before, as if the Doorway had not wanted itself known.)

There was a tower of rickety shelves pushed in front of it

that served as a pantry, holding various dry goods and cooking implements. Sorrel Flux had mustered up enough strength to slide the entire unit somewhat aside, so that he might squeeze by, and through. Although the door seemed simple enough, he was confronted with a new worry: there seemed nowhere to be a knob or handle. Just a gold knocker.

Stepping back into the kitchen, he rubbed his chin, irritated.

"Do you have another key for this one?" Flux demanded of his bound companion.

From the widened state of Lowly's eyes, Flux knew that he did not, and he set about dejectedly kicking the shelves and cursing. Tins of stale tea leaves and bottled spices sailed through the air, giving Flux some sense of satisfaction.

It was then that he noticed at his feet a peculiar slab of stone. It was set as if part of the floor, directly in front of the door. Large and rectangular, it appeared to have something written on it. Flux produced a burst of strength from his scrawny arms, and with an enormous clatter, tipped the shelving unit over and out of his way, sending grain and sugar flying everywhere.

His growing rage was staunched by the arrival of Ivy. For the first time ever she was actually pleased to see her former taster, having lost sight of him before descending into the Gray Gardens.

"Stay away, you . . . ," Flux instructed, long bony finger

pointing at the girl, marigolds blooming from his collar. He knelt down, trying to wipe the stone free of flour while appearing menacing enough to keep Ivy at bay.

The stone said simply,

Pimcaux

It was followed by a delicate arrow pointing at, and through, the Doorway.

"Yes, yes. Pimcaux. But how? *How do I open the door?*" He banged the knocker loudly.

There was a moment of stillness.

And then, slowly, very slowly, the door opened out into the room, heavy and silent.

Sorrel Flux was still upon his knees, and he skittered back to make room. He and Ivy—having forgotten their struggles—waited breathlessly to see what greeted them on the other side. (They were not to be disappointed.) Behind them, Clothilde arrived from the Gardens, having made great strides in following Ivy through the castle.

Ivy waited, transfixed. She was overcome with a feeling of deep longing, a suffocating homesickness, at once familiar and like none she'd ever felt. Much in the same way where in Ivy's dreams, particularly as a young child, her heart beat a loud rhythm inside her. Only now, she suddenly realized, it was not her heart at all, but her prized red bettle that thumped rest-lessly in one of the inner pockets of her tasters' robes.

It was beating and jumping so insistently that she let her eyes leave the Doorway to examine the peculiar thing.

Sorrel Flux stood and turned—and if he was surprised by Clothilde's presence, he did not betray it. He was more used to her flitting about in a white gown, though, for he had become quite acquainted with Clothilde over his many years of service to Vidal Verjouce and had been sent to the Hollow Bettle by the Director expressly to keep her at bay. Verjouce had feared she would get to Ivy first—and indeed, this seemed to be so.

Flux half smiled at this and was about to say something unpleasant when he was surprised by the force with which he was knocked to the ground. Marigold petals fluttered about like confetti. He had seen nothing but a streak of white and, oddly, smelled something cold and crisp (the mountaintops? he wondered)—and now here he was again on the floor, in a great amount of discomfort.

"Ivy, quick—" Clothilde flew to the Doorway and held out her hand. "This way!"

Flux, who thought at first perhaps his back had been bro-ken by the white beast, soon found that he had just had the wind knocked out of him. The experience, however, left him in a new, less generous mood. He called out the first thing that came to him—taking a chance and hoping it would buy him the time he needed to get himself on his feet, and out the Door.

"I don't suppose she's mentioned your father, Ivy. Has she?"

His words, delivered with his trademark sneer, had their intended effect.

In the dining room, an interesting juxtaposition was occurring.

Within the weeds and the clouds of insects that had sprung up from the woven panels of the tapestries, two very different men were engaging in a classic argument of good and evil.

"Is this your work?" Verjouce asked Cecil, referring to the sudden prominence of plant life surrounding them. The carpet beside him had sprung a bog, complete with oozing puddles and odd-smelling flowers. A frog hopped over the foot of the feared Director of the Guild, chasing a dragonfly. From somewhere beneath the murky waters, large bubbles issued.

"Hardly," Cecil replied evenly. "I just helped it along."

"Never one to take credit, were you, Cecil?"

"I suppose you would see it that way, Vidal."

"I wish I could say your humility was charming. But it's not. It's merely old-fashioned. And boring. And because you chose the old ways, you find yourself here in chains."

Verjouce strained to turn his scarred face to the Outrider, still transfixed and standing confused by the entrance.

"Get over here and help me out of this chair!" he hissed at the hooded figure.

"The old ways? Is there really any other choice?" Cecil asked.

A darkness flitted over Verjouce's face.

"You never saw it—the evolution. Things change, Cecil, and it was long overdue. What is your way? Old and forgotten—that's what it is. Dust and dreams—just like the old man. Poisonry is a natural evolution of apotheopathy, just as smoke is from fire. My powers have far exceeded anything that Verdigris was capable of!"

"You have stolen his best work and claimed it as your own," Cecil stated flatly.

The Guild's Director leaned in slightly, straining at his bonds. "If you wish it, there is still a place for you at Rocamadour—I will see to it."

He lowered his voice to a hiss.

"It's your last chance, Manx!"

"There is no room for treachery in my way—old or new."

"So be it, apotheopath," Verjouce spat. "You have chosen defeat."

"Perhaps. But you know as well as I that Verdigris is still very much alive. You failed at your ultimate task, Vidal. He will return, the king. And he will come for you."

The Outrider had by now successfully stripped most of the vegetation from the blind man's body, and Verjouce stood, shaking his cane at Cecil, strips of bindweed falling from his freed arms. Rearing now to his full height, he made an impressive figure—even beside the Outrider.

"No one will save Verdigris, you fool. And without the help of the Noble Child, he is not long. After your old and crippled king is gone, where will you be?"

He steadied himself upon his dark cane—bettle blazing on its top.

"See to him," Verjouce ordered. "By the time I return."

The Guild's leader turned his ghastly countenance to face Cecil.

"There's a little girl who needs my attention." His smile cracked across his face in all his awfulness.

Chapter Fifty-eight

The Wind

L et us return now for a moment to the wind—that rascal. How much trouble had it caused over the years it blew across the land? Although the season was almost behind the long-suffering citizens of Caux, the Winds had but one more mischievous act to accomplish.

The particular gust in question was nothing but a small upstart where it began, upon the mountain. But as it traveled down the valley to Templar, it gathered speed, and by the time it whipped across the Marcel—where Gudgeon had resumed his windowside vigil—it had become a rather muscular wind. It was enough of a force to knock down some of the sturdier street stalls and send a cascade of toadstools rolling about the Knox, little polka-dot tumbleweeds.

But it was not done.

The wind whipped through the narrow cobbled streets of the city and kicked dust and debris into small spiraling swirls in its wake. Bolstered and chaotic, it rose again into the sky, where it was soon to end its bullying in one final, dastardly strike.

But before this particular wind readied itself in the skies above the castle, Ivy and Flux below, in the kitchen of the king, were both being treated to their first view of the treasured land of Pimcaux. A golden light poured over them, making Ivy look very much like a priceless statue but somehow doing very little to enrich Flux.

Sorrel was reminded what a great pleasure it was to be departing Caux, to start anew. But first he must rise again to his two feet (he would hold the brat personally responsible if there was any permanent damage) and propel himself past that awful woman's red skirts. He would sadly miss not having the bettle boar as dinner.

Clothilde was standing at the threshold—in the Doorway itself—holding out her arm to Ivy, imploring the girl to join her. Flux took particular pleasure in noting that Clothilde clutched her side, as if in some amount of pain, and that her normally ivory complexion had discolored to an ashen tone. Her skirts, too, were filthy and tattered. He had never before known her to show signs of such weakness, and her suffering was something Flux planned on savoring when he found the time.

"Red is definitely not your color," Flux quipped.

"Don't listen to him, Ivy!" Clothilde begged, ignoring Flux. "You must trust me. I promise, I'll explain everything to you—just hurry! We must go!"

"So she hasn't told you about your father after all." Flux relished this bit of information. He always did enjoy being the bearer of bad news.

Ivy was immobile. Pimcaux was pulling on her. What she saw through the Doorway, although a mere scrap of a vision, was stealing her heart as it had done to so many others before. But Flux was distracting her. He was moving, too, she was vaguely aware, rising onto his knees and pressing the rest of his scrawny body up with his hands, slowly.

"Curious, the subject hasn't come up." He looked peppily from woman to girl, enjoying himself.

"Ivy, his words are poison—do not listen to him!"

"Well, I'll have the pleasure of telling the child, then, if you will not."

Sorrel Flux turned to his former charge (if indeed Ivy could be considered that, as he never really did much of anything at the mill house to help her) and opened his mouth, allowing his tongue to wet his dry lips. But suddenly Sorrel Flux's face—and shoulders, and entire robe of marigolds—drooped. The flowers withered away in an instant, petals dropping, dried and crumbling, at his feet. For behind Ivy, Flux saw the one man who still held power over him, the unmistakable silhouette of his former employer.

Ivy turned to see Vidal Verjouce standing at the entrance to the kitchen. And at the sight of Verjouce, Flux cowered—much like the hounds earlier. Gone was all the pleasure he was taking just minutes ago in Ivy's misfortunes.

"Verjouce!" he yelped.

Vidal Verjouce was indeed a sight to behold.

And with Verjouce came the upstart wind—very much as if he had conjured it up himself, for his dark purposes. It blew wickedly through his hair and threw his robes against his long body. He stood tall, and brandished his cane in the air.

But the wind did not stop at Verjouce's hair.

It blew past Ivy and Poppy and, as if Verjouce himself had sent it directly, assaulted Sorrel Flux, lifting him off of the ground entirely and slamming him against the Doorway's frame. For the second time in his measly life, he felt his breath leave him.

But his former employer, with the wind at his bidding, had inadvertently done him a great favor. He was now within the open Doorway and passage to Pimcaux, and this realization caused his trembling to subside somewhat.

"A pity to miss the family reunion," he rasped, pushing roughly past Clothilde and stepping further into safety.

"Ivy! Ivy—" Clothilde called desperately from the Doorway. "You must come at once!"

And then Sorrel and Clothilde were gone, the wind causing its final damage—slamming the Doorway shut before Ivy could do anything to stop it.

She stood stunned, the golden image of Pimcaux burning itself into her memory and, as it turned out, into her eyes.

Chapter Fifty-nine

The Prophecy

Ivy ran to the Doorway, but it was too late—the ancient magic used to make it had sealed it tight. To her horror, the writing upon the bearing stone beneath her feet was fading before her eyes.

She turned slowly to face the wicked Director. In the absence of the Wind, the room had taken on an unnatural stillness.

"It is time for me to do what I should have done eleven years ago—had your mother not interfered." Verjouce smiled sinisterly. His hand gripped the enormous bettle at the head of his cane, and he slowly raised it, pointing the sharp tip at her. With the softest click, a hidden barb emerged from the cane's end—the reason behind Sorrel Flux's panic. In a flash, the Director advanced across the remainder of the room, and Ivy had but a moment to feel the comfort of her own bettle as it beat its steady rhythm in her fist. His face betrayed his

378

satisfaction—his eyes were nothing but hollow pits, and up close now, Ivy felt a wave of revulsion overtake her.

"How strange—so much suffering brought upon me by someone so small." He reared on her with a deadly grimace. Before him stood not a child, but the source of his disfigurement and pain. "You—the source of my suffering! The Noble Child!" He spat. "Because of you I was blinded—betrayed by that wretched Prophecy. Betrayed by you. Behold my face, child, these scars. It is as if your very hands plucked out my eyes! But I can see—yes, I can see. I see the Prophecy has failed, and you along with it. I see your doom." His stale breath reached her, and she gulped for air. Ivy thought of her uncle. She hadn't finished what she came here to do.

But something quite unbelievable was happening in the palm of Ivy's hand, and although Verjouce was beginning to detail in sinister fashion the particulars of Ivy's demise, she barely paid him any mind.

Her bettle. She had practically snatched it from Flux's grasp at her uncle's tavern. It had been recovered from the icy depths of the mountains, returning to her in the mouth of a bettle boar. It had lit the way at times of darkness. Ivy's bettle, flawed and hollow, was jumping and glowing in her hand with a magic of its own. In a fit of brightness—Ivy needed to shield her eyes with her other hand—the red bettle jerked and pulsed. And jerked and pulsed. Along the line of the central flaw, a sparkling light charged from one end to the other, and back again.

And then, with one giant lunge, it broke.

Or more aptly, *broke open*.

From inside the jewel emerged the most unusual and beautiful of creatures she had ever before seen. It stood for a moment on her palm, pausing. And then, to Ivy's complete and astonished delight, it unfolded its red transparent wings, glowing like little stained-glass windows. The creature filled her entire hand and fanned its wings tentatively. A spark of light shimmered still from the bettle, brighter now, coming from the creature's very center.

Ivy's bettle, it seemed, had become something not unlike an exquisite and astounding butterfly.

Although hers was the first, it was far and wide not the only such hatchling.

Vidal Verjouce was stopped in his tracks as the grip of his cane wobbled and cracked and flew away from his grasp. With the handle shattered, the cane clattered uselessly to the kitchen floor, leaving the blind man without aid. The caged bettle around his neck escaped its filigree binds and bobbed in the air above his head, flickering, joining Ivy's. Batting the air beside his head and feeling about for his bewitched cane, the Director suddenly and for once looked like the blind man he was. A howl escaped his snarling lips.

Ivy ran around him as quickly as she could and out into the Gray Gardens.

But what Gardens they were! No longer contained by the dark magic that deprived them of color, they shone with the brightest palette of the many shades of bettles that had gathered there, like a tangle of stringed lights. They flickered and beat their wings, and still more came.

They congregated on the fountain and infused color back into the silver olive tree. The gray rosebushes popped to life more vivid than any rose before, with an unearthly scent to match. Upon the queen's favorite tree, the poisoned apples withered and died, dropping to the ground like hollow husks.

Inside the castle, as Queen Nightshade still slept beneath a cushion of oakmoss, the crystal bettles in her crown jumped and sputtered to life, flying their maiden voyage around the forested room. In the final panel of the magic tapestries, hundreds of colored specks began their own hatching process, and soon the dining room was alive with dancing light.

In fact, all of Caux was experiencing this unusual phenomenon.

The vast stores of bettles at the Tasters' Guild were all

evaporating, to the great dismay of the subrectors in charge of their safekeeping.

The king's hoards all hatched.

And in the mines—high above all the land, the miners, too, were confounded by their jewels' transformation.

The night sky was filled with their luminosity as they streamed out of the mountaintops and down the Craggy Burls, like a giant rainbowed river. All eyes of Templar were on the mountains and the dark sky, and everyone below was struck motionless by the glorious light—more magical and thrilling than any fireworks display.

The following morning, it was generally agreed that the glittering bettles provided the most beautiful sunrise ever before witnessed. And heralded by this sunrise, a new day arrived upon Caux and, with it, loud whisperings that the ancient Prophecy—the near-forgotten one, that spoke of a Noble Child—had finally begun.

Chapter Sixty

Reunion

In the days that followed, Peps and Gudgeon spread the word that the dark reign of the Nightshades was finally over, and a great sigh of relief spread first across the ancient capital city and then quickly throughout the land. As if emerging from a long and fitful sleep, the people of Caux turned again to kindness.

The celebration Queen Nightshade had been planning took place after all, with one big difference. There was to be no execution of Cecil Manx, Master Apotheopath—or anyone, for that matter. Ever again. The holiday once celebrated by the Good King Verdigris, and tainted by the Nightshades, had regained its earlier charms.

On the evening of the Festival, the softest of breezes blew through the old city. The streets of Templar were laid with fragrant boughs that released a deep and refreshing scent. Candles glittered in goblets on every available ledge, and the waters of the Marcel flowed with twinkling lanterns. Citizens of Templar came to make merry and celebrate the end of the Nightshades' regime.

"Ivy—what happened to your hair?"

Upon first seeing Ivy, Rowan—in fact, everyone—exclaimed at the sight of her. Her blond hair had taken on an usual hue of pure spun gold, which extended to her eyes, where metallic flecks caught the light like gold dust.

"I think it happened when I looked through the Doorway," Ivy confided in Rowan.

"What did you see?" Rowan whispered in awe. "What was Pimcaux like?"

Ivy shrugged.

"Nothing but fields of yellow flowers as far as the eye could see." She would remember the stolen glimpse for the rest of her life.

"That's all?" Rowan couldn't hide the disappointment in his voice. He wasn't sure exactly what he'd been expecting, but surely something more spectacular than that.

"Rowan," Ivy continued. "They were cinquefoils."

Rowan was quiet with the realization of how much magic that meant.

The view of the Templar festivities from Peps's window was spectacular, and not to be outdone, Peps was host to a fine celebration of his own. Ivy was joyfully gathered with Axle, Cecil, and Peps while Rowan caught her up on the goings-on when she had followed Flux to the Doorway.

Axle was using his pocket-sized pincers, Rowan explained, to begin to free Cecil from his binds, but the ridiculous knot held fast. The Outrider shook off his confusion and proceeded to do his master's bidding and very soon was upon Ivy's uncle. Just then the last—and nearly forgotten—member of the party made his appearance.

With a parting of the air Shoo arrived, to the elation of his troubled friends. He flew at the Outrider and, as if the old bird had been waiting for this moment since their last meeting, threw himself at the task of blinding the Guild's servant. The old crow caused the Outrider to retreat in a panic, and stumbling, he fell into a patch of stinging nettles, howling in agony. From there he lurched into the newly formed bog, where he met his end by way of a giant pitcher plant—the kind that prefers meat—that had since made a home for itself there.

Ivy's eyes widened at the thought of being slowly digested alive in the belly of the man-eating plant, but Rowan continued with his story.

Familiar with Ivy's sleeping potion, Cecil and Axle revived their friends at the table with the antidote they found growing in a convenient clump of weeds.

"Simple parsley," confided Axle, smiling. "A common

antidote for many poisons. That's why you'll often find a sprig of it on your dinner plate!"

Rowan, upon waking, was quite unsurprised to realize he had failed to detect the nightman's skullcap.

"I am sorry I had to slip you that sleeping potion." Ivy sighed.

"No problem." He grinned at Ivy and continued.

Peps at first had been somewhat alarmed and disoriented to see his brother Axle beside him but, after dusting off the lichen growing from his chin, quickly recovered his sense of hospitality.

With the help of Trindle and several of his regulars—the restaurateur had been notified by Gudgeon of the Outrider's arrival and brazenly followed him to the palace—the group secured the remainder of the party. The royal family, along with the Diarist, were stowed temporarily in the basement amid the heaps of Verdigris relics.

Everyone was quite happy to return to the trestleman's quarters under the bridge and reassure Gudgeon that indeed all was well. After the initial surprise of meeting Peps's reclusive brother had faded, Gudgeon happily brought everyone a restorative cup of tea and a hearty breakfast to follow.

Rowan smiled, having finished his story.

"But where is Shoo?" Ivy looked around, eager to see her old friend.

The group fell silent.

"When the tapestry withdrew, he went with it," Cecil explained.

"What? Went where?"

"It's hard to say, exactly. Into the tapestry itself. It was woven with some potent Verdigris magic, you know. You can see tomorrow—I'll take you there. He is perched upon the shoulder of the young lady in the last of the panels. He looks, I might add, quite pleased with himself."

"As he should be," Axle agreed.

"Shoo. I'd hardly be here, or anywhere, without him," Ivy realized. She felt a sudden sadness, and her mind drifted to Pimcaux. The thought plagued her that Sorrel Flux, that awful yellow man, was somewhere there, spreading disaster in his wake. He was there, and she was not. Verjouce was right, she had failed the Prophecy.

The party was getting louder, and Peps was beaming and enjoying himself immensely. He would tell the tale of the castle and the Nightshades' downfall a hundredfold that night—not bothered at all that he had slept through most of it.

Axle, Cecil, and the two children moved to the relative quiet beside the window.

"You are meant to go to Pimcaux, Ivy. And you will get there somehow," came Cecil's thoughtful voice.

"But how? The Doorway is sealed again. I saw the bearing stone fade away."

They watched the candles float by beneath them on the Marcel's surface. Then, before her, where she stood at Peps's mullioned window, Ivy heard a faint tapping. Against the old thickened glass, fluttering in the night, was the small red form of a butterfly.

"Ivy, I'm sure—isn't that your bettle?" Rowan exclaimed as it flew in the open casement.

Ivy smiled and watched as it elegantly stretched its magnificent wings.

"Your mother gave you that bettle," Cecil said softly. "She was conflicted, but in the end, it was you she cared most about."

Ivy thought of Clothilde then, the last glimpse she had of her.

Axle cleared his throat. "When your mother was born, Ivy, there was great hope that it was she who would save Caux. I think she wished too hard for this legacy, your legacy, and lost herself in it."

"Flux was going to tell me about my father," Ivy said quietly.

"Flux? His words are spiteful and made only to injure," Axle growled.

The red bettle flew in a lullaby of flight, its soft glow bobbing and weaving. Mesmerized, Ivy followed its curious path to the darkened rear wing of Peps's vast apartments. They were beside the west pier, where the Knox was anchored to the

bedrock. There, beside an old cornerstone more pale and ancient than the rock surrounding it, the bettle settled down, beaming brighter as it fanned its wings.

They all peered in, the empty stone somehow familiar.

"What's that?" Rowan asked. "Is that a bearing stone?"

"There's nothing," Ivy said, running her hand over it.

"Look!" Rowan would not be discouraged.

And sure enough, as the four stared at the blank face, a faint script—a mere scratching on the stone's surface—began detailing itself as if written by an invisible hand. Axle became quite serious.

"In the writings of King Verdigris there exists talk of another Door." He hesitated, catching Cecil's eye. "But it is vague, dismissed as a rumor. The pages are missing, sadly. Torn from the binding long ago, and most likely lost or destroyed."

"Another door to Pimcaux!" Ivy's heart began beating furiously.

Rowan was silent, remembering his vivid experience with Verdigris's writings—not entirely pleasant.

"So it is written."

They watched breathlessly as the invisible engraver completed the last flourish on the bearing stone.

373 knarls to Pimcaux

" 'From darksome abbey where betrayal breeds, a second chance perhaps succeeds,' " Axle recited in a hushed tone.

"Does this mean what I think?" Ivy asked excitedly.

"Yes," Cecil said darkly. "There is a back door."

"But where? Do you know? Shouldn't we go at once?" The renewed hope Ivy was feeling was tinged with trepidation at her uncle's tone.

Cecil and Axle looked at each other, and a grim expression overtook their features.

"It is very dangerous, I am afraid."

"It doesn't matter—" Ivy was just thankful that she was being given a second chance.

"And there is the small matter of the resumption of your studies—"

"Uncle Cecil!"

"Ivy, there are great and potent forces determined to see the Prophecy fail. Your path as a healer is your salvation. You need this knowledge to combat what lies ahead of you."

"Er, do you know where this back door is?" Rowan asked. "It just says 373 knarls." He had a sudden bad feeling in his stomach.

"It's no place for Ivy," Cecil muttered.

"I shall be her guide," Axle said resolutely. "The thirteenth and final edition of my book is done. I wonder . . . There's probably great need for a *Field Guide to Pimcaux*!"

Ivy thought for a moment.

"And Rowan can come, too?"

"But of course—we shall need him the most."

"Why?" Rowan was pleased at this news but confused, too, since his expertise in most things was questionable.

"Because the back door is in Rocamadour."

Final Words

After the Festival, plans fell quickly into place.

There was an enormous and well-fed gathering at Trindlesniffter's, and amid the frothy beers and vintage brandies much was decided upon. At both Trindle's and Peps's boisterous urging, a vote was taken, and it was decided that Cecil Manx—Master Apotheopath and servant to Verdigris—would stay on in Templar as Steward of Caux. News spread from the restaurant to the crowded square beside it and from there to the dinner tables of the long-oppressed Templar families. Soon, upon the lips of all Cauvians were new, lighthearted words, words such as *apotheopath* and *Prophecy*, rather than whispers of torment and tyranny.

But mostly news spread of the king, the Good King Verdigris, and of his possible return.

Ivy returned to the palace with her uncle to see Shoo. As they stood in the shadow of the masterworks, Ivy regarded the final panel. Cecil reached for her hand, and she leaned against his long cloak.

"You see, he seems quite happy," he observed.

"Still"—Ivy turned, not wanting her uncle to see the tears beginning to come—"I'd rather he was here with us."

"He is. In a way."

Ivy reached forward and touched the crow, the firm weave of the tapestry returning nothing to her fingers but a cool, slightly scratchy texture.

"If I know Shoo, this is not the last of him we'll see," Cecil counseled.

In the basement, Cecil and Ivy met the few remaining long-suffering staff of the castle. Still secreted away in the corridor were vast quantities of Verdigris treasures, the antiques so despised by King Nightshade. Amid it all, and surely to his great horror, slept the deposed king and his small entourage.

"The cart is ready, sir," a stable boy informed Cecil. "And, as you requested, the most stubborn of mules to pull it."

"Well done. May their trip be long and bumpy."

Cecil and Ivy went about the task of reviving the Nightshades. Arsenious was made so uncomfortable by being roused in a room full of antiques that he agreed most instantly to his punishment and exile. But the queen, after feeling for her crown and finding it missing, shrieked and hissed.

"What is this treason? This insolence? How dare you hold us!" Further investigation led her to the realization that her hollow ring was also absent, and, stripped of her poisons, her complexion settled into a fiery flush.

Cecil had brought fistfuls of parsley into the cellar, but it had no effect upon the Royal Diarist, who was, in fact, not asleep.

"What's wrong with him?" the queen asked, poking the man's arm several times with a sharp finger.

"He's dead," Cecil replied somberly.

"You killed him!" Queen Nightshade turned on Ivy.

"Nonsense!" Cecil admonished. "It's quite obvious it was something he ate."

At this, the former king looked crestfallen. This was even worse than losing his favorite jester.

"I was quite fond of him, you know, Artilla." He delivered a look of disappointment at his wife. The Royal Diarist had kept him company for his years on the throne and had always had a kind or encouraging word for him. The queen, looking first from Ivy and Cecil and then to her husband, sagged imperceptibly. She bit her lip.

"You will be given safe passage to Kruxt and from there to the Outpost Islands. More, I assure you, than you gave your predecessor."

"After the many kindnesses we've shown you, apotheopath," she whispered.

"Apotheopath? Is that the fellow?" Arsenious scratched his chin, peering at Cecil. He seemed cleaner. The former king sighed resolutely, staring down at his clubfoot. There was a strong sense of poetic irony, he felt, in this situation. And being a poet, he thought of a poem. Luckily for all in attendance, however, several burly townsfolk arrived just in time, prepared to escort the royals on their way.

"Do not touch me," the queen ordered, head held high. All were in agreement, since the years of Aqua Artilla had infused her very skin with the scent of poison.

Proudly, and with only a mere falter to her step, Queen Artilla walked before her husband and out of Templar, a town she always despised.

The Deadly Nightshades eventually alighted upon Brax, a small island off of Kruxt, with little by way of luxurious accompaniments. There the cruel former ruler of Caux found an appreciation for the simple life—his feet were happiest when walking barefoot in the white sand. When not on the beach, the former king spent most of his time fruitlessly chasing flying bettles with a butterfly net, hoping to enjoy them in a tonic as he once did.

One odd remnant and reminder of the potent Verdigris magic they endured was this: Artilla Nightshade could never really stop the occasional weed growth on the top of her head. Frequently, she would call for her husband's help in plucking

persistent and unsightly common dandelions from her scalp—
a process that she found as painful as it was unpleasant.

But what of the Guild?

Axle, the undisputed expert on the land of Caux, knew
this: the Tasters' Guild was strong, very strong, and the city of
Rocamadour was impenetrable.

Vidal Verjouce had escaped easily during the confusion
and celebration that the coming of the bettles brought.

Back in Rocamadour, beneath the shadow of the black
spire, he sat in his dark study (for a blind
man does not need light). He felt
for the pages in his desk.
Finding them in their secret
drawer, he sat with them,
trancelike. The magical
papers of the old king
were his alone. From
them, a faint scent of smoke
and fire.

Verjouce replaced
the papers in their
hiding place and
summoned his sub-
rectors.

There was another way.

Appendix

A lost section from Rowan's

FIELD GUIDE TO THE POISONS OF CAUX

of course, should under no circumstances be consumed

(see diagram B, part (c))

for its woody parts impart at once a sense of extreme well-being complicated by the very real fact that all indeed is not well; in fact, it is generally assumed you will have a mere 8 hours of life left

(see height and weight charts, pp. 4073—74 and it is of utmost import to factor into one's calculations whether the weed was dried or fresh).

Vital organs: liver and heart.

(see NIGHTSHADE, DEADLY, Purple worship, Belladonna, Deadly Evening

ANTIDOTES:
No known

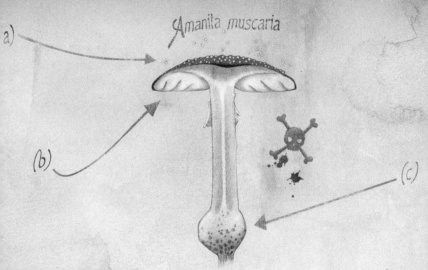

Amanita muscaria

a)

(b)

(c)

right coloring, not dull-red like many masquerading—and harmless—look-alikes. *Look alive!*

Note gill detail. Also, see p.403 for good tea recipe. See also good crumpet recipes pp. 811, 1701

...uard hairs. A true *Fly Agaric* will possess these when ripe.

As every citizen of Caux knows, some plants are good, some ...d, but all are powerful when harnessed. And it is another truth ...these plants' real essences are again awakening, after a *long*, ...d at times fitful, sleep. It is up to the reader to recognize this ...w existence, for with true knowledge of plants comes extreme ...ver. Power, even, *to be king*.

About the Author

Susannah Appelbaum comes from a family of doctors and philosophers, which instilled in her both an early fascination and a great deal of caution with bottles marked "Poison." The idea for the Poisons of Caux trilogy was born when she lived in an old woodcutter's cottage in the French apple country as a child: "Out the door were ancient forests, wild boars, and new and inviting foods to taste."

Susannah worked in magazine publishing for many years and now lives with her family in New York's Hudson Valley and in Cape Breton, Nova Scotia, where her garden prefers to grow weeds.

The Hollow Bettle is her first novel. To learn more about the author, please visit www.susannahappelbaum.com.